TWENTY FIVE MILLION GHOSTS

D1428343

Twenty Five Million Ghosts

Steve Aitchsmith

Matador
9 Priory Business Park,
Wistow Road, Kibworth Beauchamp,
Leicestershire. LE8 0RX
Tel: 0116 279 2299
Email: books@troubador.co.uk
Web: www.troubador.co.uk/matador
Twitter: @matadorbooks

ISBN 978 1788033 145

British Library Cataloguing in Publication Data.
A catalogue record for this book is available from the British Library.

Printed and bound by CPI Group (UK) Ltd, Croydon, CR0 4YY
Typeset in 11pt Aldine401 BT by Troubador Publishing Ltd, Leicester, UK

Matador is an imprint of Troubador Publishing Ltd

For the missing.

In Flanders fields as poppies blew,
tomorrow's fathers failed and grew
the nature of this flimsy world
beyond old certainty and held
    this history to be a place
    where those who gave today in haste
    are not forgotten but forged as
    distant sacrifice to a new
styled life. Here survived souls remain,
seek solace, understanding, strain
to see or feel the missing sons
who are spent, yet prowl familiar
    in their silent watch. Keep some faith
    with the fallen we still recall,
    loss borne and held eternally
    in Flanders fields where now peaceful
ploughs enduring emptiness yield.
We in melancholy loss and
they, rewarded by memory,
keep some cloaked life that blurs the day
    and obscures the view of this realm
    unimagined. None died thinking
    bright futures, as they lay stinking,
    sure they died for mundane reasons:
family, friends, do the right thing –
we welcome these vague gallant ghosts,
shadows who cannot be today;
they broke the chain of creation.
    We feel them and mourn more than them;
    The present that will never be,
    we see their seed continue now
    in our sad and empty spaces.

John 'Jack' Adams

The ants began the aggressive expansion of their territory, thereby invading mine, in May. At first they were not a major problem, just one or two marauding about the conservatory in that purposeful yet random way they have, their light black bodies highlighting them against the white uPVC and making them easy to spot.

By June they had developed their incursion into a scavenging line intermittently raiding in an organised and energetic column. There were two columns really; one line in, do whatever it is that ants do when they forage, then another line out. It was an impressive display of order and precision, like a marching army. Brave and disciplined, too; no matter how many I squashed they just kept coming, immune to the horror of the splattered remains of their nest mates. Ants really are quite formidable.

This house near Brighton, slightly tumbledown, isolated and surrounded by woodland, is my final retreat. Final retreat or last stand, however you might want to regard it. Some people, and I'm one of them, have a need to obtain respite in occasional quiet sanctuary from the world that confuses them and provokes them into resigned despair at the general foolishness.

I'm not a real recluse, my wife usually works away during the week and my daughter stays at her university much of the time. At weekends when they are with me, I can pretend to be a standard family man. Monday to Friday I'm Mr Crusoe in a dilapidated old woodman's cottage and free to exist in the last defensible camp I plan to inhabit.

I don't feel as old as I am on paper. I've always said that chronologically I'm sixty something but inside, in my head, I'm twenty-two. I'm lucky enough to have my health and fitness, I look younger than my age – I like to say about thirty but everyone else says a young fifty, what do they know? I can still run a good distance and I'm as strong as ever. So far I'm not really experiencing any joint pains, except in my back but that's a penalty for being tall. In fact, the only dark clouds over this not unpleasant way of life are an endowment mortgage that will fall short, with no real idea of how I will pay it without borrowing again, the occasional concern over what might happen with the woodland and a mother terminally ill with bowel cancer in a London hospice.

I don't own the woodland. It extends to a few hundred acres that apparently don't have an owner. I've had a few enquiries from some fat gut ripping, profit hunting developers. The forestry commission don't have it and the last capitalist lackey that enquired, seeking to confirm Joni Mitchell's prophesy, told me that it may be Crown land set aside for future national use, whatever that might mean.

I don't need to worry about money, I have a decent though not great income from investments and residual Government payments for past services. Commitment to uniformed public service and a weather eye on the

FTSE pays dividends. I say that I became financially secure by playing footsie with the state.

My parents were surprised when at the age of twenty I left a secure job in insurance to join the military. After a couple of uneventful tours of Ireland and some small foreign adventures which were not very adventurous, I sidestepped into a small joint services hush hush unit that basically went around the globe stealing other people's information.

Later, as technology improved, the stealing could be done electronically from the UK thus saving on transport costs. It's the sort of stuff that Britain pretends it doesn't do but nonetheless still has to be done. I never really got involved in the blood and guts stuff. My life has involved the occasional unpleasant rough and tumble but that has more to do with being brought up in the East End than with any uniformed service.

On the plus side, the army, and later the police, spent a small fortune providing me with university courses and over a period of years I accidently collected a shed load of letters after my name. After a couple of years of sneaky and barely legal intelligence gathering, I moved into policing and then teaching and eventually made my final tactical retreat to this secluded home that many people would consider lacks the basic heating, water and sewage essential for habitability but which I enjoy.

On reflection, I probably did more physical fighting when policing than I ever did in the army. London policing can be a bit more hands-on and bundle around than is generally thought. Teaching can, at times, be more like policing than many would be comfortable with. That might be why there's a surprising amount of movement between the two. A lot of teachers become police officers and more police than you might imagine become teachers.

So I live like this, part defensive isolationist, part content family man, part retiree, part woodman and part world weary ex-services patsy. I am the quintessential grey ghost, observing and noticing things while hiding behind the twin disguises of cynicism and anonymity. My income, made up from a small military pension, a huge police pension and a tiny teaching pension that together augment investment, keeps me solvent.

Now, of course, I have my new war to fight, I've solemnly declared hostilities against the ants. One of them actually bit me the other day so they will die. Destruction to the ants, that's what I say.

Despite my determined assault with chemical weapons, the ants proved resilient. I bought and spread about some powder, the packet of which claimed that the ants would take the sweet but poisonous deception to their nest and then all die horribly, just as they deserve. Certainly the powder disappeared so I assume it was taken. There was no observable resulting depopulation, if anything they seemed to increase in number.

My new war notwithstanding, I left the scene of battle so that I could journey to Hackney, the location of the hospice. My mother and the redoubtable Dave Thompson would expect me and I wouldn't like to disappoint them. My mother is dying and this matter of fact approach is my defence mechanism. I need to see her for my own peace of mind but I know that I'll appear to others as just the dutiful son managing the passing of the old generation while maintaining his own progress forward.

Dave is an interesting man and I always enjoy meeting him. Or 'hem' as he would insist. Not long after I first met hem I asked hem about hem's regular use of the word hem.

"It's a gender neutral pronoun," hem said in hem's soft Irish brogue, a voice that always managed to sound both caring and fiercely defiant of the world in general. "English doesn't really support the language of inclusiveness; language reflects culture, like the Eskimos having sumptingteen different words for snow, and the culture from which English originates is like most European cultures in its exclusiveness. So I've borrowed the word hem from some Polynesian language or other. It's used when the gender of the person referred to is irrelevant. So hem is the bus driver but he or she is my father or mother."

I've tried to use it but gave up because of the need to explain it to people, so I returned to the inherently sexist pronouns most of us are more used to.

Dave is always, in my opinion, challenging the world around him and this was just another example. The thing is, like most things that Dave says, it actually makes sense after you decipher his words and think about it for a while. It often takes some careful thought because when he's explaining things he tends to talk as if he's reading an academic essay.

I suppose it's why what we now call the LGBT community half-inched some words from the language to describe itself, like 'gay' which until quite recently had a much wider usage. The existing language failed to support the concept and so words had to be created, imported or usurped. It might even be why I sometimes resort to colloquialisms from my childhood when they explain what I mean but I don't really want to use a pejorative slang term, like pinched, that suggests something unacceptable.

I voiced this idea to him once and received his usual thought provoking individualistic reply.

"Community is it, well… maybe," he said. "We usually give communities a geographic location. At the same time, we have to consider the Jewish diaspora which is also a community but without a specific location – Israel is more of a safe haven than a place for all Jews. So yeah, I suppose they are a community if they want to be. But would every gay person identify hemself as part of a community? I don't know. I do know that's it's OK to appropriate for new usage any word from the English language if it can be placed in new contexts for alternative use generally, it's the flexibility of English that gives it such strength as a global language. I also know that communities develop to protect those within them but also tend to exclude others, so we're back to exclusion again aren't we? Oh, and yeah, you use colloquialisms, even though what you said is not a colloquialism, because it's easy. It's just lazy and stops you properly reasoning out your thought, you're better than that."

That's Dave for you. He infuriates me with his constant questioning and refusal to take anything at face value and I love him for it.

The fact is that he is the most intelligent and thoughtful man I've ever met. He's as hard as they come from his early life spent boxing and drinking before he found his way into the Roman Catholic priesthood. It's an unlikely transition but then again maybe not for a man who is as comfortable in a punch up as he is in a high level academic debate. Strictly speaking he's Doctor Dave (of philosophy, not theology, interestingly) but doesn't like the title.

I don't call him Father either, I'm not RC, and he seems happier with just 'Dave' or sometimes 'oi you'. He's the perfect counter balance to the rarefied atmosphere that can surround clergy of any denomination. He's also a reassuring character in a church reeling from global revelations of child abuse.

While the church hierarchy purports to protect the vulnerable and support the offenders in their weakness, Dave just says, "prosecute them, cut their bollocks off and kick them out." Dave struggles with the 'turn the other cheek' part of his faith.

The train journey to London from my hidey-hole is languorous and presents little of great interest. There is some pretty countryside on the first leg towards Victoria and some unusual buildings but the view quickly gives way to modern box housing and the landscaping of an overcrowded network of roads, services and airport.

As the train rumbles into London itself, the housing becomes older and more care worn although a bright and tall new world, often gleaming and shiny or adorned with squares and streaks in primary colours, is sprouting its oddly shaped towers amongst them, like a group of boisterous dandies disturbing the exhausted old architecture.

The easy transfer to the underground delivers one into the sardine world of the commuter, tourist or urban wanderer moving and standing in confined spaces with shoulder to shoulder crowds. Trying not to press against anybody is a complete skill set in itself.

To reach Hackney I find it's best to abandon the tube at Whitechapel and move onto the bus network. I've watched this area evolve throughout my whole life. The underlying villainy of the predominately white working class East End in which I grew up gave way, in Whitechapel and some other areas, to an incoming Islamic culture that currently dominates the area, complete with street traders, Muslim proselytisers and often eastern attire.

The significant but shy Jewish community that existed alongside us seems to have remained with the new Whitechapel and moves around the current culture with a little visible friction but more or less smoothly. However, whereas the Jewish groups largely assimilated with the previous majority group, in public at least, that does not seem to be the case now.

I wonder if it ever occurs to the Jewish people here that they were resident in this area first. When Oliver Cromwell, in need of profitable industry and the skills that go with it, reversed the expulsion of Jews enacted by Edward 1 in 1290, returning Jews settled close to the walls of London in this then rural undeveloped area. The working English were attracted by the opportunities this created and joined them soon afterwards. Longshanks created the vacuum that centuries later allowed Jewish and English workers to rush in.

London social norms change within just a few miles, it's the only place I know where one might walk all day and move through half a dozen or more different cultures. There is one common and rarely commented on thing about these places, it is something barely noticeable and apparent only in its absence. There is a whole strata of human society that has become disappearingly rare, everywhere; it is the very old, the vulnerable old.

When I was young, the confused, weak and vulnerable elders were common. It was expected that we small kids would help them as and when required. We would carry their bags, run their errands and visit them in their homes to suffer stewed tea, stale biscuits, life threatening poor hygiene and fascinating tales of yore.

They were an often confused and cantankerous bunch, at the same time they were made interesting by their exciting stories and advice. On the not infrequent occasions that they wandered into roads, forgot about ovens and fires or just got lost, this was not seen as an issue and they were just helped or assisted by whoever was at hand at the time.

As the journey draws into Hackney itself, the vocal and confident Islamism of the Whitechapel Road gives way to a black and white ethnicity of the centuries old Anglo Celt culture amalgamated with Caribbean arrivals just decades ago. The two groups were surprisingly compatible and the older people rub along together, with a little of the old racism sometimes erupting. The younger people seem to have merged into a newer mixed culture developed from the older two, it's an interesting place.

Unlike in parts of south London, where much of the young white population copied the accents of the Empire Windrush newcomers, or at least a London version of it, in the east the black population largely adopted the traditional cockney voice of those already there. I like Hackney. Recently arty types of all ethnicities have begun a colonisation of the area and this lively and eccentric group only add to the area's vibrancy with their gentrifying and amusingly fashioned presence. I've seen this bunch sporting Victorian waistcoats, coloured hair, rag doll make up, Edwardian beards and more. Wonderful. It has to be said they can be a tad insular, sticking to their own people but still a welcome subculture.

I hear that many local housing estates are plagued by gangs and drugs but they're really not apparent unless you search for them. I hope the new black/white artists develop into a local culture that washes over the nihilism and pointlessness of the gangs. London is nothing if not constantly dynamic.

Moving amongst all of this are the ubiquitous homeless and dispossessed. There's something disturbing about a society that so readily accepts the helpless and hopeless throng that sleeps rough and begs its sometimes aggressive way among them. Not old enough to fall into the hidden world of the geriatric ghetto homes and in need of too much help to actually contribute, they are simply ignored and left to fade into the social background.

Everybody in London originates from immigrants, some long ago and some more recently. The indigenous peoples were overpowered and effectively displaced millennia ago as Rome exercised its cultural, military and social hegemony over the land. Since then, every new group has just fed the constant growth and evolution of the place.

So it is, that in the modern Hackney, the black/white and developing arty ways of life sit alongside diehard pockets of the older society to form the local core culture. This being London, any number of small enclaves of other traditions and people pad out the social dynamic. Every large city entertains diversity but London is the finest example, challenged only, perhaps, by New York.

I tend to refer to the world in which I was brought up as the original culture. I know that's not true but it was dominant for a long time and it makes an easy shorthand for me. When I say it, I really mean the group of people that made up the London workers. They came from famished Ireland, enclosed Scotland, the played out mines of Wales, the over farmed home counties and as refugees from various European conflicts and oppressions. All of this, from pre medieval times onwards, to eventually man the Victorian commercial infrastructure and create additional riches for the wealthy.

They coalesced into the early Victorian bunch that tried to reassert themselves after the world wars but were so impaired that their social demise was inevitable. In terms of vanishing cultures, it was historically one of the more pleasant disintegrations, wartime violence notwithstanding. Most of the war survivors got richer, better educated and obtained greater rights. As more waves of immigrants arrived to replace the workforce, the originals moved on to better things.

This didn't stop some of them from complaining that their culture had been cleansed and marginalised by the new people. Many sat in their comfortable suburban semis and moaned about the lost world. It's something that is silly, really, but it's easy to be nostalgic for an imagined golden past.

In the eighteenth and nineteenth centuries the Irish poured into Britain to dig the canals and build the infrastructure of the industrial revolution. In their wake the Romans returned, no longer the terrifying legions of the Caesars but by then emasculated as an imperial power and now characterised by an ornate and wealthy church.

Somehow, the expansionist church of Rome had long ago established itself as a political power in Ireland but in the process had become so particularly Irish that it is reasonable to speak of Irish Catholicism as a connected but individual branch of Rome.

Mainland Britain retained some suspicion of Catholicism but had begun to move towards the discomforted but ultimately tolerant, though slightly reluctant, realism that would distinguish it as a modern nation.

The Roman/Irish church brought with it a group of Nuns. An Irish nun is a formidable creature that enforces the required behaviour of Rome, Ireland branch, with an assertiveness that will intimidate the strongest of people. Unrelentingly rule enforcing, they engendered fear of hellfire while demanding respect and obedience from the navvies that toiled, lived, loved and died in building the infrastructure of British growth and industrialisation. The nuns administered to the medical and welfare needs of the expat Irish, they provided the welfare the employers didn't, couldn't or wouldn't. Irishmen were cheap and plentiful and it made no economic sense to do more than just pay them their wages. Their welfare was their concern and not the problem of the employers.

The nuns were well regarded by both those they came to care for and the local community. Despite their fearsome and fiery reputation, local working class English took advantage of the care the nuns offered. For their part, the nuns happily but sternly gave that care. It's not clear to me how all of this was funded but it must at least have had some fiduciary support from the Catholic church. While recent revelations have damaged the reputation of the church, especially in Ireland, these were simpler times and many people took their Christian duty seriously. The nuns built a hospital in Hackney and called it St. Joseph's hospital and hospice.

The post-war arrival of the welfare state led to National Health Service involvement in St. Joseph's and it became purely a hospice in the modern sense, where the dying receive gentle palliative care and their passing is managed. Nonetheless, the Church of Rome, Ireland, maintained its substantial involvement in the place.

Today it is staffed by doctors, nurses, nuns and priests. Some of the nuns and priests are also doctors and nurses. The denomination or religion of the NHS workers is irrelevant. The patients are of any or no religion. Dave is the priest in charge of pastoral assistance to the patients and their families. That's how I got to know him.

St. Joseph's site is just off Hackney High Road. I don't think it's the original building but it is old, at least parts of it are. Much of it is the heavily built sooty brick that for many years characterised large official buildings in London. Some of it was destroyed in the second war and I'm told that for a while it operated out of prefabricated buildings in the grounds of the remaining old monolithic structure.

Now it is that mixture of modern steel and glass that seems delicate in comparison to the robust looking older masonry with which it is integrated. The entrance hall reception area displays some old and faded sepia photographs of the founding nuns and a smallish crucifix adorns one of the walls. Other than that, the only indication of church involvement is an obviously RC influenced chapel. A small sign beneath a statue of the virgin Mary proclaims this chapel to be multifaith and suitable for use by people of all beliefs who wish to quietly reflect.

Scurrying back and forth throughout the building are still some nuns and occasionally a priest. They are working hard but it doesn't really assist the multifaith claim. I think they'd be better off proclaiming their own faith but making it clear that their ministrations are not limited to Roman Catholics. The current position can make the place look a bit shifty and incompetent, since it's clearly RC trying to pretend it isn't but without hiding.

I'm sure the intention is to make everybody welcome and it's preferable to the believe or burn for eternity approach. I'm never very comfortable with aggressive religious presentation and anybody who claims to hold the one and only truth worries me. I'm born Anglican which means I go to church once in a while, rarely, and hold a not very well defined faith in a church that has an introspective tendency to bicker internally and to appear disinterested in explaining its mission. I would describe myself as an agnostic who leans towards faith. In view of my history it is probably not surprising that I'm really quite conservative in that respect.

Dave wanders around chatting to everybody in the hospice, making people feel more comfortable and reconciled to the reality of the place. It's what he's good at and it is a remarkable soft skill that is natural to him. Only the truly strong and tough can be that effortlessly gentle. With me he's blunt and to the point but that's also his skill, he just knows what works for me and that I have no interest in euphemisms. I've seen the ugly world and so has he. We can talk in a straight way that wouldn't work for many.

Should you ever wish to have whatever faith you hold challenged, feel uselessly helpless and be made angry at the same time, visit a children's hospice.

To reach the ward in which my mother is cared for, I have to take a lift to the third floor, pass the children's complex and walk several long pastel painted corridors to the ward.

Small groups of kids stampede in and out of the complex as they seek play and adventure. Many of them are just as noisy and obstructive as they are supposed to be. Some of them are so ill they are unable to leave the complex to explore the wider building. All of them will die decades too soon. Life-limited condition, such is the modern euphemism that is applied to their circumstance.

It makes me angry, they are just kids. Nobody has any right to call them life-limited. It's just wrong, that's all. They will die, that's the truth and the simple fact of the situation and I balk at any attempt to make it sound cutesy. This is a little burst of frustrated powerlessness that assails me every time I pass them. I'm old enough and experienced enough not to expect a fair world but that doesn't prevent the surge of silent anger. Death has no right to stalk the young and fate has no business neutralising such potential and promise.

It contrasts sharply with the happy noises that regularly filter out of the place. I've seen death in most of its forms, all of them ugly. I've learned that people can come to terms with any horror but it defeats me how anybody can cope with working there.

The feelings engendered by passing the children's complex diverge sharply from, and in a way assist with, the more normal ordeal of entering the geriatric ward. At least this is the proper way of things and the clean, aseptic atmosphere is strangely reassuring.

The spotlessly white uniformed attendants in the ward greeted me brightly as I entered and ushered me towards the bed where my mother lay. If anything, the ward always seems too white, overpoweringly white. It's almost as if somebody decided to recreate some early Hollywood idea of the anteroom to Heaven. Obviously, that was not the intention but the place was and is a little too clinical for its purpose. Still, at least the people here are at the natural end to their lives, nothing here to be angry about. Here lives only sadness, maybe mixed with regret and, hopefully, fine memories.

Somewhere in the building must be rooms for people of other ages, neither too young nor properly old. I expect they supply their own anger. I suppose that age based segregation of the dying serves some useful purpose.

My mother was in a bed towards the end of the ward, near the full length windows. The headboard end of the mattress was raised in the semi sit up position and a small flat screen TV hovered in front of her held by an arching metal arm. Everything was white except the black casing of the TV. The clashing colours made it look as though it were floating in the ethereal mist surrounding the queue awaiting Charon's services.

A clear plastic tube ran from her left arm into a small yellow box on the side cabinet. A constantly green light and an occasionally flashing amber light indicated something to somebody. In her right hand my mother held a small pen like device, her thumb hovering over a button at the top. In this way she could administer her own morphine as and when she needed it. As I walked towards her I noticed that she pressed the button about every five seconds or so.

A mother's smile calms every child, whatever their age. I kissed her gently on the forehead. She looked gaunt and pained in spite of the smile, the last four years had seen her undergo operation after operation. Each invasive procedure left her weaker and more dependent on care.

About a year ago the final operation and chemo left her too weak to continue and she was sent home. The regular visiting nurse was charming and efficient and helped her enjoy as much time as possible in her normal environment. Then her legs began to swell, they grew heavy with fluid and limited her movement. She was able to struggle through everyday life for several weeks but eventually the nurse arranged for her to be placed in St. Joseph's.

I remember talking to Dave about her at this time. "It's a shame about the legs," I told him. "It's just one more thing that she has to suffer." I'd met him two operations ago, when my mother was placed in the hospice for assessment. He sought me out, I'm not sure why but that's the way he is. He has an almost supernatural instinct that identifies who he needs to speak to. We got on well and developed a friendship from the start.

"It's always the legs," he said at the same time as he made me coffee in his small office at the back of the chapel. "Always the legs. They say it's to show you that you can't run away. That's true but I think it's also likely to be a holistic failure of function in the whole body. In prolonged illness the legs fail first nearly always." That was typical of him; accept the clear truth of the folk tale but offer the probable scientific reason for it as if he were making a daft suggestion.

My mother had not really been watching the TV. Some Australian soap, with no sound, played out its storyline unobserved in front her. Beautiful young people being unhealthily intense and judgemental about their teenage relationships, soaps are nothing more than dramatic stereotypes where thespians perform the imagined lives of people and a culture that only exists in the prejudices of the viewers. I know from watching TV that a popular soap set in the East End is a stylised theatrical representation of what the place might look like if most of the old culture hadn't swanned off elsewhere and most of the new immigrants stayed in their homes. I suspect all of the other soaps are the same 'not quite but slightly' misrepresentation. Oops, thinking about Dave may have accidently caused me to talk like him.

An observer might find it odd but my mother and I tend not to speak very much. We sit in a comfortable silence much of the time. What conversation there is tends to be factual and informative and we rarely, if ever, discuss anything abstract.

She was born into poverty and worked from about the age of three. She collected coal in barrows, small ones I assume, and walked them through the streets to households that had paid her a halfpenny to do so.

Ha'penny coal pushed through dangerous streets for people who should have given her food and shelter and fetched their own bloody coal. That's the pre-war East End in a nutshell. Those rich enough to do so used their relative wealth to abuse the destitute, even the children, although the people doing it would probably be shocked if they knew I considered them abusers. They most likely felt that they were helping a poor child earn her way, sod her education and innocence.

I suspect that some things that we do now will be looked on in horror by future generations. I don't know what, maybe the way we treat our elderly. The way we deprive them of liberty when they get confused, consign them to horrid practical care in segregated homes, subdue them with drugs and prevent them from doing the things they want. And why? Because they may be a danger to themselves with their forgetfulness and confusion. By that reasoning we all have moments when authority would cheerfully deprive us of our freedom. Just who do they think they are to make this judgement?

I've visited a few of these homes for various reasons. They are like something described by Dante, filled with the hopeless and soulless remnants of once lively people, now drugged to ensure compliance and forcefully regimented to a timetable that suits the home's management. Large halls filled with the silent dazed and dribbling living dead overseen by the poorly paid and minimally skilled making profit for a disguised and uncaring business. I know that I for one would rather die a few years earlier than live a pointless existence devoid of all that makes life worth living. I have no intention of spending my final years sitting in a chair drooling.

I look on old peoples' homes as mainly, though not always, benign concentration camps for those so old or frail they'd slow the frenetic world they now obstruct. Part of me is outraged by the contempt in which we hold the elders. I've expressed this view to people who work within the homes and invariably they have stated that they are just doing a job in a role sanctioned by law. Who knows what the future might make of us? Ways of thinking change and nothing is good or bad forever: The ancient Egyptians practiced incest and until relatively recently Europe considered slavery OK.

The influence of her formative years meant that my mother grew up believing that the strata of society one was born into was immutable; the rich man in his castle, the poor man at his gate and all of that infuriating rubbish. The result was that she felt that as long as you followed the rules made by an unequal and advantaged but benevolent ruling class, did not cause trouble and worked hard then one's life would always be tolerable and well fed.

I hold views that are the opposite of that and it's difficult for us to discuss them. She holds her views self-evident and in a way it's cruel to challenge them. Her views and approach to life enabled her to survive and even prosper slightly as a grateful recipient of largesse in a world she was unable to challenge.

She and my father provided me with food, clothing, shelter and a sense of security, I witnessed their struggle to do these things. My father was nearly always working and yet there was never quite enough money. I vividly recall my mother weeping because she had accidently burnt a ten-shilling note, so tired that in her stupor she threw it into the open fire with some rubbish. We lived on bread and dripping for three days after that. These things motivated me and the sense of security they worked so hard to achieve for me provided the confidence not to fear the rulers.

Therefore, I hold that one must fight for oneself, that the ruling classes are mostly self-serving crooks, and bending rules and making trouble when necessary are essential prerequisites of one's own independence. Oh yes, I almost forgot; reliance on the state limits one's freedom and creates dependence on people who do not necessarily have your best interests at heart. Every penny of benefit granted by the authorities is payment for the surrender of a slice of one's own liberty.

That's why we never really discussed politics or any other abstract matter. Another reason is that I have inadvertently progressed to post grad academically and she spent about five years in school before work, class expectations and millions of tons of bombs interrupted her education. Although she made herself sufficiently literate, it resulted in a limited spoken vocabulary which always inhibits expression. I have often wished we'd talked in more depth.

In conversation with her I would always revert to my childhood tongue, it is a variant of standard English that in many respects is like a creole. I'm referring to the real London voice, not the ridiculous mockney favoured of some TV celebrities and shows. Like all such localised languages, it depends on the culture where it resides and that culture is more or less in accordance with my mother's views, except that it's acceptable to cheat and steal a bit. I would no more use complicated language to my mother than I would write 'fuck' in an academic essay. In actual fact, I have written 'fuck' in an academic essay but it was relevant, honest.

I'm glad the culture was effectively dismantled by the blitz and subsequent Government policy. The traditional working class culture was shit and that's all there is to it.

None of this should suggest my mother was stupid. She had an enquiring intelligence that often failed to properly express itself because she lacked the verbal tools and the educated confidence to do so. When I was very young she would tell me bedtime stories she had invented but she never wrote them down.

She should have because her written word was better than her conversational voice. She could write coherently and express ideas she would not or could not refer to when talking. She read endlessly and this enabled her to write excellently using a decent and varied vocabulary, somehow she never made that small step from written Standard English of a good quality to the spoken version. Her deeper thoughts poured out onto paper. I suspect she resented the world that had beaten her into the views she held but feared to voice it.

So it was that we sat with long silences, my hand resting on hers, the quiet occasionally interrupted by family gossip updates and comments on local matters. This for about two hours. Her hands were fascinating; she was ambidextrous, although she favoured the left, quite literally sinister by preference I once told her but she didn't appreciate the joke.

Creepily, if the mood took her, she could write two separate narratives, one with each hand, at the same time. Being a little superstitious, this frightened her a tiny bit and she didn't do it very often. Being completely devoid of all superstition I was and am fascinated by it. I'm sure it's a known condition and it is on my very long list of things I'll research if and when I get the time. My daughter is left handed, although I'm right handed.

When she was small I saw her write a name label with one hand while drawing a decent sketch of a cat with the other. My heart melted a bit to see mum's genes forging their slightly supernatural way into the future.

My mother and father met just before the war. My mother was a precocious ten year old and he was a grown up fourteen. By the end of the second world war she was in her mid teens and he was nearly twenty. They had both grown up fast, he in the blitz and on the battlefields of France and Germany and she in the blitz and the home front. It defined them as people.

My mother was prone to some depression, never treated because this was in the days when you were expected to pull yourself together and get on with it. My father was intermittently prone to rages that he quickly controlled but when I was a child he sometimes beat me. This occasional violence stopped when I was about fifteen, largely because I hit him back. When I did, he looked at me for a few seconds as a small red trickle ran from his nose.

"Not like that," he said, wiping his nose with the back of his hand. "Get your body weight behind it and follow through, that should have knocked me down."

I don't think he realised how the violence affected me, to this day I hate violence and at the same time will engage in it without hesitation if I'm pushed into it.

He is not a bad man and insofar as he requires my forgiveness for the occasional beating, I happily give it. There was never any permanent harm and it was never prolonged. His life had taught him to respond with force when he considered it necessary. He is a tough one, there's no doubt about that. When he was seventy five he was mugged by a twenty five year old druggie. The mugger wasn't exactly a physical powerhouse but he wasn't shockingly weedy either. My dad knocked him out with a crashing blow to the jaw. Formative life in the East End and a youth spent in war will make you like that.

A few years ago there was some sort of problem with his pension payments and I went with him to the relevant office to sort out the matter. Apparently payments had stopped without explanation. I was just there as moral support really, dad doesn't need anybody to fight his battles for him. If anything, part of my role was to ensure he didn't over react or become too aggressive. The prefrontal cortex deteriorates with age and so self restraint becomes less effective.

It is said that you never know anybody until you've seen them drunk. In vino veritas, as they say. That's because alcohol inhibits the behaviour control function of the prefrontal cortex. Old people are like sober drunks, they say what they mean and don't fear the consequences. They release their real selves. My dad was entitled to his pension and he would make sure he got it.

We sat in a council office in Stratford. The décor was 1980s bad taste wilted with age. The yellowing strip lighting was in urgent need of replacement and the whole place clearly advertised the financial difficulties of the local authority.

It was never clear to me why the pension office was in the local council building, my dad just accepted it. It transpired that a computer glitch had cancelled his payments and he was only there to confirm his identity and then the payments would resume, with interest on the money not yet paid. Fight over, I thought. The young man dealing with him obviously thought so as well. We were both wrong.

Taz Khan was a very clean cut, clean shaven, well dressed and intelligent young man. My guess would be that he was third or fourth generation British of Pakistani origin. His real name was Imtiaz but he made a point of telling us he preferred to be called Taz. In his home counties accent he explained that he was tasked with verifying identities in order to permit the payments to resume. The modern world is far more intrusive than the world of previous generations. Loss of national isolation in Britain has forced greater scrutiny of individuals to prevent improper claims and criminal intent.

"I just need to confirm who you are. Just need to check that you are who you say you are, there's no problem," said Taz brightly. He played with a new looking Montegrappa pen.

"I am me, there you are, it's confirmed," my dad responded and as far as he was concerned that was good enough.

"I just need to prove it." Good natured and used to people, Mr Khan would do well in life, I suspected.

My dad shifted uncomfortably in his chair. "Why? I am me. I've always been me and plan to be me forever. Just give me my money."

I glanced at Taz, offering a silent apology with my eye contact. Humans are very good at subtle and unspoken communication and Taz's glance back at me silently said,

'It's OK, I'm used to awkward old sods.' He leaned a bit on the desk and said to my dad, "I'm sure we can do this quickly, may I have your passport please?"

My dad leaned towards him and stated, "I don't have one. Never have had one and never will."

"A photo driving licence, perhaps?"

"I don't drive. Gave it up."

With several failed attempts to locate identifying documents of any sort, Taz was beginning to show early signs of being worn down. After what seemed ages of negotiation but in reality was only about twenty minutes, we arrived at a way around this; I would offer my passport, my birth certificate and make a written statement to confirm my dad's identity. Dad even objected to this but I told him to shut up.

A now slightly hassled looking Taz regarded my dad. Visibly out of sorts but retaining his polite and gentle demeanour he commented, "I can't believe you don't have any documents. You must have had something at some time, everybody needs a passport at some time. Haven't you ever been abroad?"

"Of course", said my dad. I knew Taz was probably going to wish he hadn't asked. My dad looked him straight in the eyes. "I've been to France and Germany."

"Well, you must have had something with you or they wouldn't have let you cross the border," said Taz as he walked into dad's trap.

"I did, I had a rifle and they couldn't stop me."

Taz looked defeated, he slowly placed his expensive pen on the desk. "Anywhere else?" He said, sounding like a man requesting the coup de grace.

"Canada," my dad barked. "Before you ask, no I didn't. We were an army collecting war prisoners to return them to Germany. We were within our Empire and didn't need anything."

As we left I shook Taz's hand and verbally apologised. Taz smiled brightly as he dismissed the apology as unnecessary. "I love these old guys. They don't take crap from anybody. No wonder they won the war."

∞ ∞ ∞ ∞

Dad's war

Edward James Aitchsmith worked the bolt on his Lee Enfield and knelt on one knee, the grounded leg at an acute angle inward to provide stability. The grey shirt of the German prisoner stood out against the green grass as he fled across the field. Other prisoners in the now stationary train were shouting. The rest of the British soldiers unshouldered their weapons and made clear to the prisoners the consequences of resistance or any attempt to assist the escaper.

"Oh shit," Ed whispered to himself. "The bloody war's over. The man's scared. Oh shit, no."

He took careful aim. He was a good shot and at this distance it would be an easy kill. Then he just moved the rifle slightly to the left, barely perceptible but enough. He fired. The round went wide. Ed then tried to work the bolt to reload but decided it was temporarily jammed. As he tried to clear it the prisoner reached the far hedge. He turned, looked at Ed and waved. Then he disappeared into the world behind the hedge. There was no pursuit. Ed cleared the bolt, all was well now. He smiled.

As he rejoined the train another of the soldiers smiled at him and nodded. The train guard officer approached.

"Shame your bolt jammed, Aitchsmith," he said quietly. "Is it clear now?"

"Yes sir. It's fine now. Just stuck for a moment, that's all."

"Well done, lad," the officer said. "Well done, there's been enough killing I think."

As Ed went to take up his on-board position at the carriage end, a German prisoner tapped his arm. Ed looked down and the German proffered a small bar of chocolate. Ed declined, the man might need that later. The German nodded and smiled at Ed.

"You're a good man, Tommy," called another prisoner in English. Others murmured agreement.

"Enough," called the officer loudly. "It's over. Your man made a lucky escape, understand?"

Everyone nodded their agreement. A few chuckled conspiratorially.

This repatriation transport came from Canada. Some of them had been captured early in the war, others later. Ed's company had been sent to collect them. They boarded the train at St. Malo after a slow Atlantic crossing, as if the ship's crew were seeking to prolong enjoyment of the now safe and U boat free sailing. It was an easy job to guard these men. The Germans were going home and the war was over, there was no reason for them to cause trouble.

As the train crossed France the happy chatter subsided

a little. Some damage to villages and towns along with the detritus of battle in some of the fields focussed the passengers. Burnt out tanks and trucks, crashed planes and abandoned big guns. No bodies, though; the dead had been removed soon after the fighting moved east towards Germany.

When the train crossed the Rhine and passed through German towns the prisoners fell silent. They whispered to each other and were visibly shocked at the extent of the damage. Whole towns completely flattened, they hadn't been prepared for that.

There was an overnight stop about twenty miles beyond the German border. Trains wear quickly and engineers needed to check it to make it safe for the rest of the journey. As wheel tappers and link checkers did their thing, the soldiers were briefed.

"It's been straight forward so far," began the briefing officer. "Now it gets less routine and some of the prisoners will change their so far easy attitude. We will have to be more alert. It has been decided that those prisoners who come from what is now the Soviet sector will be handed over to the Russians, God help them. The prisoners will realise this soon. Be aware of what this will mean to them. The Germans murdered and raped their way deep into Russia. The Russians have repaid them in kind, with bells on and then some more. I would rather die than be subjected to Russian rage. They may feel the same, they may feel they have nothing to lose so be alert. We unload all of those going to the British, French or American zones when we reach Cologne, or rather the pile of rubble that used to be the great Cologne. They will be given the means to make their own way home. We guard the remaining poor sods until we hand them over to the Russians. That's it. I'm sorry we have to do this."

"I hate them," another soldier said to Ed. "You saw Bergen-Belsen as well as I did, more than I did. You saw what they did, those bastards. I think we should kill 'em all. They don't deserve to exist."

"Then what?" asked Ed gently. "Then we'd be just like them, like the Russians. We've got to be better than that or this was all pointless, they have to become better than that and so does everybody else. This can't be the future; I don't think anybody can survive another war like this. I want to have kids one day. I'll knock sense and learning into them but I don't want them to have to do this, not like we did and like our dads did. Enough's enough."

It's hard to say when Edward Aitchsmith's war began. In one sense it was the day he was born, although the actual war was fourteen years away. Three things of relevance to him happened in 1925: He was born, his father had some sliver of lung removed and Adolf Hitler published his rambling Mein Kampf.

His father would attend hospital every year from now on, each time a little more lung would be removed, the gas induced creeping necrosis in his alveoli a debilitating memento from the first war.

Adolf's book, which Ed read later in life, he considered to be a remarkable piece of work. It was like the recorded thoughts of a self opinionated temper prone megalomaniac. An intelligent autodidact suffering from little formal education. The misreasoned struggle of the unguided to guide others. In a different place and time, with a different history, he might have been a good or even a great man.

Ed's early life was happy and not as difficult as many in the area where he lived. His home in Cartwright Street, near the Tower of London, just by where Cable Street meets the Royal Mint roads, was filled with six brothers and four sisters, all were older and most earned a good wage. His father earned well as a manager in the local gas works. His mother took in laundry and maintained the home. His was a relatively cash rich household. He was always clothed, never hungry and mainly warm.

With so many siblings in one house there was often minor conflict. His dad would end it with his fists when necessary but mostly it wasn't. His brothers all had some kind of military history, as did his dad. As a small child he could overhear them talking about their experiences as they got drunk. He envied them their wars, this is the common error of young boys. So often they continue the error into manhood.

When he was about eleven he encountered a hint that trouble brewed in the background of his world. A breathless friend of one of this brothers called at the door.

"They're nearly here," he said. "The Blackshirts are marching. My dad and the rabbi said I should go home but I'm going to join in the fight. Come with me."

The friend was Jewish, physically strong and one

of several local Jewish boys intending to join with the socialist agitators in Cable Street, who planned to oppose Oswald Mosley's ridiculously strutting but dangerous uniformed members of the British Union of Fascists.

Every one of Ed's brothers in the house declared they would go with him. They all left and dashed up the road. A few of them took cudgels and sticks from a cupboard near the front door.

"I'm going, too," declared Ed.

"No you're not," said his dad and lightly slapped him around the head. "You will stay here with your mother. These are bad people coming, they've nearly taken over some other countries, the fools will find we're not as easily intimidated and nowhere near as gullible."

As Ed sat with his mum, his dad went to the cupboard and took out what looked like a big shillelagh. He then strode out of the house towards Cable Street.

Because the incident touched him personally, Ed developed an awareness of the tempest that was building. He started to read about the Spanish war and how dictators were seizing control across Europe.

In his local area he started to observe things that before he hadn't thought about. The local docks often hosted ships flying Swastikas. He went to the berths and watched to see what they were doing.

Men from the ships would push large carts to Manny Cohen's yard. Manny was the local scrap metal dealer and he was making good money from the trade. The interaction between him and the Germans seemed easy and friendly. They paid in cash and took large quantities of metal back to the ships. When the German sailors left the yard other Jewish men went to it and were arguing with Manny.

Manny noticed Ed was watching and went over to him. He handed him a pound note and said, "Here you go, Ed. Buy your mum a present." Manny was known locally for his generosity towards the kids. Ed was delighted, a pound was an enormous sum.

So it was that when, in 1939, Britain declared war on Germany, Ed understood. His brothers either returned to their recent regiments or, if not on reserve, re-joined. Ed was not evacuated because his parents resisted it at this time. Ed waited in anticipation as nothing appeared to happen for months. Then it did.

The speed of the allied collapse shocked Ed's dad. As the country scrambled to rescue its army, Ed was told he would be evacuated now. His mum took him to a train that transported a lot of late evacuees to Weston-super-Mare where, in theory, Ed would be safe. Since he was capable of independent living he was put up in a youth hostel. There he stayed for just a few days.

As the Luftwaffe started to raid RAF airfields, Ed decided he could safely return to London. Even if the Germans turned on the cities he would rather be with his mum and dad than hide by the seaside.

He stole a bicycle he found leaning against a wall and set off for London. The bike was a single geared basket fronted delivery bike and hard work to ride. He didn't know the way and just headed roughly east.

He'd been pedalling for hours and it was dark and chilly, he thought it was probably about 2 a.m. He was enjoying the relief of a down hill run into a village of thatched cottages and a small green. There was a slight night mist and he thought he saw something in the middle of the road in the village as he plummeted towards it.

The thing he saw was a huge rotund policeman. The officer just stood there as Ed came to a squeaky braked halt in front of him.

"Hello lad," said the officer in a thick Somerset accent.

"Hello sir," gulped Ed.

"Now, my boy, why might you be rushing through here at this hour, you're not a secret nasty Nazi come to enslave us, are you?"

"No," said Ed and the policeman smiled. His big broad face seemed friendly. A wide scar on his left cheek and impacted knuckles on both hands suggested that he could be less friendly when called upon.

"Weston called me earlier, something about a stolen bike. Is that you, is this it?"

"Yes sir. I'm sorry." Ed looked crestfallen.

"Come over here lad," instructed the law. The policeman went to a rose bush by the side of the road. He parted the foliage and reached in. When he pulled out his arm he was holding a phone handset, the wire reaching back into the bush. He smiled as Ed laughed. "I have him," he reported into the phone. "In the morning? Good enough."

In general, evacuation from London was ineffective. The working class rough-living kids did not fit well with the lower middle class families hosting them. Their lack of petit bourgeois etiquette caused friction with the aspirational emulation of their betters by the hard working white collar middle managers.

Already the wealthier working classes were referring to themselves as middle class and slowly filling the social gaps left by the carnage of the first war that forced the land owning and long standing middle classes towards extinction. They tried to act the part and this conflicted with the baseness of these not yet prosperous snot nosed gamins.

In contrast, it is said that the London kids fortunate enough to be lodged with the real country estate owning middle classes, or even the aristocracy, fared well. The securely wealthy felt no social threat from these blunt straight forward urchins and the two groups enjoyed each other's open and unpretentious presence. The first war, with its mixing of individuals, had given birth to a mutual respect in the two peoples even though it challenged the older assumptions of leadership and service.

Ed's captor lived in one of the few occupations that permitted discourse with all social levels while providing some social mobility for the post holder. The policeman and his family sympathised and cared about the determined young criminal. Ed was fed, allowed to wash and given a bed in the family home. Mrs Policeman made Ed a packed lunch for the following morning. The lockable cell at the village police house remained unused.

The car from Weston-super-Mare arrived early the following morning. Ed and his friendly jailers said their goodbyes and he started the journey back to the town.

He wondered how the bicycle owner would retrieve it and felt guilty.

The two police officers in the car, a man and a woman, were older than he thought they would be. Most young police officers had been transferred to the armed forces and those retirees still physically fit enough to police had taken up their former jobs. He sat in the back of the car for a slow and almost silent journey. They had very little to say to him but he gained the impression that criminals under escort were normally more harshly treated.

He'd expected to be taken to the police station but was instead delivered directly to the magistrate's court. He was placed in a cell below the building.

"Don't fret, son," said the old man closing the door on him. "It won't be for long. You'll see the beak soon. Don't be frightened, just tell him what you did and why you did it."

Ed was astonished to see his dad in the courtroom. The intimidating formal nature of the magistrate's court declared its power and influence. The magistrate, an old grey haired man with half moon glasses, spoke to his clerk sitting at a desk in front of him. The magistrate was the personification of the Crown's regal justice, therefore he sat higher than anybody else in an age worn dark leather chair behind an imposing oak podium. He had to lean forward over it to address his clerk.

Ed was led to the dock, a short walled enclosure with symbolic short spiked bars on the front and sides. He watched carefully and was intrigued to see the beak smile at his dad. The clerk, a thin ferret faced man, read out the formal charge and asked Ed how he pleaded.

"I'm guilty," admitted Ed.

His hair was ruffled by the large policeman who had arrested him, as he walked past to take the witness box. The officer explained the theft and subsequent capture of the thief to the court.

"Well then, young Aitchsmith," the magistrate boomed, his voice full of a vitality that belied his obvious age. "Is that how it happened?"

"Yes," whispered Ed.

"Speak up boy," the main man peered over his half moons.

"Yes," Ed practically shouted.

"As if we don't have enough problems, what with that half mad little upstart trying to murder us all. Why lad, why did you do this?"

"I'm sorry, sir. It's my mum, she needs me back. I didn't know how to get to London. I have to be with my mum."

"Lad," said the magistrate, his voice still filling the room but without the implied threat that normally accompanies magisterial pronouncements. "Lad, I've spoken with your father, a man who gave much in the first war battles and who this court therefore respects. He is willing to pay restitution to the bicycle owner who is willing to accept it and not pursue you in the courts. You should be grateful. Your motives were fine but your plan was criminal. I take into account the exceptional nature of the times in which we live. I also note that the police state that you did not try to hide, flee or deny your

38

wrongdoing. It may seem a small thing, this theft of a bicycle, but it is for the rule of law that brave men are currently laying down their lives. Therefore, I owe it to them to apply the law in your case and not be swayed by the sympathy I feel for you."

"I'm sorry, sir. I should go to prison." Ed's downcast head and dejected looks provoked a small snigger from the public gallery that was quieted by a single glance from the magistrate.

"You will not, young man. If this war lasts, and God help us I think it will, you'll be fighting in it before the end. I don't want to burden you with prison before you face your future. No lad, these are exceptional times and you shall have an exceptional punishment. First, you shall paint the shopfront of Gardner's Groceries, on the sea front, for it was his bicycle you stole. You will paint according to Mr Gardner's instructions. When he is satisfied that you have done a competent job, you shall face the second part of your punishment. You shall reside with the arresting officer's family for three weeks. During that time you will complete such gardening and odd job work around the village as directed by the constable. Your father will then collect you and return you to London. You now have a criminal record, let this be the only entry on it in your life. Should you fail to complete these tasks you will come back to see me and I shall be less generous. Go now, lad. May you survive this terrible time and may God see fit to bless you with a long and fruitful life."

Ed enjoyed staying with the police family. He thanked them when he left and promised he'd write from time to time. The big tough policeman sounded a little choked up as he said goodbye and his wife gave Ed a stifling hug.

He barely had time to settle into London again when the Luftwaffe changed its focus onto the capital. His dad gave many possible reasons, such as we bombed Berlin first in response to one rogue bomb on London, or the airfields wouldn't give in so they chose an easier target. Whatever the reason, the German air force turned its full and massive capability onto the ancient city.

Too young to either enlist or work with the home guard, Ed was sent to help operate a search light on the roof of the Tate and Lyle factory in North Woolwich. The enemy squadrons would follow the Thames from the estuary to the Royal docks and then star burst across London to deliver their blows. RAF fighters harassed them mercilessly, the German fighter escorts rarely made it this far. Overhead was a real kill fest. The Germans rained explosives onto the people below. The British fighters tore at the bombers from above. The Germans didn't hang about over London. Most of them were ripped up by the RAF.

It seemed that endless waves of bombers swooped, bombed, fled, swooped, bombed, fled. A darkened London was illuminated by blast flashes and incendiaries, the sounds of the city replaced by the drone of aircraft engines and explosions with a background orchestra of fire service and ambulance bells and the crackling of combustion. The air filled with the stench of smoke and the almond smell of high explosives. The horizon glowed orange from both air and ground. Overhead the dakka-dakka dakka-dakka of fighters smashing rounds into the bombers provided the beat to this nightly sonata, accompanied by the slow and steady bamp bamp bamp of ground based anti-aircraft fire.

Once in a while an enemy plane would be trapped in the searchlights. When this happened all of the other search lights would surround the beam illuminating the target, this way it could not quickly hide by changing direction. Then ground based heavy guns would thump away at it. The airburst shells around it threw heavy shrapnel into the aircraft. When caught this way it was never long before the crew bailed out. As they parachuted down the sound of light arms being fired at the men was almost but not quite hidden by the other noise. Mainly though, the job of the search lights and ground guns was just to reassure the people that we were fighting back. They rarely took down more than one or two planes a night.

"I think they should stop shooting at the crews as they bail out," he said to his dad. "It's not fair, it's like shooting a wounded man."

"I know what you mean," replied his father. "But, they came here to kill us. Me, you, your mum, your sisters. As far as I'm concerned we should kill them all. They came here to do this evil and they should pay the price. I would even shoot them when they reach the ground. They came to murder us, let them suffer the ultimate consequence for that."

Ed's dad's lungs finally gave out and he died during an operation at the height of the blitz. It was conducted by candle light with dust filling the room as it was shaken from the walls by the blasts. At this point the bombing was unrelenting and there was no other choice but to work in those conditions. His body was moved to a rapidly filling mortuary and he was buried in a mass grave in the basement foundations of a large bombed out rubber factory. The battering from the Germans was destroying more than just buildings and people; it was also impacting on the normal civilised functions of the city. Mass graves went unmarked and unrecorded, known only to the locals and their families.

Four years into the war Ed was called on to enlist. He was given a nominal five year enlistment but told that in reality it was for as long as he was needed. By coincidence he was sent to a military camp at Weston-super-Mare where he was trained and prepared for war. He took the opportunity to revisit the policeman who was delighted to see him.

"Come down the Wheat Sheaf and have a pint with me," suggested the policeman.

"I can't," laughed Ed, "I'm not twenty one yet."

"Sod that," said the mighty lawman, "as long as you're in uniform, nobody cares anymore. If you're fighting then you are twenty one. Beside, you'll be with me and I decide who gets in trouble around here and it won't be you or the publican."

The two men staggered back many hours later. They both found it riotously funny when the policeman pointed out that the bike Ed had stolen was now rusty and useless and still in the policeman's garden.

After a year or so, Ed was getting bored with being rested at the base. He wanted some action now. The boredom was relieved for a while when his brother, Albert, was also posted to the same camp. Ed had been spending his wages on providing clothing and gifts for his sisters, all still lodged in the town. Now Albert helped that process. They didn't stay in camp for much longer and were separated by deployments within a few months.

Nobody in the camp really knew what they were waiting for. There were still some limited exchanges in North Africa, the Japanese were pretty much well entrenched on a thousand islands around the western pacific rim and the southern European theatres didn't show much promise towards stunning the Reich into submission.

We're going to India. We're going to Australia. We're going to Italy. We're going to Gib. We're going to South America. We're going to Norway. There were as many rumours as there were places. From time to time the troops from camp were used to search the coastline or chase down some bailed out enemy airman, phantom or suspected saboteur. Still they trained and still they saw equipment being stockpiled before it was trucked away only for the stockpiling to start again.

One morning Albert's regiment was gone. The tents and barrack sheds were empty and much of the armour had disappeared. Nobody had seen them leave so it must have been done quietly.

Ed's battalion was briefed by a stern looking staff officer. "Men, we move on in the morning. I don't know where. I am able to tell you that you have an essential role in achieving our victory and you will be informed of your task when we arrive or shortly before. I can tell you we will be put on a ship at Southampton. Nobody may leave the camp before we deploy."

The buzz spread around the soldiers. This was it, this was what they'd been waiting for. Suddenly it all felt a little less exciting and a great deal more worrying.

The following day they took ship at Southampton. After the hustle and hassle of boarding an entire battalion and their transport, the grey painted vessel sailed. The ship cut its way through all of three miles of calm water and docked at Cowes on the Isle of Wight where they disembarked.

"Excellent," said another soldier to Ed. "We're going to the bloody Isle of bloody Wight to bloody fight the bloody squirrels and bloody subdue the bloody local girls in the bloody pub every bloody night."

"Yep," responded Ed. "Truly a bloody engagement."

"Bloody Hell," said another. "Bloody bloody bloody." Then he walked away laughing.

The task, it transpired, was to manually heave and shove a long flexible nine inch diameter pipeline into place on the south east side of the island. Pluto, somebody called it; Pipeline Under the Ocean. They struggled to fit this end of the pipe from Shanklin, down a dangerously steep gully everybody kept calling a chine, whatever one of them is. At the sea front they stopped. When another pipe was laid behind a ship crossing the sea it would be joined to this pipe.

"I know it's not exactly what you expected, men." The officer addressed the assembled troops. "It's done now, well done, and essential. Down this pipe we will pump the fuel needed on the French beaches." There was an audible collective gasp and a few isolated ripples of applause. "Yes, that's right, the French beaches. Hundreds of miles to Normandy. While you've been working to do this, the first wave hit the German Atlantic Wall and it fell down." Cheers. "The second wave hit the beaches and pushed inland." More cheers. "The third wave recently landed and will launch an assault in several different directions, the enemy is crumbling." Loud cheers. "You ship out within hours, the voyage is long enough for you to wash and feed on board. You are the fifth wave, the fourth is currently landing, and you will be dropped, shipped, dragged or driven to strategic positions behind the enemy lines to disrupt their defence." Silence.

The memory of the first war loomed large and the assorted allies all expressed anxiety at any likely return to trench based attrition. To this end, the fifth wave would prevent the Germans from digging in and keep the invasion mobile. Already the Americans were bogged down by thick intertwined and impenetrable hedges in the Norman countryside. This in addition to major losses on landing.

The common British view of the American soldier as an overpaid preener very quickly changed. Their courage and tenacity on the beaches and in the fields earned them the eternal respect and compassion of every soldier, even the Germans. They paid for their new reputation with blood and vile death and there was consensus that nobody else could have done it.

Ed was one of five men in a small army truck, which was itself one of five. The briefing gave their orders as… skim along the coast as far as far as you can, Calais preferred, and disrupt German attempts to establish a defensive line.

"Sir, doesn't the enemy shore defence stretch along the entire coast?" Asked Ed.

"Yes," the officer confirmed. "Don't worry, it's mainly unmanned. The enemy is massing east of Calais to regroup and defend. He is already throwing armour at Caen to disrupt us. You are several tens of small mobile units that will disrupt his retreat. Don't engage a fortified defended position but other than that, mess him up, keep him panicking. I'll tell you a secret about Jerry; he's great in attack but gives up in defence if you hit him hard enough."

"Are you sure?" questioned Ed.

"I've met them before," spoke another soldier. "They're the hardest, toughest, most committed and best soldiers you can imagine. They'll fight to the last most of the time."

The trucks soon lost contact with each other. Lots of small mobile offensive units prompted the enemy to create lots of small mobile defensive units to counter them. Along the north coast the war became a series of skirmishes between small mobile groups. One such caused the trucks to split up and Ed's vehicle pressed on alone in what they all hoped was east. The skirmish had been nothing more than a few exchanged shots but that had been enough for both sides to scuttle off.

They'd been rolling along without incident for over an hour. The occasional Frenchie on the roadside did not supply exactly the euphoric greeting they'd been warned about.

"They will be ecstatic," the briefing officer had said. "They'll offer you wine, food and their daughters. Don't get drunk, leave them the food 'cos they need it and don't touch the daughters. Things will look a lot different in a few months when she's got a big belly and a couple of angry brothers." That caused some laughter. As it turned out the civilians offered nothing more than curious stares and half hearted waves.

"Can't really blame 'em," said Ed to the driver. "We didn't exactly announce ourselves and if even we don't know who controls this area they probably don't want to commit yet."

One of the others pointed out an apparently abandoned farmhouse near the road.

"We can't just break in," said the driver.

"Yes we can. Look, I thought I saw movement in an upper window. It might be the enemy waiting to ambush us, what with his sneaky shooting back and everything."

The farmhouse was a large three storied characteristically French building. Its marble front steps and large bulging roof declared it a wealthy and genteel abode. It was intact and lacked any sign of abuse. Nonetheless the dirt on the windows and the dead leaves on the steps suggested it was empty.

They forced the door and entered cautiously,

obviously empty places sometimes store a surprise. Not this time though, the small group's armed search revealed nobody. The place was completely intact with wine stocks, food, mainly now corrupted, and working bathrooms and turned down beds, albeit covered with dust sheets.

"I've solved the mystery," said one of the group while they were in the drawing room. From a drawer he held up a small minora, seemingly made of solid gold and expensive it had undoubtedly been missed by whoever removed the occupants, or maybe they just fled.

"Let's hope they ran, let's assume they give their permission for us to use their house." The driver's suggestion was agreed unanimously.

After several days of disrupting the enemy, primarily by means of not seeing them anywhere, they all welcomed the chance to clean some kit and wash some bodies. They all rinsed down their uniforms and went on to enjoy one of the four working bathrooms, the one with a huge shower. They could have used all four rooms but felt safer staying in a group. It didn't matter that there was no hot water, this was luxury to the five tired men.

The sound of an engine complaining as it was forced to work hard across open land interrupted the washing of the five. One went to the window and carefully peered out.

"Oh blimey me, blimey," he exclaimed. "It's Jerry and he's seen our truck. There's about five or six of them and they're deploying to the bund at the side of the house."

"Move, lads, move, move," instructed the driver. "We've got to get to the opposing bund before Jerry fully deploys or we're lost. We can't fight from here, we need to get the house between us."

Generally speaking, five naked men don't make an effective fighting force. The group gathered up their wet uniforms from the chairs and doors where they'd hung them. Some wrapped towels around their waists, one donned a flowery dressing gown he'd found on a door hook and another opened a wardrobe and pulled a pretty pink jumper over his head.

They rushed out of a side door looking like the cross dressing section of the invasion force. Some bare foot, some in ladies' slippers, a variety of clothing grabbed at random, all female. Clutching their boots, helmets, rifles, webbing and wet uniforms they ran for the bund at the opposite side of the house to the Germans.

They were surprised that no shots were fired at them, then they heard the laughter and one man shouting angrily. It was clear that the enemy extended a professional courtesy by not shooting at the group while they looked so ridiculous. The officer disagreed and was shouting at his men.

The group quickly squeezed themselves into their kit and took up firing positions on the bund. The wet uniforms caused dirt and leaves to adhere, a kind of quick form camouflage. Either side of the house the enemy could be seen in the same position on their bund.

"Reckon you can hit one, Ed?" asked the driver.

"Yep, easy." Ed was the best shot. He worked his bolt to load a round and took long careful aim. He then fired the only shot of this encounter which felled the officer and stilled his coarse aggressive voice. This was his first kill and Ed thought it strange that he felt nothing, not anger, not regret, not elation, not fear, just nothing. "An emptiness of being," he said softly to himself.

They expected a fusillade of shots in reply and sank into the earth to minimise their exposure. Instead the group was taken aback to see a white handkerchief being waved over the opposite bund.

"What?" called out the driver.

"We should talk," called back one of the enemy in good English, the accent uncertain but not German.

"Just one of you, come out into the open, I'll meet you. My blokes will take you down first if this is a trick."

It wasn't a devious trick. The soldiers were Ukrainian seconded into the Wehrmacht. The officer was German SS and they couldn't care less about him being shot.

"It saved us the trouble," said one of them.

They had been Ukrainian army and after their nation's capitulation were taken over to the German side to fight the Russians. They were quite happy to fight Russians.

"Not you, though," explained the spokesman. "The Russians are our natural enemy, but so too are the Germans. We hate the Russians the most so we fought on the side of our lesser enemy. We have no quarrel with you or England or France and we want to surrender to you and be put in the English army to fight the Germans."

The Ukrainians gave up their arms, it was agreed that one of them would retain the officer's Lugar purely for personal defence, they would be returned to the British line, wherever that might be, and any information they had would be gathered. They knew that they might not be able to simply join the British forces but still wanted to go. They also explained that in the initial encounter they would have fired as ordered but were too immobilised with laughter when they saw the British cabaret pile out of the house. The officer was threatening them so they would have shot him anyway if the British hadn't done it first. They thought it a good shot and congratulated whoever fired it.

The group delivered the Ukrainians, who gave some useful information about enemy deployments and reserves. Ed and his team were called before the officer commanding this part of the invasion.

"Well done, men." He had the face of a slashed joint of meat with scars and old rips all over it. "I see you're admiring my handsome good looks. Just the result of Chindit work in Burma. I got called back for this show. The Japs are more ferocious fighters than the Germans but it's all one on one stuff. The Germans fight en masse and present a more intelligent and organised resistance."

"Are we to return to skirmishing, sir?" asked Ed bluntly.

"Do you want to?"

"It doesn't really matter what we want, does it sir? We'll do as asked, whatever it is."

"You know," observed the officer, "I've noticed that it's the hardened men who answer back but obey orders anyway. Did you have much of a scuffle with Jerry while you were out and about?"

"A little, sir. Not as much as you obviously had with

the Nippon wallahs but we swapped a few shots." Ed didn't want to exaggerate their combat experiences. This man was the real thing and had experienced more than any of them would ever have to, hopefully.

"Well, what can we do?" asked the officer rhetorically. "We don't want the Germans to know that we know things the Ukrainians told us, at least not for the next couple of weeks. We can't run the risk of you falling into German hands because they will persuade you to tell them everything you know, don't dispute it, believe me, with your best intentions you will still tell them. They can be very insistent. So, our options: We can shoot you," the group feigned concern, "we can transfer you to the far east," the group showed real concern, "or we can send you back to Blighty to drink and fuck for a fortnight. What do you think?"

"I am quite thirsty," grinned the driver, "and my girl could do with some company that's not either too old or American." The officer laughed.

Ed enjoyed a couple of weeks leave. Most people assumed he'd been wounded during the invasion, even though he was obviously healthy and unharmed. He got a free drink in the Tower Arms and a couple of passers by patted him on the back. He was quite content to play the hero for the public.

London was still under sporadic attack from Nazi vengeance weapons. He didn't like the doodle bugs, underhand little weapons that cowards fire, he thought. He saw a few, one of them glided over the rear garden at roof height while he and his mum were drinking tea. The thing must have been caught on some kind of updraft because even with its engine off it just kept gliding until it was out of sight.

When he reported back to his unit, still based in Weston, he learned that he was to be posted as a driver and run a constant delivery between London and Portsmouth.

"Easy war, no?" asked the colour sergeant who posted him.

"No, but not as hard as some have it." The colour sergeant did not comment. Ed thought that the war must be going well if the army could afford to leave fit men doing this kind of work at home. He kept doing this for a few months.

Eventually he was told to attend a new briefing and that his deployment would change. He and several others, almost a full battalion, were spoken to by a young and inexperienced officer.

"Now then," the young man started, "you may wonder why you chaps have been kept here in England while you want to be over there getting at the Hun."

"The Hun? Really?" The cheeky words from a grizzled old young soldier in the audience. "We are here because the King doesn't want his prettiest boys to get hurt and you need a fuckin' nursemaid." Everybody laughed. The young officer was flustered.

"Pack it in, Jackson," ordered a sergeant in the crowd. "Carry on, sir. I'll thump any other ill disciplined idiot who fails to listen or interrupts."

"Yea, shut up, Jackson, yer old woman." This from somebody further back and caused more laughter.

"You're going to Germany." This announcement from the officer forced immediate silence. "We are already over the Rhine. Jerry has thrown an armoured brigade against the Americans. It initially broke through but the Americans have now turned it back. Our men further north are slicing into German territory, so much so that we've had to slow down. We're taking prisoners by the thousands and word is the enemy are now pouring old men and boys into the mix. We're beating the sods." Cheers. "The invasion of Normandy was an amusing reversal of history." Amusing? Nobody spoke but a few of the men glanced at each other. There was a general silent decision to tolerate the young officer's silliness. "Now we compound that by entering the land of the Saxons, the land from which many of you originate over fourteen hundred years ago. We leave tomorrow night."

Ed realised that despite his couple of actions, he'd had a lucky war so far. As the aircraft landed in Holland he feared that now he might have to really fight. This was the area of the earlier operation Market Garden, that disaster had now been mitigated by the general allied advance. The invasion was now making inroads into Germany and moving into the endgame. The Germans would not easily give up their Fatherland. They were good fighters and capable of turning the tables, even now.

After landing, the troops were drilled to shake of the stiffness of flight and then sent to makeshift camps in the Dutch countryside. They were warned that this area was only recently liberated and it was possible some enemy still lurked. Alert and well armed guards were posted with instructions that each man was to retain full combat kit and ammunition at all times. The following day they were trucked about thirty miles towards a forest and then told to advance on foot.

They were joined by a small fleet of tanks so that they were now an armoured infantry column pressing into the heart of the enemy's home. The forest was huge and they pressed on for a couple of days, ripping paths through the vegetation without a single sight of the enemy as they advanced into his homeland.

The small German village was very still. People watched from their windows but nobody came out. There was no sign of damage or fighting and the enemy forces had withdrawn from this place just a day ago. This village was not worth a fight in itself and had no strategic value.

Nonetheless, Ed and his battalion moved in battle formation, lines either side of the road, tanks rolling in the centre, advance scouts secured the ground onto which they moved and reported any problems. The sound of a firefight sent all of the soldiers to cover. The officer sent runners to the front and obtained information from the scouts. There was no major problem, a small group of SS had engaged the scouts just beyond the village and were quickly dealt with. Nobody seemed to know why they decided to fight over a packed earth and gravel fork in the road. They soon found out.

An excited scout on a motor cycle came roaring back to the main body. He let his machine fall to the floor and ran to the officer. Ed stood nearby since he'd been told to remain close to the officer in case his dead eye shooting skills were required.

"What is it man? You look like you've seen a ghost."

"Worse than that, sir. I've just seen hundreds of living ghosts."

"What do you mean? Be straight, I can see it's shaken you up but we can't afford emotion. Not here, not now. We need to stay calm."

"The camps, sir. The ones they talk about at home. The ones the papers say exist. The camps the politicians won't talk about. It's true, sir. There's one about half a mile up the road. We've found a camp sir."

The officer purloined a Jeep from somewhere, he drove it himself but ordered Ed to go with him. They raced ahead of the column which would catch them up.

At the gates to the camp stood a German SS officer. Ed started to work his bolt but was stopped by the officer driver. The officer left the Jeep and went to the German. They saluted each other, proper military salute from the German and not the silly schoolboy raised arm of the Masters of the World party.

When the officer returned to the Jeep he explained to Ed. "The German Commandant will stay in command of his men. The German SS troops have left and the only private German soldiers here are in fact Hungarian. You will stay until the column catches up. At that point you will be joined by more men to start sorting out this mess."

"Sir, surely I'm not to take orders from the German?"

"No. He has been told that you are in command. He will manage his men and act on your instructions. They will remain armed for the moment. If the SS officer declines any instruction from you, and I mean any, you are to shoot him. Understand?"

"Yes sir. Sir, did you expect to find this place, is this why we're here?"

"Ask no questions, Aitchsmith my man, and you shall not be lied to."

Ed looked hard at him. "I don't expect to be lied to anyway. I just want to know if this was expected."

"Yes," said the officer, looking at Ed respectfully. "It was. That's why I brought you. I need an intelligent and thoughtful yet ordinary man. I wonder if you know just how rare that is." The officer drove back towards the column. It shouldn't take them too long to mop up the area and then join him.

"What should I do?" asked the German.

"I think you've done enough, don't you? I will wander round. You just carry on being in charge of your men. When I've seen enough I'll let you know."

"There is a great deal of disease here, these Jews have no idea of hygiene and it spreads. Watch out for typhus, a terrible Jewish disease that they can give to people. There's a few Russians here as well, watch out for them..." Ed raised his hand to stop the German. Ed wanted to hit him but decided to do so later, there was no point in testing his theoretical lone authority. He instructed the German not to shoot anybody, not even a Jewish anybody, and started a tour of the camp.

This was a camp of death but not a death camp in the true sense. Nobody was brought here to be killed although thousands died of neglect. There was no gas chamber and no oven. This camp was for holding or transfer. It became permanent by default and murder here, with the exception of individual sadistic acts by guards, was by indifference. Thousands left here for the more proactive Auschwitz and other industrialised extermination camps. It was the lack of ovens here that permitted the evidence of human remains to be documented.

The camp consisted of double perimeter wire, guard towers with spotlights and lines of long wooden huts. It was hard to guess just how many but certainly in excess of fifty.

When he'd been waiting with the Jeep, Ed had seen some thin hunched figures milling about between the huts. They all appeared to be bald, dangerously skinny and wearing tatty striped clothing. He didn't yet have a close look at these people. As he walked towards them most fled into huts but a very few just stood and stared, a stare more like that of a petrified kitten than a curious person.

The first impression was one of order and efficiency. That didn't last for long, as Ed rounded the corner of the first hut he stopped as if stunned. At first his head declined to interpret what his eyes saw. A pile of corpses, malnourished and contorted now decomposing and fouling the air. The miasma of fleshy corruption permeates the scene of war and he hadn't noticed this before. Now it was overpowering. Soulless eyes in large fatless sockets stared stoically at the world. An obscene pile of pathetic skeletal, pale and taut skinned suffering.

"Sir, sir, please, sir…" a small woman clawed at his arm. She was starved meatless and wasted, dressed in ragged striped pyjamas and holding a small bundle wrapped in a dirty white cloth. She looked at him with the defeated unchallenging eyes common to all of the impossibly thin occupants. "She needs milk. Sir, please find her milk." She handed the bundle to Ed and slowly shuffled away, her speed and agility impeded by her starvation.

Ed warily unwrapped the bundle and within it found the body of a baby, the umbilicus ripped open with dried blood around it, nothing remaining of the cord. He guessed the infant had been dead for a couple of days, she probably died shortly after birth. How, in God's name, was a baby born here? He gently placed her on the disgusting pile of carrion and covered the tiny cadaver with the wrapping. Some things, he thought to himself, will haunt you forever. This small girl probably lived for less than a day but Ed would shed the occasional tear for her forever.

He soon discovered that the camp was loosely separated into sections based on the offenders' characteristics. By far the most numerous, of course, were those whose offence was being Jewish. They occupied most of the huts and their terrible nature was advertised by yellow stars on their thin and worn striped pyjama-style uniforms.

Ed's first thought was that it was a Star of David. Later he formed the opinion that it was not, the Nazis were not caring or thoughtful enough to permit a comforting religious and cultural symbol. It was simply two yellow triangles placed over each other as the official mark of JEW, merely part of the strict categorisation of people that marks the fundamental national socialist error, a quality mark to highlight those who differ from Aryan perfection. Or maybe the Nazis though it amusing to use the triangles to form the star, maybe they thought it insulting, who knows? They were crazy.

Various other identification insignia adorned the camp's non Jewish inmates' dress:

Red triangle, political offenders including communists, liberals and freemasons.

Green triangle, traditional dishonest or violent criminals who were often used to supply labour within the camp or to clear the dead.

Purple triangle, other unacceptable religions.

Pink triangle, sexual offenders including homosexuals and those who had sex with forbidden people such as Jews.

Black triangle, the workshy and lazy and if it sported a Z for Zigeuner they were gypsies or fortune tellers.

Ed later discovered that this was all noted in camp records, he thought that these efficient identifying marks and records underlined the insanity of the Nazis. Either they chose to create carefully documented evidence against themselves, or they really thought that these things matter and they intended to deal with the aberrations efficiently with a clear and careful bureaucracy to manage it. Nuts, eh?

As for the people in the striped uniforms, they all had a similar look; defeated, helpless, unfed, unwashed, surrendered, uncared for and uncaring.

He explored the huts, they were all the same. Rows of three tiered wooden surfaces, he hesitated to call them beds, just about large enough for a small person and crammed together to maximise occupancy. Most were still occupied by lost souls, often two or three people pushed tightly together, who observed him without expression; their wasted faces no longer possessed the muscles that enable facial movement, their teeth appeared misleadingly large in shrunken and diseased gums. Most of the people were young and probably strong before this ordeal. There was an absence of children or the elderly.

He found no place for ablutions or toilet for the huts. The huts were built on short brick columns and a glance under one hut revealed the place where human waste was dumped. One of the central huts had a small dribbling standpipe on the side, this appeared to be the sole water source for the inhabitants. Ed tried it and could not increase the water flow beyond a small trickle.

The last hut near the end was different. It was for guards and had a small section set aside for the officer. Here he found stored food, acceptable though not luxurious cots, a wood burning stove and stores of alcohol and cigarettes. A communal shower and lavatory annex provided adequate provision for bodily waste and cleaning. By the door was a rifle rack and ammunition boxes secured by lock and chain.

The Hungarian guards kept out of his way. He didn't unshoulder his rifle once during the exploration. He became aware that other allied soldiers were now in the camp and he walked back to the main gate. The Jeep officer was by his vehicle in conversation with the German officer. The tall German stood imposingly well dressed, though slightly overweight, in his carefully styled and commanding SS uniform. He sported the

Totenkopf skull shining in the centre of his properly cared for cap, the peak of which partially obscured his eyes.

As Ed reached them he unshouldered his rifle and started to work the bolt. The Jeep officer grabbed the weapon and Ed surrendered it to him, he had no intention of brawling with his own officer. He turned to the German and knocked his cap from his head.

"Do something, give me an excuse," growled Ed, his voice breaking just slightly as he stared challengingly into the man's eyes. The German wore a pistol in a fully enclosed leather holster but he did not reach towards it. Instead he clasped both hands in front of him at belt height. He looked at Ed without hate or anger or fear, he just looked blankly as if awaiting whatever was to come, just like the inmates. There he stood without resistance, devoid of both supplication and contrition.

Ed flat handed him across the face. The German continued to stand impassively.

"Come on, you sick cunt, do something." He flat handed him again and then again. The German started to lean to one side and bend forward slightly. Ed started to draw back his fist.

"No, Ed. I'm sorry but no." The officer commanding him to stop had grabbed his arm.

"Sir, you should see…" started Ed, his eyes filling with tears, then he fell to his knees and vomited.

"I'm sorry, Aitchsmith. I left you there alone because I needed a reliable man to report back to me. One capable of explaining what he saw and writing it down. There will be trials, I promise you. They will hang, be satisfied with that. The law must exact justice, not revenge, that's why we're fighting." The officer handed him a warm tea.

They were in a tent that was set up as a command post outside the camp. The armour and most of the infantry had moved on, the Germans were now in full but still fighting retreat. About a hundred men had been left at the camp to document and record the sights. Medics were still arriving. Several prisoners had already died because well meaning soldiers had given them food that their stomachs couldn't handle.

All soldiers were ordered to stop giving them anything unless authorised to do so by medics. The medics first went about supplying preventative medication to the soldiers to minimise infection from the abused souls in the camp. The inmates were being assessed and treated as best as could be done in the circumstances. A contingent of Royal Engineers arrived to dig latrines and install washing facilities.

In the first week one inmate was shot dead by the still armed Hungarian guard. It seems the poor man had wandered outside the now open gate and failed to halt when challenged by the guard. The offending Hungarian was badly beaten by two British soldiers and summarily hanged from a nearby tree. The two soldiers were severely admonished and fined a day's pay for their action. They both said that it was money well spent.

As a result of this incident the Hungarians and the German officer were finally removed in restraints and taken to a secure location to await their eventual fate. Some prisoners complained that the inmates should simply be released. It was explained to them, with apologies, that this was a war zone under martial law and they must stay. Soon after they were relocated to a captured German barracks where they could be better cared for. The allied officer commanding the camp rehabilitation was court martialled for permitting the SS to remain armed for so long.

Photographs of the conditions in which it was found were posted all over the camp. The corpse piles were still there but now covered in quicklime dust to reduce the stink and prevent infection. Every occupant of the local village, every man, woman, child, and even babes in arms, was taken to the camp and made to see what had been done in their name and in which they, by their silence, acquiesced. Each person who was old enough to understand was asked why they had done nothing, said nothing. Every person, including those who supplied goods to the camp, denied knowledge of the crime.

Estimates of the final toll, total victims of murder by neglect of those intended for murder elsewhere, rolled into the tens of thousands. It transpired that this was a remote overflow camp for the main transit camp at Bergen-Belsen and the figure was a relatively small number in comparison to the camps actually intended to take lives.

The civilians were sent away and the entire camp was destroyed by flame thrower, including the corpse piles. A well regarded British American film maker, Alfred Hitchcock, recorded this just as he'd recorded the camp itself.

After the camp was gone, statements taken and

effective systems put in place to help the prisoners, the soldiers who liberated and eventually closed the camp were formed into a special detail to repatriate enemy POWs when the war ended. In the meantime, they were to organise and prepare for the logistical challenge of this operation.

The war ended, the Germans lost all resistance, Germany was partitioned for the convenience of the occupying powers, and the POWs were returned since their physical ability was badly needed to rebuild the shattered country.

When the last of the POWs had been handed to the Russians the unit was instructed to take up camp in West Berlin. Berlin itself was firmly in the Russian sector but agreement had been reached, as a symbolic act, that each power would hold a section of Berlin.

When it became clear that the Russians would treat captured territory as their own empire, relations soured somewhat. They even closed off the supply corridor to West Berlin and the allies came close to fighting each other. Supplies were air lifted in and eventually the whole situation settled down into a decades-long armed truce.

Ed and the other soldiers were pleased not to fight the Russians. After about a year they were returned home and demobbed, with thanks, and required to pay for any equipment they'd lost.

Ed found work as a carpenter and married Margaret Adams. The war and its nasty memories he pushed to the back of his mind, except that once in a rare while he would seek solitude and quietly weep to himself.

They took up residence in east London. There were several German women in the community, war brides brought back by soldiers, and there was never any animosity towards them. Nonetheless, there remained a resentment and anger towards the Germans in perpetuity.

∞ ∞ ∞ ∞

Whenever I visit my mother I'm filled with these nostalgic reveries. So much of my early life was spent as listener for one veteran or another that events were seared into my consciousness. I'd been sitting with her for a couple of hours when she pulled her hand from under mine and placed it on top. We'd been silent for some time.

"Where do we go, Steve? Afterwards I mean, where do we go?" This was deep stuff for us. "When I die will I go somewhere, do you think?"

I looked at her for a few seconds. "I'm not sure, mum. I hope so, I feel that we do but I don't know. I just feel that there must be something else." I was tempted to just spout knowledgeably about heaven, afterlife and anything else that would comfort her. I didn't because she always knows when I'm bullshitting and she'll just say 'BS boy, BS'. Mothers know their sons. I, at least, owed her honesty.

"Do you remember that *X-Files* stuff you always made us watch when we were at Richford Road?" She was referring to the TV programme. *Dr Who* and *Star Trek* were my viewing favourites as a child. I made my poor mum and dad sit through them all. Later I was into the *X-Files*, and the fact I lived elsewhere didn't stop me insisting they should watch it.

"Yes, of course I do," I chuckled.

"I'm like that, I want to believe. Not in stupid aliens, I want to believe in God." There were tears in her eyes. We've hardly even ever discussed politics or anything else and now she's into the big questions. I thought it probably a sign that we were nearing the end.

"You took me to church once or twice, when I was little," I said.

"We would have gone more," she squeezed my hand. "They were a stuck up bunch at All Saints and made us sit at the back because they all had their own special places. I didn't see God in that church, I just saw a bunch of snobs being holier than thou and sticking two fingers up at the sinners. I don't think Jesus would have liked them much."

That made me laugh out loud, which in a geriatric hospice is considered poor etiquette. I glanced around me apologetically. A young, good looking, blonde, white attired female nurse at the central desk grinned and jokingly wagged her finger at me. It was like being admonished by the angels, which almost made me laugh again.

"He was known for his dodgy temper in churches," I said. I'm not sure she understood the reference but she smiled.

My mum sighed, "I hope there's a heaven. I hope somebody will pray for me when I'm gone. I hope that I see my dad there. I hope I meet my mum. I even hope Kim's there."

That surprised me, Kim was my childhood dog. I kissed her hand. "I'll pray for you, I promise. I doubt if dad will understand but I'll do it anyway. I just can't believe that this life is all there is."

She was still hitting her anti pain button every few seconds so I don't really know if I was talking to my mum's real self or some opiate-soaked version of her. She suddenly looked more wide awake.

"What worries me," she said sternly, "is that sign on the bus."

"What sign? What bus?" I said, a bit confused.

She looked alertly at me. "A few years ago the buses had a big sign on the advert strip. It said 'There Probably is NOT a God'."

I remembered that. A few years ago, for some unfathomable reason, a group of vocal atheists funded the bus adverts. There were some senior scientists among them, which is funny given the theological response to the statement. I wondered whether I should give that antithesis to my mum now, would it help her?

There is something mildly absurd about evangelical atheists and at this point I was cross with them for making it harder for my mum to find comfort at her end. I don't give a shit about their fearless search for the truth. They should shut the fuck up, they are upsetting some vulnerable people. See, strong emotion forces the London voice to the surface. It's guttural and filled with glottal stops with not much 'cor blimey guv'nor' and a lot more aggressive and demanding than you'll hear on TV pastiches.

I considered for a moment. "You know, they were

wrong if they thought that the scientific method gave that result."

"Really?" She sounded interested and alert. Maybe she was hoping I could solve her crisis of faith. If so, then she was wrong but I could maybe make her feel a bit better about it.

"There's no real evidence either way," I pontificated. "In the absence of evidence we're just left with the scientific method of enquiry. That works by stating something, the hypothesis, and then trying to prove the opposite, the antithesis. Every time we fail to prove the opposite and thereby form a synthesis, or new hypothesis, we reinforce the first hypothesis so it stands as the probable position. We cannot prove that there is not a God. So, by the scientific method we are left with the first hypothesis that there is a God. Which means that the sign should have read 'There probably is a God' because that's currently the only possible synthesis." I chuckled at my own sophistication. There is a lot of sophistry in discussing religion. Incidentally, that argument is the reason I'm agnostic, I consider it the only valid intellectual position.

"Shut up," said my mum.

This was Dave's fault really because I borrowed this argument from him. I've only ever had one discussion with him about religion and the existence of God. He's very comfortable with agnosticism and even appreciates the atheist position. He has no interest in trying to persuade anybody into the church of Rome and has reservations about the Irish version of the franchise. A most unusual priest is Dave.

I once said to him, "I appreciate the human need to believe in a higher power, a supernatural being, a force to right the wrongs and reward the good. That doesn't mean that it's intellectually sound to believe it."

"Oh no?" challenged Dave. I knew that I was in for one of his slightly tangential but annoyingly sound pronouncements. "In what ways can we validly believe something? We can believe it because it can be shown empirically to be true; I believe in gravity because I can see things fall. We can believe something because it can be shown dialectically; that is by sound reasoned argument. That's where science gets its 'hypothesis, antithesis, synthesis' way of doing things, evolution is a good example of that. If something fails to lend itself to either empiricism or dialecticism, we can then validly adopt it as an article of faith. Physicists do it all the time, the church does it more often. The article of faith stands until it requires amendment due to some dialectic or empirical defeat. I call this 'theology, anti theology, synthology' technique the theolectic approach to faith." Trust Dave to argue that simple belief is intellectually sound and at the same time decline to be limited by language. If you need a new word, just invent one.

After leaving my mother I made my way down to the ground floor. As I walked along the corridors they changed from smooth modern pastel shades on plaster board to old solid bare brick visible behind a not very nice cream and mauve paint job with each colour delineating the lower and upper halves of the wall. Maybe somebody felt that we slow witted visitors couldn't tell up from down. Thus, they identified them for us using the cheapest paint they could find. That old hospital ugliness is common in such buildings, what's wrong with a nice apple white?

I eventually reached the hospice chapel. A small blue robed statue of the Virgin guarded the double wooden doors. Beneath it was a small typed note disclaiming denominism and declaring a multifaith intention. I suppose Jews, Muslims, Hindus, Sikhs etc. could just ignore the suggestion of parthenogenesis if they chose to. Protestants, of course, may just decide it's symbolic and not literal. These are just the kind of things for which people have killed each other in the past, and some still do today. If there is a God, He (Hem?) must be pulling out His or Hem divine hair at the human capacity for conflict over nonsense.

The chapel was empty and I sat at the back. I was not praying, I'm not a regular begging kneeler but nor do I entirely dismiss it. I was just using the relaxing quiet to think about whatever. Just taking it easy, really, seizing the opportunity to recharge my emotional batteries for the journey home. There was a simple wooden desk at the front and no crucifix or other indication of a specific religion. The room still managed to exude that calming presence of the sublime, a numinous ambience common in many places of worship. It was a good place to just rebuild one's coping strength and carry on.

"Oh, shit," exclaimed a soft Irish accent as a notebook was dropped entering the chapel. Bending to recover it was a short stocky man, five six at most but with powerful looking arms and shoulders. He was carrying a pile of files from which the notebook had fallen. The gold crucifix on a chain around his neck dangled free as he stooped. He wiped the notebook on his black shirt, which was not ironed and had a slightly off white dog collar. He hurried past me without noticing.

"Very priest like, Dave," I said.

"Hey, hi Steve. How you? Been up to your mum yet?"

"Yeah, just come down. Just needed to sit for a while."

"Coffee?"

I accepted the offer. He made decent coffee in a pod machine kept in his small back office and I could do with the caffeine support. "I don't think she's got long now. She's talking about things she has never spoken about before. She's looking for some reassurance that death's not the end but she's struggling to convince herself."

"We all do, Steve. At the end we're all looking for some evidence that this fleeting moment of life filled with heartache and weeping makes some kind of sense, that it serves some purpose. She'll go gently when the time comes. I promise there'll be no pain, no suffering. Our doctors are too good for that; I give you my absolute word." He looked earnest, compassionate, worried.

"I know," I told him. "Good coffee, thanks. My dad will be a pain in the arse when it happens. He'll be up here causing Jeez knows what ruckus. I'll try to get him under control."

"No, no, no," Dave laughed. "I can deal with him. He's passionate and he loves her so much. He will need to crash around and shout and curse. It's fine, I'll stay with him and he can take it out on me. If he hits me I'll pretend it hurt. Is he here now?"

I laughed. "No, he'll be up later. He won't hit you but he will be loud and aggressive. It's just his way. He'll curse the God he doesn't believe in and then tell you you're wasting your life doing what you do. I apologise in advance."

"My shoulders are broad." They were, quite literally but that's not what he meant. "So are God's, so don't worry about that."

"I wasn't," I said. "Dad will cope. It will be hard for him, though."

Dave's serious face took over. "We're never truly gone, you know."

"Yeah, I know. In the memories of those who knew you and all that."

"Sloppy." That was his way of telling me off for not thinking clearly. He had to do it a lot. "Everything we do affects somebody else. A mother sings her child a song. Hem goes on to sing it to hem kids and they to theirs. It's in the collective memory and that influence lasts forever. We make somebody happy or sad and they react to somebody else from that position and it's in the collective again. Big things and small things. We are never gone because what we do, what we are, goes on forever."

"I know," I grinned. "I beg forgiveness for my lack of academic care in what I say."

He punched me lightly in the arm, at least he thought it was light. Those great big scar knuckled thumpers almost knocked me off the chair. "Yowl, that hurt."

"Weakling. I know you, you've been in the middle of it in the past. Tough up, you wimp."

I pretended to wallop him in the jaw and we both grinned. "Dave, it always helps to talk with you, thanks." I don't know why but I told him how I felt every time I passed the children's hospice complex. The anger and the rage at the unfairness.

He handed me a tissue, I hadn't realised that my eyes were filling up. He looked more earnest now.

"That even challenges my faith, Steve. There are all sorts of theological arguments to reconcile it with a caring God but I know what you mean. I share it sometimes. Theolectic explanations just seem like word play in the face of such apparent injustice. Sins of the first created man and woman? That's fine in a debate setting but it sounds like bollocks when faced with the reality of a dying six year old. I can't answer that one, I'm afraid. I just share the anger and the discomfort and the hope. It's even worse if you consider the lost possibilities. Not just the poor kids dying now but all pointless deaths."

"What do you mean?"

"Take the wars, just the last two world wars, not even all of them that went before. Did you know that you Brits have invaded over one hundred and seventy countries in your time?"

"I don't know if it's that many," for some reason feeling defensive. "It wasn't me, you know."

Dave laughed at me. "I wasn't blaming you personally. Anyway, the point is that each time, in war, young men die. Mainly young men but lots of women and kids as well. Young people who will not then go on to have children who will have children who will have children, see?"

"Sort of," I said.

"Probably not. Look, just taking British deaths in the last two big wars, and based on the average birth rate for each generation, that's a cumulative total of over twenty five million people who don't exist either because they were killed or never born. Twenty five million missing in this country alone. Europe wide it's over half a billion. Worldwide, God alone knows. There are more Jewish people in New York today than in the whole of Poland yet before the war there were millions of Polish Jews. If we assume three million and use roughly the same calculation for our own missing, that's about fortyish million who should have existed. In that at least the Nazis were successful. The world is different because of all of those deaths and non-lives. Just think about all of the missing people you should be seeing. They are all ghosts now, dead and improperly unborn alike. Don't look for the human idea of fairness, my friend, it isn't there. That's the price we pay for war. That's the price the kids upstairs are paying for being alive. That's the shocking price paid by those who should have been here but aren't." He looked angry and intensely sad.

"Did I say that talking with you helped me feel better? I may have been mistaken," I said lightly.

"You were. Be pissed off about it, Steve. We all need to be pissed off about it, that's how we'll stop it happening again. Millions, billions, of missing worldwide. Every single country: The States, Australia, New Zealand, Canada, West Indies, India, Nepal, Burma, Japan, China,

Germany, Russia, the whole of Europe, on and on and on. There's nowhere that isn't emptier than it should be. They all threw their young people into the meat grinder. Be pissed off." I both admired and was intimidated by his anger.

We chatted some more, just small talk and inconsequential stuff. I told him about the ants at home.

"Tin 'em," he said. I must have looked quizzical because he went on to explain. "Place an empty tin over a nest entrance in a sunny spot. It helps if you block up some of the other entrances. Over time, a week or so, the ants will move their larvae into the warm dark tin. When it's full, take it away and destroy it, burn it or something. The nest will be so weakened that it will either die out, move away or re-establish itself on a much smaller scale. We used to do it all the time in Ireland, when I was small. It really works. Our garden was never under the control of an ant colony. We got colonised by you dicks instead." He grinned.

We exchanged a few meaningless words and then I told him I had to be going. We shook hands, his massive paws easily encompassing my hands which are not small themselves.

"I'll be back soon, probably the day after tomorrow," I informed him.

"I'll see you then, then. I'll phone if anything happens."

"I think it'll probably be over in a week or so," I told him.

"Oh, it's a doctor you are now, is it?"

I headed for the doors. "See you later, you bloody disgrace of a priest"

"Piss off, you English bastard," he laughed.

"Prick," I called back and heard him laugh again. A most remarkable priest and a most remarkable man is Dave.

Visiting my mother always left me thoughtful afterwards. Conversation with Dave always left me pondering what he'd said. This turned the journey home into a kind of slightly absent minded surrealism where I moved through the world but not entirely in it or committed to it. I'm a natural people watcher anyway, that's what made me useful to both the army and the police. Getting into places and observing things was my forte. My usual casual observation of those around me was this time influenced by my few hours in the hospice.

On this occasion I saw them all as survivors. In some way, and against the odds, these people had come to be. Not really against the odds, after all most people survived the wars. But the point, as far as I understood it, was that those killed were the procreating generation. Take that away or minimise its function, then what? Everybody under seventy managed to achieve existence in spite of the mass extinction. Were they the descendants of cowards or tough guys? Were they just lucky? Were they faster, slower, quicker thinking? What qualities make a survivor? Probably all of these and then some more. Cowards seems a bit strong but consider this; the coward has many opportunities to have a child, the brave person may not survive to do so. My wife says I overthink things. Perhaps I'm doing that now.

The journey home was mainly uneventful. Mainly

uneventful is about as good as it gets on London public transport. A city filled with the stressed out, overworked, the barely coping underworked or unemployed, and more than it is sensible to have of untreated mentally ill wanderers is a city where things occur. Mostly those things are entertaining or insignificant, sometimes they are serious enough to be a problem.

This journey threw up its only incident on the underground. Sometimes the tube can be like a packed solid cattle truck. Most days it's reminiscent of a Japanese style push 'em all in commuter nightmare. If you tell Londoners you were on the 7.50 out of Bombay, they will know that you don't mean it was full of Indians, it was packed inhumanely tight and the only way another person could have got on would be to cling to the outside. On this journey it was empty enough that just a few people were standing and there were even a couple of unused seats.

The tube was its usual demographic soup of all ethnicities and cultures. There were even some tourists looking a bit out of place, the way tourists do. Some kind of dispute started to get louder about half way down the carriage. It seemed to be a seated older lady versus a couple of young men strap hanging near her. The woman was dressed in clothing that had obviously been treated carefully so that it would last longer, tidy and clean but beginning to wear slightly.

The two boys, one black and the other white, wore inexpensive suits. One wore an ear stud and they both looked confident and physically fit. Since we were heading into the city, my guess would be that they were junior traders. My experience of public transport is that much of the daytime trouble is caused by well dressed middle aged men. The younger drunks and narcissistic bucks find their place at night.

I don't really know why the middle aged, middle management, middle income angry ones perform during the day. I often suspect that they are the remnants of the barrow boys and hucksters who took over the city trading floors in the eighties. They must have all been busy with usury or fiscal exploitation so the apprentices were apparently having a go.

"Shut the fuck up," one of the boys shouted.

"Go away, you arrogant poorly raised yob," the woman retorted. Next to her a young woman in a cotton light green hijab seemed to be trying to ignore the dispute. Maybe she was just being London or maybe she was just pleased she was being left alone.

The thing about London is that even when everybody seems to be ignoring something, they are not. Every Londoner is aware that once you get involved you have to be prepared to go where the situation takes you. Sometimes that can include blood and rolling around. So, Londoners don't ignore things, they are just each deciding at which point they will interfere and hoping they don't have to. Some might decide they will stay out of it because they have kids with them. Some may decide to just leave and others will decide that at a specific point or event they will get involved.

"You fucking cunt slag," exclaimed one of the boys and grabbed the clothing on the woman's arm. Seven men, including myself, stood up. To my surprise the young lady in the hijab also stood up.

"That's enough, boys. Leave it now." The man who spoke was a big, slightly over weight builder or workman of some kind. The boys looked around them, decided the odds were against them and moved away down the carriage. One of them mouthed something indistinct at the young lady who had unexpectedly stood up. They didn't move far, though. They needed to save face so their retreat was enough to make it clear they'd stopped but not far enough to look as if they were fleeing.

Everybody sat back down and there was a five minute period of distrustful glances between the interveners and the two boys. At the next station the boys alighted. This way they rescued their egos even if they had to wait for the next train. I wondered if Londoners before the wars acted this way. Is this careful engagement genetic because war survivors were like this? Would our forebears have just thumped them? Would they have stood their ground? I decided I was probably just tired and overthinking things again. This being London, England, nobody said anything else and we all went back to ignoring each other except that the older lady and the young hijab wearer were now in quiet conversation. I thought this was interesting and we'd just witnessed a social barrier being breached. Good.

For the rest of the journey home I retreated into my own head. This is an autistic skill I value greatly. I know the world's out there and I keep a sentry watching for any serious outside event that requires me to actually interact with it. Apart from that, I'm quite content within myself, thanks. It's where I can think.

Because of the day's events, I was thinking about my

family, my mum and dad especially. I was thinking about Dave's comments and I was thinking about the meaning of life and death. Introspective and depressing stuff, really, but also kind of interesting. Without any obvious reason Albert came to mind. Albert was my dad's oldest brother, he lived to over one hundred. He probably popped into my consciousness because he died in St. Joseph's several years ago and Dave knew him when he was there. We discussed Albert once, he had an exciting life, although I knew him when he was older and he rarely talked about it, except for bits of information and minor anecdotes.

He did talk in depth with Dave. When he learned that Albert was my uncle he told me his story, Dave has a bit of an eidetic memory so I'm sure it was retold reliably. Everything he said fitted with the little I already knew.

∞ ∞ ∞ ∞

Albert's Wars

Albert Stephen Aitchsmith was born at the end of the nineteenth century, two years before the death of Queen Victoria. His father and mother had recently moved to Cartwright Street, not very far from the Tower of London. He was their first child and they were pleased to know that he was robust and healthy. Most children didn't make it beyond their fifth birthday.

Albert's father was always able to find employment in offices or public organisations thanks to his quick mind and remarkable ability with mental calculation. Young Albert was schooled in the local church hall by volunteers who sought to enfranchise the young poor.

In his world at this time you were either rich, borderline poor or destitute. The financial gap between the destitute and the struggling poor was slim, the gap between them both and the rich was huge. Which you were had very little to do with ability and was primarily dictated by the social and economic position of your ancestors. For most people the objective was to work hard in order to remain merely poor and avoid impoverishment.

As he grew up, this inequality grated with Albert and he formed some radical opinions. For instance, he held the view that the economic system was designed to perpetuate privilege. More than that, he held that since any wealthy ruling class needed to rely on a buffer between their full life and the empty existence of the lower masses, who they required to serve them and work for them, they must create a managerial class in between. To do this they must identify and train those intelligent enough to manage but thick enough to not realise their overall function, which is to permit the ruling clique to maintain their luxury.

To Albert, this explained why the ruling and lower classes contained both highly intelligent and dog brain stupid individuals but the managing classes were of a homogenous conservative and unquestioning but capable functioning intellect.

He watched with interest as the Bolsheviks slowly gained support in Russia. He spent a lot of time in the public library, recently opened by a wealthy philanthropist, and studied their world view. He did not find himself in complete agreement with the Marxist ideal because he felt it ignored the ultimately decisive influence of human nature.

Human nature, he believed, prevented achievement of full equality and equitability in society. He veered towards the less absolutist view that equality of opportunity would level the social playing field and allow the capable to thrive and the incompetent to be humanely managed and well treated. He suspected that pragmatic socialism was the way forward and the inevitable end point of capitalism versus collectivism.

When, in 1914 a mixture of poorly drafted treaties, nationalistic lunacy and the perceived financial interests of rich families threw first Europe and then the world into war, the fifteen-year-old Albert saw his opportunity.

Dulce et decorum est pro patria mori, thought Albert. The nobs of the managing classes and the idiot sons of the ruling elite actually believe that twaddle. If, he reasoned, he were to be there and do his duty, as seen in their eyes, he may be able to make the connections and contacts necessary to make the money that would enable him to advance socially. After all, he decided, any truly pragmatic socialist should realise that the way to make money moral is to give it to those who will use it properly, in this case himself.

His father enlisted, against his mother's wishes. Although in his late thirties, the older man was snapped up for his mental math skills and sent straight to an artillery regiment. His mother complained bitterly that she would struggle to cope with the growing family, now boasting four sons, even though his wages would be sent straight to her. Albert's father explained to her that it was his duty to offer his skills to the Crown in this moment of need. Albert wasn't entirely sure how seriously to take that explanation.

For his part, Albert waited until his father departed for his regiment and then went straight to the recruiting office himself.

"Are you sure you're seventeen, son?" asked the recruiting sergeant.

"Yes, I might look a bit young but I'm seventeen."

"The navy takes boys at sixteen, did you know that?"

"No. And I don't want to join the navy, I get seasick."

"So did Nelson." The sergeant grinned as he said it.

"I'm seventeen and I want to join up," insisted Albert.

"Yes, my fine young lad, of course," the sergeant boomed for the benefit of the officer supervising the room. He beckoned Albert to lean close to him and continued in a much lower voice. "We don't really need to take boys, not yet anyway. Maybe in a few years, ignore that rot about it being over by Christmas, this'll last years. Son, if you insist then I will sign you up. Don't be daft, go home to your mum and help her for a few years. They'll be plenty of Hun left for you in a year or two."

Albert had the head smarts of a person much older than him but the emotional smarts of a teenager. "I insist," said Albert, "I insist."

The sergeant explained that once signed, the contract of enlistment was irrevocable. Once signed up, he was in the army and nobody could undo that. The final attempt at dissuasion failed and Albert signed. He was now a seventeen-year-old fifteen-year-old, and a soldier. His first surprise was that he may not return home to inform his mum and would be immediately taken to camp, somewhere near the town of Warminster wherever that was. A fume-puking truck took him and several others to the Euston terminus where they were put on a train full of other new recruits.

He composed a contrite letter to his mother on the journey: I'm so sorry, mum…I have to go and fight so that I can impress some fool who will give me a good influential job afterwards so that I can get rich and spend it fairly for a better world and the benefit of mankind.

His mother wept.

After training Albert was attached to a battalion of the London Rifles and shipped to France. The contemptibles, the regular British army so named by the Kaiser as an insult, had fallen back early in the war. Once dug in they showed the German army that contempt often has a high price, especially if it involves assaulting a fortified British position. They had held the German advance after a few tactical retreats and now were bolstered by thousands of volunteers from home.

For their part, the French fought tenaciously and with a determination that intimidated the Prussian regiments that had started towards Paris with a light heart and a spring in their step. As they now stood face to face with an opponent as pugnacious as themselves, they were perhaps questioning their initial optimism.

Albert thought the whole war was stupid. The reluctance of both the British and French leadership to combine command and operation was even more stupid, he decided. British and French forces were further strengthened with troops from their respective empires. Brown and black faces were not unknown in Europe but nobody had ever seen them in the imperialist countries in such large numbers. They proved to be effective and courageous fighters, a fact that might have caused the ruling classes some concern. Now the colonial natives knew that they could fight white armies, where would it all end? Albert hoped it would all end in an equitable global economic model where nobody was mistreated. Such is the idealism of the young.

Albert had been in a front-line trench, somewhere near the Belgium border, for about eight months. He wondered when he'd get some leave to go and face his mum's wrath. He wrote to her often. She wrote back regularly.

Letters out were censored but not letters coming in for some strange reason. She informed him that his dad had been home on leave and would then go to a location about thirty miles south of Belgium in order to arrange a bombardment to support an initiative intended to allow the stalemated British to advance. The war planners had noticed that, in one section, the Germans kept insufficient troops opposite the British and this error should be exploited. She hoped he was well and did he need any opium or cocaine sent to him?

Opium, cocaine, heroin, along with tobacco, these were the most common gifts sent to troops. Sold in High Street stores, drug use had caused some concerned debate in Parliament. Albert noticed that many soldiers were under the effects of opiates when they attacked. This, he conjectured, is what caused some of the more bizarrely silly decisions of this bizarrely silly war.

It was all summed up for him in one daft alleged quote from a very senior British army general. Something like, "If, at the start of this battle, I have ten thousand men and the enemy have ten thousand men, and at the end I have one hundred men and the enemy have fifty, I shall have won." Great, thought Albert.

Albert's team was informed that there would be an attack several miles to the south. He decided this must be his dad's attack. They were informed that it was unlikely to impact on them but they should fire a few more rounds than normal while holding their position, just to keep the enemy occupied and prevent him taking troops from that section to support the section being assaulted.

Albert had discovered himself to be an exceptional shot. He could drop a German at a good distance, most of the time first time. The local commander had appointed him unofficial sniper. This meant he could choose his own position and fire whenever the fancy took him. His rifle was not as accurate as the custom built German sniping weapons which had telescopic sights and barrels that diminished both flash and noise. There was a ten pound reward to anybody who could capture one along with some ammunition.

Albert became aware that about twenty yards to the south a man had been shot in the head while clambering over the back of the trench to take a crap. This meant an enemy sniper, this meant a rifle, this meant ten quid. He draped himself in some muddied blankets and eased himself over the parapet, his Smelly or Short magazine Lee-Enfield rifle, was wrapped with dark muslin to disguise its profile. He'd already worked the bolt to place a round in the breach and set the hammer, so had to be careful not to discharge it accidently. He lay still in the mud, just watching.

The British threw the occasional bomb over, just to keep the enemy lively. They returned the occasional shot or mortar shell. Snipers tended to wait until a quiet spell, when men might get careless. During one such period, Albert watched intently. He saw some movement behind some sandbags in the enemy trench about forty yards to the north of him. He brought the stock of his rifle to his shoulder, a movement requiring not much more than a few inches of travel. He saw a man with a long rifle, a telescopic sight set along the length of the barrel.

Ten quid, Albert thought, as the man leaned back from the sand bags and took aim at something to Albert's right. The German sniper took care not to allow his rifle to protrude beyond the sandbags. Albert had him targeted straight away, he gently squeezed his trigger. The powerful kick of the rifle thumped into his shoulder joint and the man dropped. Albert couldn't see where the man's rifle fell, it was probably still in the enemy trench and therefore too risky to go after.

That's enough for today, said Albert's inner voice, don't push your luck. As he reversed slowly into the trench he felt a sharp blow to the top right of his head and then nothing, just a deathly dreamless lack of being. I no longer think, therefore I am not.

He woke slowly, the sensation felt like climbing up from a deep pit towards white brightness and indistinct sounds. He was mostly conscious but tried not to move. His head hurt. His eyes hurt. His nose hurt.

"Are you awake, Albert?" The woman's voice spoke English but with a guttural accent. He slowly opened his eyes.

It took a few moments for the overpowering light to subside into vision. "Where am I?" he asked.

"Safe," she said. "You are in a hospital. I am German but this hospital is in Holland."

"He's awake," this female voice was English.

"What's going on, is this stupid war over?" he asked.

"It is at this place," said the German nurse.

"This is neutral territory," explained the English girl. "You were shot, I don't know how it came to be that German medics recovered you but they did, somehow. They sent you to their field hospital with their own wounded. The German doctor sent you to us. You seem to have received a glancing blow from a high velocity round, it took off a small chunk of skull but missed your brain itself although the outer membrane was torn and there was some cerebral haemorrhaging. Here a German surgeon fitted a metal plate to your head after stopping the bleeding in your brain. The plate's good quality silver and should last forever."

"Thank you German medicine."

"Nein," said the German, "thank you Dutch neutrality and Dutch humane instincts that let us work together to piece together the mashed up remains from this awful war."

Dutch neutrality was a fact, but it was a well armed nervous neutrality. The Dutch stayed fully mobilised throughout the war and trenched their borders against any sudden entry by any of the antagonists. They worried that the prospect of outflanking each other by dashing through an unsuspecting non-combatant's land might be too much of a temptation for either side.

Albert spent the rest of the war in a POW camp in Holland guarded by Dutch troops. The Dutch had agreed to host prisoners although the relevant nations paid the costs. The agreement was that Britain and France paid for the German prisoners and Germany paid for the allied prisoners, a sound financial incentive not to take too many prisoners.

The Dutch had no axe to grind and treated all POWs perfectly well. However, it was rumoured that one or two had been shot trying to escape. The Dutch intended to take their responsibilities seriously without taking sides. It was a Dutch criminal offence to escape unless and until the escapee managed to get home, in which event it was all forgotten about. Captured escapees were likely to find themselves sent to a much less pleasant civilian prison.

Some prisoners were housed in the fighting countries, mainly those who were important or useful, a little personal insult that Albert didn't notice. The rest were held by Holland and Switzerland as part of their agreements to maintain their distance from this butchers' exhibition.

Albert wondered for a long time how he came to be in German hands. He was on top of his own trenches when he was hit, surely the British medics should have got to him first. Eventually, he pieced together the events that had led him here by questioning anybody who could help him.

Soon after he had been shot in the head the Germans started a small shelling of the British line. Somehow he had survived this unscathed and just lay apparently dead as the enemy made a rush at the trench. A staff officer's report later described the small attack as unseemingly rapid, disorderly, without clear presentation of attacking troops and unfitting for any respectable army. The Germans were initially successful and the British fell back to their reserve trench. While they regrouped and prepared a counter attack there was a short lull in the fighting.

A couple of German soldiers took the opportunity to grab a smoke and decided to rest on the blankets they could see on the trench edge. To their surprise Albert was underneath and, as one of them sat on him, he gasped. Since they were not actually fighting at that moment and the discovery was unexpected, they reacted like people instead of soldiers at war. That was why they called over some nearby medics who checked him, decided it might be possible to save him and whisked him away. Even in war, real humanity will reassert itself at any given opportunity.

It was the Dutch guards who told them the war was over. The guards' view was that nobody won but that Germany got the rough end of the peace treaty so probably the French could claim victory.

"The French will be really upset that you helped them," joked one of the guards and everybody laughed.

Albert returned home to a hug from his mum then a clump from his dad followed by a hug. His illegal enlistment was never spoken of again. His dad found work with the gas company who were ecstatic to have a quick-witted figures man. Albert was offered work with the same company but declined. With trepidation he informed his parents that he wished to stay in the army. To his surprise they readily supported him.

"Now this lot's over, there will never be another one. Go and police the Empire, that's all you'll be doing," said his dad.

"Yeah, and after twenty six years I get a good pension and can retire on a good wage for doing nothing for the rest of my life," Albert explained this as his plan. Then he found out that POW and rehabilitation time didn't count towards the total so now he would have to soldier until 1944 to earn his money. He was content with that.

He became very comfortable within the army. His war record and natural ability led to offers of promotion which he consistently declined. His post-war service provided him with travel around the world and a wealth of life experience.

His views remained basically leftish, the pragmatic socialist continued to look on the world and think it socially broken. He failed to be impressed by the Russian experiment and saw it as nothing more than one elite seizing power from another. In his view the majority of workers became bonded servants under the reds.

His battalion was deployed, without firearms, on the streets of Britain itself during the general strike. He drove a London bus and gave as good as he got to trade unionist insults. On the rare occasions that a striker tried to use force on him he simply produced the pick axe handle with which he'd been issued and the threat subsided. He was happy not to be deployed to the industrial north or Wales.

His contact with the radicals supporting the strike was not without consequence. Towards the end of the twenties he announced to his surprised mum and dad that he intended to marry. His bride to be was a former suffragette turned socialist agitator who he met by dragging her away from his bus while he was breaking the strike. They must have both enjoyed the struggle because they agreed to meet later. After several meetings he proposed to her and she accepted.

So it was that the soldier married the disgraceful lefty and she married the imperialist flunky, they were both very pleased about it. Albert came to further examine his evolving socialist instincts and his wife, Dorothy, came to settle happily into the life of a soldier's wife. They had three children, two of whom survived to adulthood.

When the second war broke out, Albert was in Australia taking part in exercises. The soldiers called it pub crawl training although the command team insisted it was escape and evasion in an urban setting. Very few soldiers were found by the Australian army, who were looking for them around the centre of Sydney. For some reason it just never occurred to them to check out the pubs.

After an initial whinge about Gallipoli the locals were happy to drink with the Poms, especially since the Poms were buying. For their part, the Pom soldiers respected the Aussie military whose courage and endurance had impressed everybody in the trenches. Most of the time was spent laughing and joking, playing a few silly pub games and occasionally betting on any fights that broke out. The troops considered the operation a great success.

At debrief, Albert said he'd found shelter with a friendly smiling man he'd met in the local public toilet. This nice man was willing to let Albert use his spare bed and bathroom, for which he was grateful, even though the man had an annoying eye tick that looked as if he kept winking at him. A few chuckled at the fictitious debrief information and some made a dodgy comment or two.

The command team were not stupid, they knew the reports were false. They just went along with it, with the exception of the man who tried to say he'd been disguised as a police kangaroo and kept in a police cage all the time. To him they explained that Australian police do not use kangaroos for anything and then sentenced him on the spot to twenty one days regimental punishments. Nobody tried to be a comedian after that although inventing stories became progressively more difficult. Eventually one smart chap explained he'd sat in a pub drinking and assimilating with the locals. He was commended for his resourcefulness.

At the end of the debriefing they were informed that they would now be moved to Darwin in the far north. The objective was to protect Australia from any attempt by any other power to take advantage of the recently declared war. It was feared that an unidentified somebody might think to snatch some territory while Britain was busy elsewhere. When things settled down and Australia was fully mobilised they would return to Europe to defeat the Germans.

Oh, that again, thought Albert.

On the ship back to Britain, Albert was called to the officer's mess to speak with a staff administrating Rupert, that being a general nickname for any upper class officer seeking safe privileged passage through the army.

"Well, Aitchsmith, you are fortunate." The officer supplied him with tea and scones. "The War Office has agreed that if you wish to manage a civil defence unit or two at home you'll be permitted to serve a few years after this war to make up your time."

"I do not, er, wish, sir." Albert looked a bit cross.

"Why not? You are not young and this will be an active war," explained the officer.

"It's not very active at the moment. Has anybody even fired a shot yet?"

"They will, and when it starts it will be a lot more mobile and faster than the last lot. Your experience is needed, very much so, but age alone will slow you down.

We value you, you see." Rupert passed the butter for the scones.

"No," stated Albert. "I will see this out, even if it goes over my time, and afterwards I'll take my pension. I don't mean to be rude, sir, but how I plan my service is my affair and nobody else's."

"Fair enough," conceded the administrator. "One last thing, you don't have to answer this but I've read your record and I'm curious. You were wounded in the trenches and then a POW. Your service before and after has been exemplary. Why, just why have you turned down every promotion that's been offered to you? Why are you still a private?"

"Oh. Well, sir. It might not make sense to you, with respect. You see you're from a class that assumes privilege and advantage. I expect you went to an expensive school and, when it was necessary, had private tutors. You probably then just eased into university and then a commission. It's what was expected. It's what you felt that men like you do. I don't intend to be offensive, I'm just trying to explain. The class I'm from, well, it's a bit of a result if you have food every day. I will never rise to a rank that will undo the social disadvantage I started with. Therefore, I see no reason to take on the responsibility of managing men, except in the field where sometimes I have to do so just to keep them alive. The point is, sir, I'll follow orders but won't try to get above myself. It's not that I think it's fair, it's just that I've learned I can't challenge it."

"One day, Aitchsmith. Maybe one day, I think things will change. Thank you."

Albert's views had mellowed some. He still considered himself a pragmatic socialist but now also thought of himself as a humane liberal capitalist at the same time. He was now a pluralist, believing that both ideas had merit and could be balanced against each other.

He'd grown suspicious of absolute solutions, that's what this war and the last one were about. He thought that pure socialism was a childish philosophy; it merely replaces a paternalistic ruling elite with a paternalistic state. This way the child could still turn to the parent, now the state, for sustenance. It absolves the individual of responsibility and can only work with a coercive approach to manage those it purports to represent.

He thought that pure capitalism was a heartless philosophy: Every man for himself and devil take the hindmost; succeed or starve. He questioned the idea about the dictatorship of the proletariat, that was just substituting one ruling class with another. Mob rule was inevitable but it needed to be managed though democratic structures. What was needed was universal suffrage, that stopped the political cycle moving on to rule by elites and tyranny.

It was the voyage that made him think so deeply, lots of sea and time and not much to do. The officers worked hard to keep the men busy with drills, exercise and games. There was one moment of excitement when lookouts spotted a submarine. Everybody was called to battle stations and the escorting destroyer moved towards the suspected enemy.

It turned out to be a neutral American which surfaced to show itself and thereby avoid accidental conflict. The captain popped out of the conning tower to wave.

The war kicked off properly during the long voyage. The ship disembarked all troops at Plymouth and then put back to sea for Dunkirk. The locals mistook Albert and the others for Dunkirk survivors and cheered them wildly.

The troops were then sent to the far north west of Scotland, presumably to prevent anybody from stealing the whiskey. They spent a pointless and chilly twelve weeks being drilled and having their fitness assessed.

Albert and five others were ordered to find transport and rush down to an isolated pub near some loch. The publican had phoned to say he had an unknown customer with a rucksack and a funny accent. They entered the pub with bayonets fixed and the publican pointed out the man.

Faced with six bayonets obviously meaning business at the on guard position, the man smiled. "I say, chaps." The accent was pure posh rich Rupert. "What is this? I'm on a walking tour before I'm posted. I just wanted a drink, that's all."

Albert offered apologies, after checking papers, but the man would have none of it. He entirely understood and was pleased to see the impressive big chaps the Hun will have to face. He offered to buy drinks but Albert declined, much to the disappointment of the others.

"That is not a funny accent," he said to the publican. "That is a posh accent from England. That is a posh officer from England. Mind you, thanks for the run out, we were bored." The posh officer laughed for some reason.

"That's fine, you're welcome," said the Scotsman. "It's a funny accent around here. Come back for a drink when you can."

"I can't believe you didn't recognise the accent. Not just trying to drum up drinkers, are you?"

"I'm insulted. Come back with all your friends and we'll talk about it."

Albert spent a few years guarding shores, being shipped to various parts of the Middle East or North Africa but all without seeing a single German. They did see two Italians in Libya but they were deserters and happily gave themselves up. The poor Italians were in a confused position for this war. Most of them had serious reservations about Mussolini but at the same time, country is country even if it is wrong and doing stupid things.

The Italians never really fought with much heart. That wasn't because they can't, it was because as a people generally, they didn't really want to be doing the things they were made to do.

After too many boring years of postings, missing the fighting and guarding things, Albert's battalion was posted to Weston-super-Mare and told they were being held in reserve. Something was in the air, quite literally, as they were trained on light anti-aircraft guns, a kind of double barrelled ack-ack.

Albert met up with his youngest brother, Ed, in the town. They did some family stuff to look after other siblings taking refuge in the seaside community. This went on for a little while before Albert and his mates were all confined to barracks. He had seen the vast amount of ordnance and essential goods being stockpiled and allied troops being held in obscure locations. He had an idea that soon he'd be back to shooting people. He regretted that, he just wanted to complete his time and earn his pension. Still, war is a harsh reality and he'd been lucky so far. In a big war like this that couldn't last.

It was apparent that the perimeter of the camp was patrolled and guarded by Ghurkhas. This was an unusual thing, a regiment among the fighting best in the world being employed simply as guards? Because his age, length of service and good reputation gave him a special status, Albert asked to talk with the commanding officer.

"Sir, we know something's going on and we know we'll be briefed in time. It's just that a few of the lads, me included, find it a bit odd that the Ghurkhas are being used to guard the camp."

The officer looked at him with something approaching respect. "You're a bright and observant man, Aitchsmith. I wish you'd accept some promotion. I trust you but I need your word that you'll tell nobody and I'll explain as much as I can."

"Yes sir, I give my word." Albert meant this, his word really was his bond.

"The troops camped here shall soon be shipped into mainland Europe. That's why we're in isolation at this time, to prevent any possible leak of information. You will be sent into the final assault against the most powerful and capable enemy we've ever faced. The smallest thing might derail this enterprise. If we fail then we can look forward to decades or more of war or even defeat. Nobody comes in and nobody goes out. This is so important that any breach, any entry or exit will be dealt with extremely. I mean that the person will be shot, there and then. Could you shoot one of your mates sneaking out for a pint, or one of the locals sneaking in to sell cigarettes or milk? You might even know them. The Ghurkhas will shoot them, they don't know anybody here." The officer looked stern.

Albert thanked him, confirmed he would keep his word and returned to his barracks. He informed the others that he couldn't tell them anything except that they'd be shot if they tried to leave camp. They understood.

The troops were warned that they had four hours to prepare and would then leave. Most men hurriedly penned final letters and completed short wills as ordered. The letters were all taken by a team of staff officers and the troops informed they would be sent to families and loved ones after the operation was public knowledge.

They were told to take just the clothes they wore, battle dress with no insignia, and personal weapons. Everything else would be supplied to them. They were then taken by truck to a railway station in Devon where they were loaded onto a train and taken to Southampton. There they were crammed onto a Navy transporter with landing craft strapped to the side.

"Oh shit," said one of the men. "Oh shitty shit shit, we're going to war."

"I think we're going to France, my friend," Albert replied. "I think we're going to take the fight to the enemy."

"I think we're going to wish we were somewhere else," said another man and a few people chuckled.

Full briefing for the troops took place on the ship once it had sailed. In groups of about one hundred they were addressed by their officers.

"Men, we go to Normandy where we turn the tables on the Nazis and end this nonsense," the officer exclaimed and then waited for applause that never came. He looked disappointed but continued, "as we sail we join up with thousands of other ships, squadrons of fighters and gliders towed by bombers will be overhead, fighting ships will clear the path and pathfinders will clear the beaches. We're going to hit them head on and then hit them again and again until they curl up in agony and surrender Berlin to us. We're going to break the bastards. Every nation on Earth that counts is with us: The whole of the Empire, the Dominions, the Americans and even volunteers from neutral countries are with us. The French Maquis resistance will disrupt the Germans from within and the French military in exile will storm ashore with us. The Free French will deal with the Vichy traitors as they see fit, we follow a plan to liberate the great country and smash the evil nation." He sensed that most of the men thought he was being a little too theatrical and decided he should tone down his performance.

"Do they know this or will they do something unexpected, like try to stop us?" The man who spoke was a short, stocky northerner with patchy white hair and boxing ring features. A colour sergeant standing near the edge looked towards him.

"Ha," responded the officer. "We will use the landing craft that you've all seen, they will be managed by Navy people, we will charge the beach, take the defences and then press inland when instructed. Our teams will march on the town of Caen and deny it to the enemy. It is tactically essential and once we have it we have Normandy. From there we press on. The landing craft have been fully tested by other troops for function and effectiveness and will work well."

"So why aren't the testers doing this? None of us have even been in one before. Are we just the cannon fodder to open up the front?" The northerner looked defiant.

"That man," roared the colour sergeant. "This is not a bleeding discussion; these are bleeding orders. You will stop spreading alarm and despondency and listen to the officer. You will bleeding listen and bleed as you are bleeding told to bleeding bleed. Do you bleeding understand?" A few people laughed.

The officer laughed as well, he raised a hand to quiet the sergeant. "Thank you, sergeant. I think the point's fair. You don't need training on the craft, other people will get you on, get you there and get you off. Once told to do so you just need to attack up the beach, take the defences and then make a brew. I know it won't be that easy. We will lose a few, we will encounter obstacles, mines, wire and booby traps. You are not cannon fodder but you are the first wave. It's always hard for the first wave. You have been held in reserve for years, each one of you known for your courage, ability and simple straight forward soldierly fortitude. I know you won't let us down. You will invade in your normal teams, your team commander, officer or NCO, will direct you. If it helps, I'm not going to sit back here and watch you do your thing, I will be in the first craft and charge ashore with you." Albert thought that deserved a small round of applause and started one, a few others joined in. This man might be a bit of a twit but he was brave.

They had sailed just before night. By morning they were almost there. The seas were rough and there was a thick mist hovering over the sea up to a height of at least fifty feet. Shadows of the other ships in this vast armada floated in the cloud surrounding them. From the shore it would have looked like a huge number of sleek grey predators slithering towards land out of the eerie white fog. Anybody able to see above the mist, a hill based shore battery for example, would have seen the masts and towers of the big ships cutting through the billowing cloud.

Even with the most effective briefing, an individual involved at an operative level in something this size will rarely be fully aware of what's going on or where. Albert knew that an incredible floating harbour had been towed over for the ships to use. He knew that the various countries would be hitting different beaches on a front a few hundred miles long. He knew he'd been told that the enemy would defend every inch of that stretch of coast with heavy batteries and large troop numbers. His experience told him that was not possible, they simply didn't have enough men or resources to defend every part of the coast to that extent.

He later learned of the desperate battles fought by the Americans and Canadians at their beaches. He became aware that much of the British beach faced less severe, although still formidable, opposition. He discovered to his joy that the part of the beach his team hit faced only token opposition. As the front of the landing craft crashed down and the boat commander told them to attack, he and the others charged ashore against no wire, no mines and just a few rounds fired at them from a handful of Germans a little inland who then fled. In total, this little bit of beach suffered just two casualties as they secured their beachhead. Albert also knew that luck like this wouldn't last.

Their armour and heavier guns were brought ashore. Further down the coast he could hear the boom of ships guns supporting attacks on more hotly contested landing points. Because it was obvious that the other beaches would take longer to conquer, the British here were ordered not to advance yet but secure their position and send out scouts to identify local enemy positions. The allies appeared to have complete and sole mastery of the air and not a single enemy aircraft approached Albert's location.

About six hours after securing their landing zone, Albert and his gang were in proud possession of their twin barrelled self-motorised ack-ack, an eccentric looking engine carrier with a gun on top. The weapon itself seemed to be a pair of old two-and-a-half-inch two pounders merged into a single double barrelled effort, he'd seen them in the first war. They were now reinvented as an anti-aircraft, or AA, gun and cobbled onto what appeared to be an old tractor body with some thin armour at the front. The allied phonetic alphabet at this time used the word 'ack' for A, hence the name ack-ack.

Albert knew that the gun, or guns, actually originated from an 1890s cavalry transportable field weapon called a Pom-Pom, but thought it best to keep this to himself. He was sure it had been improved since then... he hoped. What next, bows from Agincourt?

The pom-pom, now ack-ack was a typically British re-engineering solution. Limited resources applied with sound engineering principles providing an effective but slightly Heath Robinson result. The barrels rifled and firing at a rate of two rounds per second were hardly comparable to the excellent German Spandau. Still, the thing was mobile enough to deal with an unknown aerial threat and with two barrels that meant four rounds a second exploding into the target.

Without any aircraft to actually shoot at they spent their time checking and rechecking the weapon, their lives might depend on it later. All along this section infantry and armour were ready and eager to press on.

"We launch straight at Caen," the peripatetic staff officer informed them. It was nice to see that, in this war, the staff command and leadership people were actually working in the battle zone. Albert hoped that this might prevent some of the dafter decisions that were made in the last one.

Most of this advance was like a Sunday drive. No opposition and no problems. Local people cheered them as they passed farms and small hamlets. They were becoming overloaded with wine, bread and cakes. About five miles from Caen they encountered the first serious reply from the defenders.

An unexpected spattering of mortars halted them. Armour moved forward, infantry went into battle formations and mobile guns searched the air for the still non-existent Luftwaffe. The tanks didn't get far when the lead vehicle just exploded. This halted the column and then small arms and automatic fire came from everywhere, rounds were plinking off of the front armour, the gun base and the side skirts. Albert's gun team was five men, including the officer. They leapt from the gun and ran for cover into a nearby barn. The confusion and disarray of battle descended immediately.

The hundred yard dash for the wooden building left them in the dishevelled and messy state of fighting soldiers. They couldn't do much to assist what was now a close quarters battle so they decided to stay put and get back to their gun as soon as they could. They were not well armed, as a gun crew the officer and men all carried revolvers. They had just one rifle between them and that had been left on the gun carrier in the haste to stay alive.

They soon crept out of the barn and took up position by a nearby hedge. A small group of Germans appeared, moving at a crouch about thirty yards away across the field and seemingly trying to outflank some infantry. The crew opened fire with revolvers, the inaccurate low powered weapons were completely ineffective. The Germans issued the ultimate soldiers' insult at this, they glanced at the group, one of them laughed and then they ignored them.

"Let's get back to the gun, we can use that on them. The bastard laughed at us." Albert's suggestion caused the officer to look thoughtful and then nod. They quickly dashed back towards the carrier. When they were fairly close to it the small German group realised what they were doing. Rifle and automatic fire started to spit around them. Albert thought he preferred the initial insult.

They clambered onto the gun, it appeared unharmed. They released all the safety features, pulled the slides to put rounds in the breaches, swung it round and fired a five second burst. The result amazed them. The rounds were designed to either airburst or explode on impact. They were about six inches long, tipped with hardened steel and contained explosive cores packed with small ball bearings. As the rounds impacted around the Germans they exploded and threw up sods of earth. As the air cleared it was obvious the Germans had been torn to pieces. Albert felt bad about that but they had been trying to kill him.

"Right," declared the officer, "from here on in we use this as a battlefield weapon. There's no aircraft so we're going to become a great big mobile artillery."

"Don't fire bursts longer than a few seconds," cautioned Albert, "that last burst almost tipped the carrier over, we were designed to shoot upwards."

"Well done," the officer congratulated him on the observation. "When we can we'll see if the engineers can do something to prevent that."

A few infantry dashed down the road and grouped behind them.

"What's happening?" The officer shouted the question down to them.

"I'm not sure, sir," one replied, "Jerry has panzers up ahead so I think we'll probably get orders to fall back soon, for now we're using you for cover if you don't mind."

The officer was about to respond but one of the gun crew yelled down, "it'll cost you half a crown an hour, three bob if you want a seat."

"I'll telegraph my bank manager," one of them replied and both groups chuckled.

"Panzer," somebody shouted. In front of them, about a hundred yards away stood the horrifying black spectral Tiger tank. Its gun was facing left but, as it slowly advanced, the turret was swinging round towards them.

"Give it what we've got boys, if it doesn't work, well it's been a pleasure and thanks for being great."

"If it does work, I'll remind you that you said that," shouted Albert. As the others laughed the ack-ack gun fired, a burst of five seconds. Rest. Another burst just the same. The same amazing result. The Tiger was ripped open at the front and the crew visible only as mince meat in the open and mangled crew compartment. Fire spread rapidly in the now useless metal war monster.

"That's bloody horrible," somebody said, "those poor sods."

"As soon as we can, anybody, spread the word to the other crews. We've got a new weapon that we didn't even intend," shouted the officer.

Caen raged for nearly two months and came close to trench warfare. The French town was bombed heavily in attempts to break the German's tenacious defence. Armoured columns crashed together and as always individual infantry fought to the last. This was an atavistic clash of tribes, stone age humanity with the ability to throw more than stones, basic uncivilised and cruel domination of one clan by another.

Albert and his crew were permitted one day of rest after the local victory. They did not enter the shattered town but camped on the outskirts. The day was spent cleaning and servicing the gun. Ammunition was replenished and the engine maintained and fuelled.

In the moments they had to actually rest properly they noticed towns people, mainly women and children but some older men, had come from their homes with wine and cheese. Albert was touched by this; these people had suffered, much of it at allied hands as the place was mauled and pounded to get at the Germans. Still they came with gifts.

The soldiers readily accepted the wine but all declined the food. There is little more uncomfortable to a French person's ear than an English person torturing their beautiful language. Nonetheless, through poorly accented French and broken English, with a little Franglais thrown in, the troops expressed their gratitude but would not take food. Some soldiers gave the town's people their own rations. It's anybody's guess just how they survived the ruthless bombing, civilians should have evacuated beforehand but the Germans wouldn't let anybody leave.

They were soon reassigned. These mobile guns, never intended for this use, had become an important part of war planning. The senior staff saw them as able to support infantry or tank groups, vulnerable but more agile big hitters able to pin down the enemy heavy armour. As such, they and three other guns were to make their way several miles south east and join up with the Free French.

The officer briefing them for this new adventure was a hard bitten and harsh looking man, a veteran of both wars and never willing to give an inch to the enemy. He saw a natural friend in Albert and greeted him warmly. Such men are capable of great affection once their rock hard exterior has been negotiated.

"We're winning," explained the officer, "but the Germans are very good and keep falling back to regroup and counter. I hate to say it but they really are quite impressive." The men nodded, nobody had ever said the Nazis couldn't fight. Part of the problem was that they could fight very well indeed.

The officer ensured that sandwiches and tea were supplied to the men, then he continued. "You chaps are assigned to help the Free French column moving on Paris. The French insist that it must be their forces that liberate Paris but they are conscious that they are an army returning from exile and therefore lack some things in logistics and resources. We are supplying those for them. You will be there so that the column can deal with enemy armour or built up defences. We don't expect the Luftwaffe will be able to support the defenders, but just in case there will be reconnaissance aircraft above you so that we can send bombers or fighters if required. You will do as the French request and obey lawful instructions from their officers. If the French start executing Germans, or even their own collaborators, don't interfere but don't join in either, refuse the order if you have to and you'll be supported by us. It has been made clear that the French will enter the city as liberators. You may enter after they have done so and invited you to join them."

The little convey set out at dusk. By morning they were with the French and heading fairly rapidly for Paris. It was rumoured that the Germans might surrender it without a fight. The French were adamant that would not save them, these men were angry and looking to avenge their nation's defeat; if the German's would not fight, they had best flee.

Whatever the truth of the rumour, the three panzers lurking about fifteen miles west of the city hadn't heard it. They burst out from inside fire gutted village houses where they'd secreted themselves. They poured machine gun fire onto the infantry and one of them fired its cannon at the mobile guns. As two of the guns returned fire, one of them was hit and exploded. Albert and his crew were hurriedly turning their weapon to aim at the tanks. Albert felt a sharp blow to the top left of his head and then nothing, just a deathly dreamless lack of being. I no longer think, therefore I am not.

He crawled to consciousness from the familiar pit of emptiness. As his eyes adjusted to the light he was aware of two men in white coats standing by his bed. One of them wore German uniform under his whites and the other British. The German uniform collar had remnants of stitching where badges, presumably swastikas, had been removed.

"I've been here before," croaked Albert. "I woke up to prettier faces last time. Is the war over or do both sides just worry about me a lot?" Both doctors laughed.

This time the doctors were able to explain to him everything that had happened: The exploding gun had sent huge chunks of shrapnel flying towards Albert's gun. Two of the crew were killed and he was hit in the head. The tiger tanks were destroyed and the column pushed on. He was recovered by a British and French medical team following the column. The Americans provided transport teams for all wounded and they brought him to this field hospital in Caen.

The military hospital was attached to the civilian hospital in order to use surgical theatres and other resources. Although most of Caen was flattened in the battle, the hospital received minimal damage because some brave staff managed to get a large red cross flag onto the roof. That didn't stop all hits, though, and some damage was done.

The German explained that he was a military doctor captured in the initial invasion. As a highly skilled trauma surgeon he was offered the choice of incarceration in England or work in the field here. He chose to work but only if he was treating soldiers from both sides. When Albert was brought in the doctor was called from the POW field hospital to see if he could save him. The doctor said he was so impressed by the plate fitted to the right side of Albert's head that he'd fitted another on the left.

"I'm astonished that you are alive," said the German. "You fought in both wars, no?"

"Yes," said Albert. "And I had to argue to persuade them both times."

"You are stupid then, no? Or brave, or maybe it's the same thing. You'll be fine after a few weeks. No more wars, eh? There are better things to do in life."

Albert spent three weeks in the field hospital, a long time in the circumstances. He enjoyed the ministrations of the French nurses and the conversation of the German doctor. When he was discharged he bought a bottle of wine from a nurse and gave it to the doctor.

He was returned to England, Guys hospital in London. He learned that Paris had been declared open by the German governor and fell without much damage. The Free French and resistance inside the city had meted out some severe instant justice to occupiers and collaborator alike.

The German governor, Dietrich von Choltitz, had been ordered to defend or destroy the city. He refused and surrendered his occupancy to the returning French after he declared the city open. Albert felt the man probably deserved some kind of monument in Paris.

Maybe the French felt the same but obviously couldn't do such a thing for fear of public anger. Although the French were ruthless with the Nazi SS and French collaborators in the city, Dietrich von Choltitz and his troops were regarded with some small respect.

After all, he had not only saved lives but had preserved a beautiful and soul repairing city. After the war von Choltitz admitted he'd fallen in love with Paris and wished he'd been born a Parisian.

He also lived with his regret at not opposing the Nazis in the early years. He offered posterity no excuses and said he felt ashamed and offered himself as a warning to the future.

Albert was called to his battalion HQ to meet with a senior staff officer. He entered the room with perfect soldierly indoor marching and sat correctly when requested.

"Well, Aitchsmith, what are we to do?" The officer was about sixty, physically fit and imposing with a first war walrus moustache now turned grey. "The King is concerned that the world may have insufficient silver reserves to keep putting plates in your head. Mr Churchill suggests that you be held in Threadneedle Street as a reserve wealth fund. Your head must be worth hundreds."

Albert chuckled at the joke and resisted the urge to stupidly ask if both the King and prime minister had really said that. "I thank them both, or you, sir, whoever said that."

"I have authority here in my hand," the officer waved a sheet of paper, "to enable forthwith the payment of your pension. It includes a lump sum injury allowance and an additional annual sum added in compensation for your wounds. Should you remain in the army I have ordered that you will not be posted to any theatre of war ever again. It's up to you, pension or cushy office job, which do you want, you awkward, impressive, unswerving, loyal, insane bugger?"

Albert took the pension; he had achieved his goal. He warmly shook hands with the officer who wished him well and expressed his pleasure that Albert survived.

This being the army, it took two weeks to complete all of the relevant rigmarole to retire. He left the army before the war ended with his pension and his sanity. No small feat, he silently opined to himself.

∞ ∞ ∞ ∞

The day before I was due to visit the hospice again, the landline rang at about 5 a.m. Two hours earlier, I'd woken up and, in my half sleep, imagined that outside a misty white cloud enveloped the world. I imagined that my mother was saying goodbye. Morning mist, that's all it was but I knew this was the inevitable call.

"Hello Dave," I said without even waiting to verify who it was. I would have sounded weird if it was somebody else.

"Psychic, Steve." He sounded soul drainingly weary and a little emotional. "You know what I'm calling for."

"Yeah, when was it?"

"A few hours ago. It was quiet and easy. No pain, no struggle. It was time to let go and she went peacefully." He sighed.

"It's a littler earlier than I expected, I should have visited yesterday. I could have but I just chilled out here. I'll get dressed and drive in to get my dad." I never mean to sound cold but I can deal with anything without allowing emotion to slow me down. It's not that I don't care, I do care enormously. It's just that uniformed work, army, police, it teaches you to throw a switch in your head. It switches off your feelings and lets you perform; that's how you can do what you need to do. The feelings dam up. There's normally a release later. If the switch is left on for too long the release can be spectacular.

"It's OK, Steve." Dave's touch on humanity, his feel for people and events, his simple understanding strength reached out. "Don't feel guilty, these things are not fully predictable. It's a bit earlier than any of us expected. I've sent a cab to get your dad, we'll pay the fare."

"You don't need to do that. I'll reimburse you when I get there. I'll be there as soon as I can. Can I park?" Driving and parking in London is a massive challenge, that's why I normally use trains and buses.

I heard him half-sigh and half-chuckle. "Sort out your family at home first. I'll stay with your dad. Don't take any chances, drive carefully. Settle yourself down first, have a cup of tea and eat something before you leave. When you get here come into the car park at the back. I'll let security know that you're authorised. If there are any problems, don't kick off with them just get them to come find me. There won't be any problems."

"It's OK," I said. I explained that Dawn, my wife, was working in Devon for the week, something to do with early years education planning, and Alexandra, my daughter, was fully involved at her university because exams were approaching. "I'll phone and let them know." Then a thought struck me: "Hey, were you with her all night? There's no way you sit with everybody and do that; it's a hospice, people are passing all of the time."

"I told you," he said. "I knew Albert, I like your mum and dad. Besides, it's for you."

I didn't really know what to say. "Thanks." I was moved by this. I hung up and started to make a cup of tea.

Alexandra will be devastated even though she's expecting the news. She has my skill, if it is a skill, at throwing the switch. She's probably seen me do it for years. I hope she's able to release it slowly and avoid the painful emotional flood. Being a bit of a psychology wiz, she once said to me "Emulate the sociopath but not for too long, the emotional suspension is a fake in the rest of us and as long as it's recognised as such you can let it all out safely." True enough; only people with empathy even need to use this trick. I'm sure she'll be able to do it. It bothers me a little that I may have taught her to bottle things up. Still, Dave told me to not feel guilty, so I won't.

I rolled into London at the height of the morning rush hour. That's a misnomer, long lines of vehicles spewing poison and moving at less than walking speed, that's hardly rushing. The traffic started to build while I was still on the motorway. Unless there's an accident or spillage or something, the long lines of vehicles tend to keep moving. Not smoothly, any number of inexplicable sudden little jams build up and then release into fast traffic again, all for no apparent reason.

London itself is a different proposition. The entire world seems to be heading for the centre. Stop, start, stop, start, stop, stop, stop, start, stall. Great stuff, constant gear changing, clutching and braking. I hadn't experienced this for years. It always made me wish I had a vehicle with automatic transmission. For some reason I always bought manual transmissions the same as nearly everyone else. Being fairly big and needing plenty of space, I usually keep big cars. The ten year old Defender that I currently own coped well but was not exactly a luxurious ride. I swung the big green four by four through the rear gates to St. Joseph's, the lone security bod just waved me in. I made my way to the reception area.

The middle aged matronly looking lady at the desk checked a list. "I'm sorry for your loss," she said. "Please go up to the ward. Somebody will meet you there."

The children's complex leaked the sounds of morning as I passed it. Tired voices chattered and crockery clinked and chinked. This morning I did not feel the usual stab of anger and powerlessness. The switch was on, I was emotionally armoured today. At the door to the geriatric ward there waited the same young nurse who had told me off last time.

She had the most engaging smile and presence. Slim, well shaped, about five seven and just lovely. Get a grip, you embarrassment, I said to myself. She must have been in her mid-twenties, I guess.

"Please come with me," she said and led on. We walked about twenty metres further down the corridor, me trying not to stare at her backside wiggling through her white dress, then she opened and held a door so I could enter. I twisted a bit to get past her without any physical contact. This girl was stunning and probably used to the glances of guys who are too old but refuse to admit it. I thanked her, smiled, silently apologised for my objectification of her and she left. I hope that her good looks aren't a disadvantage in her career. She seemed confident enough to cope.

My dad and Dave were in the room. Dad was seated on one of several red plastic chairs lining the walls. Dave stood just to the side of him.

"She's nice, isn't she?" said my dad. Oh yeah, I thought, I'm sure she dreams about an aggressive nonagenarian like you sweeping her off her feet with his walking stick and whisking her away with his bus pass. Dave came over and warmly shook my hand. He led me to a chair, where I sat.

Nobody, as far as I'm aware, really knows Dave's life history. I suspect military and possible special forces of some kind, I've met enough of them to recognise the type. He stood in front of us as if he was about to deliver a debriefing. In a way he was, the debriefing at the end of my mum's life. My dad's rheumy old eyes were full. Occasionally a tear slid and zig zagged its way down his age lined face. I patted his arm.

"Ed," he said. My dad seemed to sit up straight at the mention of his name. "Ed, you did the right thing in arranging funeral services before the end. That ball is rolling and Jay will deal with everything." Jay, it transpired, was the undertaker, funeral director as he preferred, that held the contract for services my dad had paid for in advance. They were always ready for the worst, my mum and dad. It was probably the war experience that made them both stoical and practical about these things. I inherited it from them but, in me, it's a learned response, they lived it and were nurtured into it by life. As Dave said, our influence goes on forever.

"Funny," said my dad, "I'm thinking about Albert and Findlay, not Marge." Findlay was another of my dad's brothers. He had six in total and four sisters. My grandad and grandma on that side seemed to churn them out endlessly. Dave, being Catholic, was probably used to big families but it's unusual in Anglicans. It gave my dad's early life a lot of personal and economic security, there were ten or more good incomes going into his house just off Cable Street. Most of his brothers got involved in the famous riot and one of Findlay's boasts was that he 'smacked' a Blackshirt. My dad was too young and his dad wouldn't let him go. Then, after grandad hypocritically went to join in, dad's mum made him stay in the house.

Dad had sometimes mentioned Findlay before. He was responsible for the Polish cousins I've never met and wouldn't even know if I did. He was quite a lad, Findlay. He died in the Korean war after doing the usual family thing of joining in when he didn't need to. Too many wars. One too many for Findlay.

∞ ∞ ∞ ∞

Findlay's Wars

In 1907 Findlay William Aitchsmith was delivered into this world at the hands of a severe, rude, self opinionated Irish nun who also happened to be a qualified midwife and whose abrasive character hid an intense love for humanity.

St Joseph's hospital, maternity section, stood separate from the hospice building where many people spent their final opiate soaked days. The nuns prayed earnestly for their souls. Those who were not Roman Catholic and declined the offer of conversion were bluntly told they would go to the hellfire such intransigence invites. The nuns prayed for them anyway.

Findlay's parents were neither Catholic nor stupid. They gratefully accepted the medical skill, especially since it was free, and simply ignored the evangelism. They did not attend any church and considered themselves Church of England only so that they could complete the relevant line on forms and official documents.

Findlay was seven years old when his dad went away to war. He returned five years later with a couple of new scars and damaged lungs. He had inhaled a small amount of mustard gas during the Battle of the Somme and now suffered from reduced stamina. He hadn't been a front-line fighter, his role had been as artillery spotter; he would lay up in some forward hole and identify shell landings. From that he would do the math and use a field telephone, when it worked, to advise new elevations for the big guns.

He was quick with mental math and good with advanced calculations. He fought his war with a slide rule and log tables, his math killed more Germans than any gun. He had two infantry soldiers attached to him. They could protect him from snipers, spotters were a prime target, and also act as runners or wire fixers when the telephones broke.

He returned fit enough to work and continue to father children, he considered himself fortunate. It was clear to the now twelve-year-old Findlay that his dad was different. He'd become quieter, less playful and often wanted to be alone. Findlay didn't mind too much, his dad still hugged him, sometimes his dad wept a little as he hugged him and that frightened Findlay a bit.

When his father died in 1942 Findlay and his adult brothers were unable to attend due to military deployments. His sisters, his mother and young Ed provided a family presence as the man was hurriedly buried in the basement of a bombed out building. Later, Findlay was unable to confirm whether his dad had been properly reinterred in a more appropriate location. He may remain beneath whatever building finally ended up on the site or he may be in the City of London cemetery mass war grave.

Findlay was the brainy one. He was most unusual for the area in his likes and interests. He was an East End boy and could fight as well as any of them. He preferred not to, his special pleasure was poetry, writing and history but was good at every other subject as well. He believed that practical skills were as essential as academic success and taught himself joinery from books. His skill with window frames was in great demand from his relatives and neighbours.

He won himself a place at the grammar school where he comfortably achieved a school certificate at such a high grade he was accepted by Edinburgh University.

His dad was pleased he would study in Scotland, he felt it was appropriate given the family history included Scottish origins. Even better, the university fees would be paid through a bursary fund set up by a unified Scots/

English Quaker educational trust. Its noble objective was to provide working class boys with an education commensurate with their ability.

Findlay did once suggest that it would be even more noble if it considered including girls as well. Findlay was slightly belligerent that way, not that it prevented him from taking the charity. He graduated with a first in History and Philosophy. To fill his spare time, he learned German, French and Russian. He planned to learn Japanese if he ever found the time.

After university he found work with the civil service. If he had any career plans they were not transparent, not even to him. He liked the idea of advancement but intended to learn his job first and worry about that later.

In the early thirties he was taken from his role assisting Government ministers and moved to the war office. There he was instructed to meet with a person he should only ever refer to as 'Leader'.

"Without knowing your name I'm not comfortable and I don't really like referring to you as Leader, it feels like I'm in some way surrendering my thinking to your whim." Findlay spoke from a luxurious leather armchair in the Athenaeum club. Opposite him in a similar chair sat Leader. They both held brandy glasses although Findlay drank none of his.

"Good," said Leader. He was no longer young, maybe in his mid-sixties or perhaps just a good living late fifties, it was hard to tell. Overweight and with a clear lack of anything resembling exercise, he'd be lucky to last another ten years.

"Good?"

"Not your discomfort, that is not the intention," Leader sipped his brandy. "It is good that you are not intimidated and speak your mind. I believe our choice is correct."

"I intend no disrespect, sir," said Findlay. "I am here because I was ordered to be here. I do not know what you want nor why you want it. I will not cooperate fully without full information, I am prepared to listen but I am confused and not a little concerned. I am content that there is some level of legitimacy behind whatever this is but I will not blindly agree or consent to anything without sufficient information. If this means I fail some kind of interview then I'm sorry, thank you for the brandy and with your permission I'll return to my duties."

"Excellent," responded Leader. "Failed? No, not failed. Passed with flying colours perhaps. I should not give you my name and you don't need it. I am the managing director of what we call the secret service, special operations, spook group, intelligence service, clever buggers club. We are the Secret Service Bureaux."

"I don't know," responded Findlay immediately. "I thought it was something like this and I'm not sure. I think that since I'm not sure my answer must be a polite no. I'm not really interested in intelligence work and I have no real interest in politics other than in how it impacts on my life."

Leader looked thoughtful for few seconds. "I understand," he said. "You know, you remind me of a young man I met many years ago. He was of humble origins and as sharp and bright as a pin. Like you, he was his own man with a strength of character that dared challenge the limitations of his birth. I didn't care for him but that was for personal reasons. As a man he was like you; a gem, brave, resourceful and intelligent. You'd be perfect for the work, it's not what you think it is, there's very little danger and even less fun. We apply intelligence and analysis to information. You'd be perfect."

"Nonetheless, intelligence work is really not my cup of tea. I like analysis but prefer it to yield concrete results in the real world. I really dislike the idea of just collecting and collating information in order to try to second guess world leaders and events." Findlay thought this might end the matter.

"Your pay will double and you will still earn the civil service pension. You will be free to give it up at any time without penalty, except we'd expect your future silence of course," said Leader. "The work will exploit your language skills and knowledge of history and its implications. It will be varied and you will have a high degree of autonomy, we've found that's best."

"May I think about it?" Findlay asked.

"Take my card. It'll give you my name, the first time I've ever given it to anybody, but remember that this conversation never took place."

Jonathon Metcalfe, Lord Sedgwick, MBE. So Findlay knew the name. That meant nothing, of course, but to him it indicated that he might be able to work with these people. Two weeks later he phoned the number on the card and said he'd take the post, if it was still on offer. That's how Findlay came to work for the intelligence services.

126

Findlay took to the work. His brief was foreign regimes, he was not required to consider home grown problems such as Mosley and his ilk. He studied the rise of Franco, Mussolini, Stalin and Hitler. It was fascinating to him. For the next few years he built huge dossiers on these people and was a frequent visitor to Germany, Italy and Russia. Not Spain, though. Franco had declared that he would kill any spies he found in Spain and that meant only the special operations people sent anybody there, Findlay was always transparent and obvious in his visits. He was an analyst, his role was to interpret and extrapolate into imagined potential future actions, not to sneak or fight. His work was best done with open discourse between him and his targets and access to less open information obtained by somebody else.

Findlay did not settle down in life. He had a few girlfriends but showed no indication of marrying.

"Do you know this?" He once asked one of them, a teaching fellow from one of the Oxford colleges, "Hitler, Mussolini, Franco and Stalin all basically believe the same thing. They are all worker focussed, accept wholly or in part the arguments of Marx and see the dictatorial rule of the working classes as a natural progression, as long as they lead it. The only thing they differ on is that Stalin believes it is an international thing and the others believe it is nationalist only and threatened by the internationalists. They even all use Jews as scapegoats, although Hitler seems to actually believe it. For the others it's a useful explanatory shorthand, it saves their supporters from having to think things out."

The inevitability of war became clear to the intelligence services before anybody else, except that interfering though surprisingly prescient old bugger, Churchill. It came to Findlay's notice that the troublesome, though somewhat admirable, Churchill was receiving information from somebody in the civil service. It was the only way the man could know some of the things he talked about. This was not Findlay's area and he simply passed his suspicions on to the relevant section by way of memo.

The creation of the Soviet/German non-aggression pact preceded and enabled the German invasion of Poland. The Russians took the opportunity to steal some Polish land from the other border. A matter of weeks later Britain declared war on Germany.

This coincided with the death of Lord Sedgwick. Sedgwick died in the bath from a heart attack after too many brandies and a rich meal. Findlay was part of the team that was sent to search his property to remove anything that might be relevant to the service, either benefiting or embarrassing it.

Findlay did find some medical papers that indicated the late Peer was early stage syphilitic. He destroyed them, he saw no reason to impugn the man's memory. He was admonished by his section head for the act. There was no other action taken because it was felt he erred out of loyalty to the individual rather than malice. He was informed the section already knew the medical condition of Lord Sedgwick since he had advised them.

Findlay and the section settled down to collect and

analyse information from the war. Bletchley Park had been activated and Findlay thought about applying to be posted there. After some thought he decided his language and other skills would better serve the London office, Bletchley was really a mathematician's game.

The war started with a period of quiet inaction by both sides. Many people hoped that it would fade away, nobody wanted a return to trench stalemate. Findlay and his section knew better, their analysis was that Germany would do something unexpected to avoid entrenchment. They didn't know what because German sources were disappearing fast and the Nazis knew how to play their cards close to their chest.

When things did start to happen they happened fast. The stunning blitzkrieg smashed into Western Europe. France and Britain reeled and gave way to the swift, modern, ruthless armoured military brilliance that was thrown against them. Lovely, brave, beautiful, passionate France fell quickly. It was not for want of determination or courage, nobody could stand against the spectacularly proficient new German war machine which was without precedence or apparent weakness.

For their part the British fell back to Dunkirk to undertake the undignified and panicky scramble to reach home.

"If they keep pushing and come after us immediately then it's all over, we can't stop them." This was Findlay's depressing statement to the review group, nobody contradicted him.

Afraid of entrenchment, the Germans hesitated at the British fortified position in the channel port. Their uncharacteristic lack of resolve permitted Britain to rescue its forces and regroup in England.

In an early attempt to regain the initiative, a British expedition to create a front in Norway was completely defeated. The country stood in an impasse with the mighty German forces. Britain's reputation for military defensive competence caused the Germans to pause at the moat of the English Channel. They decided, correctly, that any successful cross-water invasion required air supremacy.

At home, politics moved just as fast. Findlay was aware that many members of the Government wanted to offer terms to Germany. Findlay's analysis was that Germany would accept terms advantageous to itself and the British Empire would become a vassal to the Third Reich. One Winston Spencer Churchill prevailed in the executive dispute, became prime minister, dismissed any suggestion of armistice or truce and prepared his war cabinet.

"My whole life has prepared me for this moment," Churchill is reported to have said in his office.

"That bellicose old sod will fight a good war but I wonder who will survive it," said Findlay in his.

Then things started to happen in the service. A new head, who Findlay never met, was appointed. New sections were formed, including one to implement an active network in France and the Low Countries. Several people were moved to new offices or sections and Findlay was instructed to attend the prime minister's office.

Findlay sat across the desk from Churchill. He could not detect the usual aristocratic arrogance that normally broadcasts from such men. On the contrary, Churchill seemed warm and friendly. A little overweight but Findlay thought this made him look cuddly rather than gluttonous. His eyes were not threatening nor were they arrogant. Findlay formed the impression that they were caring and possibly sad but also indicated a certain steeliness of character. This man could be a loyal and emotional friend or an implacable enemy, that was Findlay's analysis.

The prime minister glowered at him. "Why, Mr Aitchsmith, do you think I might want to see you?" The voice, soft though a little growling, revealed a slight difficulty with sibilants, but was also warm.

"Prime minister, sir, I don't have enough information to even guess. Something to do with the war, obviously. A new posting possibly. I'm sure you don't speak to every civil servant so this must be something that affects you or your office directly." Findlay decided that this man required blunt focussed responses.

"A memo, Mr Aitchsmith, a memo about me, sir." Spoken with an amused anger, a most unusual style of speaking.

"Yes sir. I did submit a memo suggesting that you may be unlawfully receiving confidential documents from another section of the service for which I worked. I neither deny it nor regret it. I suspect it was true, or why else would you now speak to me? With respect to you, sir, I do not apologise and in the same circumstances would do the same thing. Frankly, sir, I would have thought you have bigger things to occupy you at this time." Findlay merely looked the man in the eye.

Churchill was silent for a moment, then he laughed and thumped the desk. "You are the man I need, Aitchsmith. Your damned impudence, your damned refusal to back down and your damned insistence on doing the proper thing. I commend you, sir. I have a job for you, reporting directly to me or my secretary. I wish to place you in serious danger, Mr Aitchsmith, and I think you will accept it."

If Findlay were to advise anybody on meeting Churchill, he would recommend they avoid historical matters, especially those being made at the moment. Churchill went on at interminable length about the Molotov-Ribbentrop pact of non-aggression. He prattled on about Bismarck and the Russian revolution before Findlay raised a hand to stop him.

"I accept the post, sir. I will do my best." Findlay would have accepted anything just to make the man shut up.

The post was to reside at the British embassy in Moscow and then use this ambassadorial position to openly infiltrate the court of Joseph Vissarionovich Stalin. It was Churchill's view that within a year or two either he or Hitler would treacherously breach the pact. When that happened, he wanted a man on the ground to influence the Russian dictator. Findlay agreed with the analysis.

Sidney George Reilly, a British quadruple agent from the past and eventually executed by the Russians, had worked for whoever paid him enough. He had also produced excellent reports and they were still on file. Findlay collected them and spent time reading them all.

This way he hoped to form the mind set he needed to operate in his new role and also gain some understanding of the Russian mind set.

While Britain fought for its life and, with the aid of its Empire, punched it out with the unrelenting and frighteningly capable German forces, Findlay was flown to Moscow. Over the next eighteen months or so he became a common sight at the Kremlin and met Stalin several times. He was liked and free to visit the seat of Soviet power whenever he wished.

In June he was summoned to the man himself. He found him sober, not always a certainty, and agitated.

"Findlay William, welcome." Stalin stood by his desk and Findlay remained standing as well.

"Joseph Vissarionovich, a pleasure as always." Findlay felt there was something different about this meeting. The great Stalin was a short, broad-shouldered man with the common Russian look of too much Vodka. His white suit was crumpled but clean.

"We are not a nation of drunks, Findlay William, but it's true, I enjoy a manly drink." Findlay was taken aback by Stalin's words, was this man psychic?

"I didn't mean…" started Findlay.

"Ha," Stalin's victorious cry. "I was right. Findlay William know this, a man in my position has to guess his opponent's mind; I have to read the person to guess at their thoughts."

"I'm not your opponent, sir. I am your ally as far as I can be."

"Humph," said the monster man. "I've killed

millions, did you know that? I did it deliberately and would do so again to maintain the proletariat led land I have the honour to speak for." Findlay started to speak but Stalin raised his hand to quiet him. "You represent the relatives of the bastards we killed to free ourselves from tyranny. You represent the capitalist land of a Royal possession. You are not my natural ally, Findlay William. You are, however, my ally of convenience and you will be deployed as such." Stalin smiled, "I like you on a personal level."

"Sir?" questioned Findlay. This level of personal attention from Stalin was rarely good.

"I really do like you, Englishman. However, don't think I forget that in 1917 your land sent troops to try to rescue the Romanovs. Don't worry, they just marched about for a while and then went home, busy elsewhere, you think?" He laughed at his own joke. "Now though, now, things are different. You have to know that today the pig Nazis have invaded Mother Russia, a full six months before I planned to invade them, the cheating bastards." He laughed again.

"I didn't know," said Findlay. "I should contact London for instructions, sir."

"No." There was no arguing with the great proletariat leader. "No, you will be deployed to a front-line unit of my army. I like you, you speak Russian well, an unusual skill in an Englishman. You will observe my troops and report back to London and tell them to send me the items I will tell you that you have decided we need."

"You tell me what I decide?" Asked Findlay, chuckling.

"Yes, my friend Findlay William Aitchsmith. It is the burden of the great to think for others. Before you start to tell me that you are not a soldier, don't bother. It is decided."

"Sir, I'm not sure that…" Stalin again raised his hand to quieten him.

"Know this, loyal Findlay William," the Russian dictator spoke softly and with reverence. "We are a pragmatic and determined people. Did you know that Lenin was financed in his revolution by the Germans?"

"Yes, I did."

"To maximise that benefit we exacerbated already existing anger in the shtetls, Jews are always easy targets to focus mindless simpletons to a task. We produced propaganda to motivate our people and even passed it to the funders, the German Royal command. We are always pragmatic, see. The Germans really bought into our propaganda, so in a way we paved the way for the Nazis."

"I know," said Findlay.

"Now the penguins are coming home to nest." Findlay tried not to laugh at the mistranslated saying. Stalin continued, "I actually feel bad about what the Germans are doing to the Jews, possibly as a result of our accidental instigation. We'll free any we find, unless we have a use for them. You see, the Deutschepricks actually believed it. We expected the ordinary people to do that but not the leaders. At first we thought they were just being manipulative in the same way that we are pragmatic."

"Same thing," ventured Findlay.

"No," laughed Stalin. "We are only ever pragmatic, they are manipulative and you are manipulated for pragmatic reasons." With that the great proletariat leader strode out of the room laughing softly at his own wit.

A tall Russian military officer replaced him. "Greetings, friend. You will come with me. I have orders to shoot you if you try to run, contact London or refuse me. I don't want to, I want you to see our great army so that you can convince London to send us weapons. It will be a year or more before our weapons production is where it needs to be. Please be assured that we will do our best to keep you safe. You are our friend but friends do as they are told." Findlay thought it best not to respond to that.

The Russians supplied him with a genuine British army field uniform with captain rank on the epaulettes and it fitted him perfectly, how they got it is anybody's guess. The battle dress had no regimental insignia on it. They explained that he should wear uniform so that everybody would recognise him as an observer and understand he was not to be used in combat.

He was allocated a mentor, assistant, minder called Aleksandra Ivanovna Barantceva. She was about twenty six, spoke with a Cossack accent and held some kind of senior rank. She was also stunningly pretty even in the baggy Russian uniform. Her long dark hair was allowed to hang loose but she bunched it up under a cap when she wore one. At about five eight she was shorter than Findlay but showed no discomfort at her lack of clear physical strength. He became very fond of her.

When he arrived at the front, just short of the Polish border, she informed him that Russian forces had been pushed out of the part of Poland they had occupied.

"Our job is to delay," she explained. "We will slow them down, pay the price in blood to prevent their usual fast advance. When that is achieved they will find that their supply lines are too long, their army too small and their resources insufficient. We slow their blitzkrieg, force them into entrenchment and then hit back. They have no idea of what a winter on the Steppe is like. We will sacrifice as many lives as we need to and we will not make the mistake of trying to rescue the civilians. We will avenge them later."

"I see," said Findlay in Russian. "You blood curdling beauty," he said in English.

"I speak English," she looked amused.

"Oops," said Findlay.

"Oops," she responded with an engaging smile.

They were in continuous managed and controlled retreat. As they fell back they destroyed everything the enemy might find useful. The peasant villages were left to their fate, wells were poisoned, crops were burnt and factories blown up. Not a bean, not a vehicle, not a cup was left for the enemy to take advantage of. The Germans rushed headlong onwards into the vast empty Steppe.

Findlay and Aleksandra Ivanovna often spent time in conversation. At first it was just explanations of what additional resources the Russians needed. After a few weeks their relationship evolved and they started to exchange personal information.

When she wasn't ordering suicide missions or butchering Germans she was teasingly coquettish with him. He felt the stirrings of need in her presence. She knew this and made it clear she reciprocated. To Findlay's frustration the war was more pressing for both of them. The other Russians were amused by the Englishman and his crush.

Findlay was beginning to think that he should return to Moscow in order to report to London. Did London even know that he was here? He wanted to ask London to arrange arms and food for the Russians. They were working military miracles with limited ordnance.

The Germans, if reports were true, behaved appallingly. Aleksandra Ivanovna informed him they were murdering men and children, raping and torturing women and girls and destroying whole villages. Findlay had some respect for the Wehrmacht and didn't want to believe the stories. However, he saw one captured German and he sported the insignia of the SS; Hitler's personal regiment of psychopaths and deviants, the stories were probably true. The German was shot in the head after interrogation.

Findlay planned to request his return to Moscow the next morning. He settled down to sleep as best he could. The tarpaulin roofed temporary dugout he and several others occupied helped keep some of the wind at bay. Each day seemed to be colder than the last and nothing could keep him warm, except possibly Aleksandra Ivanovna Barantceva but she was leading a battle.

Just before dawn he was woken by the others shouting and scrambling outside, there was shooting and several explosions. As Findlay started to rise a massive blow to his head returned him to unconsciousness.

When he regained some sense he realised he was still in the dugout. Rough hands pulled him to his feet and put him on a wooden chair, where did that come from? His hands were tied to the arms. He shook his head to clear it. He realised that on a chair next to him was a battered looking Aleksandra Ivanovna. He tried to talk to her but could see she was barely conscious.

"Who the fuck are you?" Said a German voice.

"My name is Findlay Aitchsmith," he answered. "I am a military observer posted here by Britain to advise the Russians."

"You speak good German," said the voice. The owner then identified himself as Hauptmann Johann Waldheim, Wehrmacht intelligence attached to the SS advance assault group. "I recommend that you tell me everything. Remember I have access to intelligence information and I am familiar with British intelligence. You should tell me the truth. Your next interview will be with the SS and please believe me when I say that you will like me much better than you will like them. I know who you are."

Findlay told the truth. He explained how he was attached to Moscow to influence Stalin, he didn't mention Churchill. He explained how the mad Stalin sent him here and he explained how he was just looking for an opportunity to slip back to England.

Waldheim explored his story and was eventually convinced. He had some water brought to him and told him he would now leave him to the SS. He assured him that he would advise the SS that he was best retained and did not need to be further interrogated.

The tall strapping brown haired lunatic who replaced Waldheim looked good in his black uniform. He looked like he was attending a ceremonial event not a front-line war position.

"Aitchsmith, you do not need my name."

"I didn't ask for it," replied Findlay.

"You will be handed to the Wehrmacht, for some reason they want to keep you and I have no need for you. As for her," he indicated Aleksandra Ivanovna, "I'll think of something soon." His grin was theatrical, like a pantomime villain.

"She should come with me," suggested Findlay. "She's of no use to you, you've obviously overrun her position. The Wehrmacht will find her useful in assisting with German occupation. She has language and organisational skills that will be useful."

"You want to fuck her, yes?" The Nazi nutcase leered. "Too late, English. Half my unit already have. The whore moaned and wriggled like nothing you've ever seen. She serves no further purpose other than to show you that you should never seek trouble with us, ever."

With that he drew his pistol and shot Aleksandra Ivanovna in the face. She fell backwards onto the floor, the chair sliding and scrapping slightly on its rear legs as it tipped over, then he put another two rounds into her head. Findlay sat in stunned disbelief as the madman walked out showing no emotion whatsoever.

The Wehrmacht were very apologetic to Findlay about Aleksandra Ivanovna. Waldheim took charge of him. "These monsters, what can I do? This insanity will pass. When the Nazis have built their Reich, and they will you know, the lunacy will stop. Germany has given itself to them and now we have to accept their blunt ruthless ways. They will give way to sensible and more cultured leadership in time. Once they have established their dominance and made themselves masters of everything, they will stop."

"That's reassuring," mocked Findlay. "I promise you, Johann, I will find that bastard and I will kill him. If that means you now have to shoot me, be my guest."

Johann was a good man in a bad situation. He had Findlay removed to several miles west of the Polish border and placed on a farm.

"I've never farmed, I know nothing about it," he protested to Johann.

"Yes you have," Waldheim informed him. "This farm has been stocked with some animals and some Polish women, farmers, to manage it. I have to report your location and advise my superiors that you have given your bond to remain on this farm. I have to tell them that you have the relevant skills and are an experienced farmer. If I cannot do this then I must hand you to a rear based SS unit for reassignment, do you understand me?"

"Only too well. Yes, actually, I have farmed all of my life. I know how to milk a chicken and grow sheep and everything."

Waldheim chuckled at him. "Please don't leave the farm. Keep your uniform, sew a red patch onto the arms to show that you are a prisoner. It's about two hundred miles to the nearest town and you have no motor transport, don't be silly."

"I will, Johann." Findlay looked serious, "Johann, get his name for me. Let me know who he is so that one day I can look for him. Whoever wins this war, none of us will want a psychopath like that around."

Johann touched his shoulder. "Forget him, Findlay. This world has gone mad and crazy men like him are everywhere. Part of me hopes I get killed so that I don't have to see it afterwards. Good luck."

Six Polish women ran the farm, ranging in age from twenty one to thirty six, all of them attractive. None of them spoke English, German, French or Russian and so over the next couple of years Findlay became fluent in Polish. They taught him to farm and they became good friends. Their men were all missing, some known to be still fighting for the Polish resistance and others just gone.

People being people, whatever their good intentions, over the years Findlay fathered four children, one of whom died at birth. It is not true to say that he enjoyed a harem, he was just a healthy man with six healthy women, no outside influences and no outside moderation, the Germans didn't even visit the farm again, and nature has its own way of doing things. Between them they raised the children as best they could.

Findlay left the farm only once. About a year into his detention he decided to search some of the local area to see if he could find a motor vehicle or even a bicycle that he could use. The farm didn't have any horses or other useable transport, just chickens, ducks and small scrawny goats. Most of the time they grew potatoes and cabbages. Findlay made spears and a crossbow to protect them and their livestock from wolves. Even so, they lost at least two animals a week to predators. It was depleting their stock and making the farm unviable.

Leaving the crossbow for the women and armed only with a spear, he made his way towards the south west. There was no real reason for the direction, he just reasoned that he was less likely to encounter the enemy that way; most movement was east/west across the northern part of the country. He felt a little ridiculous in his uniform and tatty boots with a savage's weapon. On his back he carried a home made pack with some small pans and a twig stove. He'd find food and water from the land.

He walked a full two days and saw nobody. This land was mainly virgin woodland and often difficult to pass through. He found only one burnt out country house, plainly a wealthy abode at one time. Searching the ruins and the surrounding land yielded nothing. He noticed that there were what appeared to be bullet strike chunks out of one of the house walls. Every ruin has a story and he'd never know this one.

On the third day, Findlay resolved to start back after one more day walking. He hoped that his sun and stars navigation hadn't got him lost. In the early afternoon he settled to rest and brew up some roasted acorn coffee. He still had some boiled squirrel from yesterday and decided to lunch. He leaned back onto a long mound that was grassed but with no trees or bushes.

No trees or bushes? He realised the significance of that, this mound was fairly new. He examined it and it appeared to have no military function. He dug a little at the base and the smell of carrion, once known never forgotten, assailed him. He hadn't dug far, just a few inches, when a small mummified hand, a child's hand was exposed. He stopped. This was a grave. This was a mass grave. For whom? Whoever had put it here hadn't even bothered to dig deep. The mound must just be earth covering bodies dumped into a shallow ditch. He stood looking at the mound for a while and then just continued his walking.

A few miles further on he heard cheerful German voices. He approached with caution ensuring he was hidden by foliage. Peering from beneath a fallen tree he saw a work party guarded by at least six armed Germans in black SS uniforms. As he listened he realised that one of the uniformed guards was Polish. A traitor, then.

He watched. The workers were all male, all thin and all wearing striped baggy uniforms. He watched carefully and he realised from yellow stars on their stripy tops that they were all Jews. They worked hard using long handled shovels to dig a long shallow ditch the purpose of which was clear to him because he remembered the mound. The dirt was being piled onto the far side of the ditch. All of the workers looked gaunt and painfully thin. He could see no feeding area, no toilets and no transport. After about an hour he needed to move as his limbs were stiffening up.

Just as he started to crawl away one of the guards shouted incoherently. All of the work squad moved into a huddled group about twenty yards from the ditch. The sound of a truck growling through the woods was evident.

When it arrived it disgorged first about a dozen SS all armed with rifles. Then about sixty women and children climbed or were pulled from the truck. Findlay had never seen such a defeated and accepting look as these people obediently followed the instructions of their kidnappers. Even the children seemed devoid of mischief or hope.

They were all lined up and shot at the ditch in six tranches, none of them reacted or even voiced objections as this happened. Group after group stood placidly facing into the ditch as they were shot from behind. Findlay even formed the bizarre view that some of them were trying to fall in positions convenient for the murderers.

The SS climbed back aboard and the truck left. At a shouted command the workforce moved in to start piling the earth removed from the ditch onto the corpses. Some of the bodies were still twitching and he could hear a child whimpering weakly beneath the bloodied pile. They were covered anyway. The workers were now carefully watched by their guards to ensure they did not hesitate in their task.

Findlay was stunned and stealthily left the murder zone. He was barely prone to extreme language but on this occasion he just thought, those fuckers, those fucking fucking fuckers. He wanted to kill them all.

"There will be a time of retribution, mark my words," he said to nobody there.

When the war turned it was not noticeable on the farm. Things continued as before until one day a car containing two Russian officers drove up.

"Who the fuck are you?" one of them said to Findlay.

"Why do people keep asking that?" he responded.

"Who the fuck are you?" repeated the surprised Russian.

Findlay explained as best he could. The mention of Stalin's name was enough to ensure his protection, and that of the women, from these people. For their part, the Russians explained that the Germans were in full retreat and on the other side of Europe the Americans, British and allies were squeezing the Reich to a well deserved death. Findlay was ordered to remain on the farm while they passed the information to Moscow. He was told that if he left the farm he would be shot.

"Why does everybody keep saying that as well?" he asked. As they left he quietly said, "it worked Aleksandra Ivanovna Barantceva, you slowed them down and they died of it, well done you beauty."

A couple of weeks later two highly amused NKVD men, the Soviet secret service come thought control police, sat with him at the farm table. The apparent leader said, "London and Moscow confirm who you are, it seems Churchill is delighted. So too is Stalin. You have some powerful friends Mr Aitchsmith, nobody on this side will do anything bad to you."

"They're not exactly friends," Findlay explained. "I think of them as demanding friendly bosses." The NKVD poured more vodka to show they understood.

What really provoked their sense of humour was the

kids. "All yours, eh? You English dog in heat, kept your weapon ready throughout the war, didn't you?" They roared with laughter.

Findlay was sorry to leave the children; he really did love them. He obtained assurances that the women would be respected and well treated. He was advised to rush home to Britain immediately because the Polish men would return soon and they would be less than impressed by him, secondly and more importantly because Stalin said he should. He obtained an absolute assurance of safety for the women and kids and then made his sad goodbyes. Everybody, including the half drunk NKVD men, wept.

The Russians supplied the transport to get him to Moscow, from there he flew home courtesy of the RAF who swooped in specially to get him.

"Three kids," laughed Churchill. "You dog…"

"I've been there with the NKVD and quite frankly I don't need it from you. I loved those little ones, I still do and if you think I'm going to sit here and let you…"

Churchill raised a hand to stop him. They sat in the office from which the prime minister had despatched him to Russia. "I apologise. Of course, you are suffering. I have to tell you that it's unlikely the Russians will permit the children or women to travel here. We'll ask but I'm confident they won't allow it. They'll occupy Poland for years, you know. I'd like to expel them but the cabinet and house will oppose that so it won't happen."

"I know," said Findlay, his anger subsiding slightly. "I've left full details of everybody I met with the section.

There's a German I'd really like to meet again. He's SS but I don't know his name."

Churchill looked at him for few moments. "I know the story. We have him, his name is Friedrich Jagemann. The Russians caught him hiding in an old barn and crying like a baby. We also have Johann Waldheim, he asks after you. He seems a decent chap but will still have to pay the price for helping the Nazis. He was wounded in an exchange before he was captured but he'll be fine. He told us about Aleksandra Ivanovna Barantceva," he consulted notes so that he would get the name right. "I had a section supervisor brief me on everything that happened to you."

"Johann's a good man, he did what he could but obviously not enough. I want to have the SS officer for myself and I want to give evidence at the trials." Findlay sat up as if that settled it.

"You can't have him," said Churchill. "I'm sorry but he must stand trial. If I'd been you I'd want him as well so I do understand. His guards have been instructed that you may not see him, should you attend the trials. You have some evidence of the mass murder of Jews so you probably will be called on."

Findlay gave his evidence. He gave general evidence of mass murder, specific evidence of SS murder and character evidence for Waldheim. Jagemann was hanged soon after his trial, in which he claimed that his acts were sanctioned by law at the time and therefore he was simply following lawful orders as was his duty. Findlay was permitted to observe the execution as a favour obtained for him by Churchill from the new British Government. When the Russian team objected Churchill had Stalin inform them that he also wanted Findlay to attend and the objections ceased.

Johann Waldheim was acquitted and released. He wrote a letter of thanks to Findlay and invited him to Germany as his guest when things improved.

Stalin also wrote to Findlay. Findlay was surprised to find the dictator understood people's fears and concerns better than he thought such a man would. Stalin thanked him and apologised for sending him to the front, he hadn't intended him to be captured. He also gave his personal assurance that Findlay's children would receive a good soviet education and do well in the communist state. He concluded by informing him that Aleksandra Ivanovna Barantceva was declared Hero of the Soviet Union and her parents informed of and thanked for her courage and sacrifice. They ask if Findlay would write to them.

Findlay did write to Aleksandra Ivanovna's parents, he told them of his admiration for their daughter and concluded by telling them that she loved them and often spoke of them. That of course was a lie, she never mentioned them, but a justifiable one, Findlay thought.

He also wrote to Stalin. He begged that Stalin release his children to Britain along with the women. He added that if Stalin was unable to do this, then he thanked him for ensuring they are cared for. He wanted to berate the dictator but with his kids still in Soviet hands he didn't feel able to. He received no reply and never heard from or about the children again.

Findlay could have retired at that time. He was promised a good pension and an early honourable release from service. He declined. He did take a year sabbatical during which time he finally learned Japanese.

When the Korean war burst into the world, he quickly learned Korean; it is similar to Japanese in some ways but with a heavy Chinese influence. It is a distinct discrete language but recognisable to any linguist as an amalgam and adaptation of several far eastern phonologies. He requested a posting to the war zone and was embedded with an American squad interrogating prisoners.

The world is filled with stupid moments. As Findlay left a feeding station one night, he was run down and killed by a passing Jeep, the young American driver had been looking at some girls and didn't see him. The medics who desperately tried to save him said he just kept muttering some Russian sounding name over and over before smiling, reaching out and dying.

∞ ∞ ∞ ∞

Standing before my dad and me, Dave, the debriefing priest, explained how all post-death matters were in hand. My dad was pleased to hear that there would be no invasive post mortem examination of my mum. The doctor here would issue a death certificate and the coroner's involvement was just a paper exercise. He explained that doctors wanted to check over my dad before he left and then another cab would take him home and, if necessary, somebody would stay with him until he was certain he could carry on.

"I'll take him home and be with him," I said.

"No you won't and no you won't," Dave ordered. Normally, that level of control thrown at me would meet with a forceful response. Not today though, I trusted this man and if he had something else in mind he had good reasons. The beautiful nurse returned and led my dad away, I swear she winked at him as she invited him to follow. I laughed as he shuffled a little dance step and fell in behind her. I called out to him that I'd phone him and get to his flat as soon as I could.

"My dad seems to be behaving himself," I said to Dave.

"Hmm, maybe," he replied. "He had a bit of a curse and rant before you got here. I've fed him and he's nearly cleaned out my coffee supplies. Actually, he's impressively fit for a man of his age. I think he'll be OK now. I've phoned the coroner and hem said that hem is content just for our paperwork so Jay will come for your mum. Do you want to see her?"

"No." No hesitation. I wanted to remember her as she was when she was animated. I had no need to observe an empty shell looking a bit like my mum. Maybe that was the effect of the switch but I don't think so. It's a decision I made when I realised my mum would die soon.

"OK," said my priest. "Steve," he put his hand on my shoulder, "it's OK to let some feelings out if you can. I do understand what you're doing now. Remember that eventually they explode out of you. I know you're doing the thing we do, people like you and me."

I thought that was a curious thing to say. Definitely some kind of uniformed history there. This was the time

151

and place, I decided. "Dave, where did you serve, who were you with?"

"Ah, observant bastard, eh? I know, we recognise each other, those of us who were stupid enough to think we were tough. I did wear the Queen's uniform and I did go to some places. I was one of those who had special indulgence, that meant I didn't need to serve in Northern Ireland. That's not uncommon for soldiers from the Republic in the British forces. I did go elsewhere, though. I did some things and saw some things. That's all I'll ever tell you. It's also why the church doesn't send me to certain parishes outside the UK."

There was no more to say. I nodded my comprehension to him. He just patted my arm and suggested we go down to his office in the chapel. He said he had something to show me. Several inappropriate and unkind jokes swam into my head, mainly about priests showing vulnerable people things in secluded places. This was just the black humour and the schadenfreude of all services threatening to show itself. It was probably because of the stress of the circumstances and what we'd just said to each other. He knew, he just raised his eyebrows as if daring me to say it and led the way to the chapel.

We walked in silence and entered the chapel. Dave made some coffee from whatever he'd been able to salvage from my father's looting of his supplies. While he was in his little office I took up residence on a chair at the back.

"Always at the back, eh?" he said as he returned. "There's no easy escape, you know. Cancel that, there's no escape in the end. Sit at the back, near the door, if you like but what happens, happens and will happen whatever you try to do about it. Don't fool yourself." Typical, on a day like this he's identifying my psychological need for an escape route at all times. In hotels I always walk the escape route, in cinemas I identify the exits, in rooms I don't control I sit near the door and normally with my back to the wall. On the other hand he might just be using this as a disguised and devious prod towards faith, he's quite capable of that.

He gave me coffee and I noticed a vanilla A5 envelope in his other hand. He gave it to me. "This," he solemnly declared, "is a letter from your mother. She asked me to give it to you. Don't read it until you get home."

"Wow, when did she…" I was quieted by his raised hand.

"Fuck off," he said.

"Oh, very priestly again," I said.

"Shut up," he said, this an order.

"Have you read it?" I enquired.

"Yep, she wanted me to."

I just looked at him. I felt my eyes start to fill up but quickly had it under control again. "OK," I replied.

"When you've read it," he spoke in a low authoritative voice, "you'll have a lot on your mind and will want to visit the area where you were brought up. Do that but I suggest that before you try to act on the letter, if you do, you should tour your old childhood places, see the people who aren't there."

I chuckled softly, "Dave, that's even more Irish than usual."

"Twenty five million, remember. They're still there

and everywhere. Call me at any time. When you're ready, come back to see me if you need to. You are my friend and I'm pleased to have met you. We have differing views of God and man, and you of course are wrong. Be a friend and call on me anytime for any reason, you're safe with me. I'll be at the funeral." We hugged, a rare thing for me and he seemed a little uncomfortable with it as well. That might just have been the height difference, though. I left and took the long journey home. I really don't remember a thing about it which is slightly worrying considering that I was driving.

I didn't read the letter immediately. I wanted to but at the same time I didn't want to accept it. This letter was my mum's voice from the other side and I didn't want to accept the finality of her death by hearing that voice. I knew I would, of course, but for now it was as if I could keep her alive just a bit longer by not reading it. This is nonsense, I know that, but we all are guilty of stupid thoughts when we're emotional. The switch was still on and I was a little worried about when the dam would burst. Now would be a good time since I was all alone and isolated. It stayed on.

By way of distraction I examined the ants. The little blighters were everywhere. I captured a few to examine them. They were black and not particularly big. Certainly not wood ants, they tend to be fairly large and build huge mounds of wood pulp that stink of formic acid. There was no noticeable smell with this species and they were more like the small ants I remember in London.

I hunted around and found several entrance holes in the lawn. A couple I blocked but a few others I dug into a little bit. I then poured boiling water into the depression. The water was quickly absorbed and I poured more. A cruel assault intended to cook them and their larvae, I saved some water to make myself a cup of tea. I imagined that they would reduce their activities as a result of my wet weapon of mass destruction. I called it the aqua bomb.

Combat against the insects done for the moment, there were no other excuses. I sat to read the letter.

∞ ∞ ∞ ∞

Letter from my mother

Steve,

I'm sorry to leave you this way. I doubt if we'll talk about much before the end so I've decided to write down some things you should hear. Our time together was not that bad, really. We had some fun and we had love. Nothing's ever perfect but I succeeded in bringing you up and giving you a half decent start. I have the need to tell you about the war and what happened.

My father saved my life when I was eleven years old. He saved me but it ultimately cost him his own life. It was 1940, September I think but I'm not sure. London was being demolished by wave after wave of bombers and I was right in the middle of it in Old Ford. I've told you a lot

155

about that time but there are some things I didn't tell you and one thing I still can't.

The Germans had become very good at hitting us quickly. Normally the bombs would start falling within a few seconds of the siren warning. This night we ran for the Anderson shelter as soon as the wail began to wind up. My paternal grandmother carried Joe, my small brother, and my dad ushered me quickly in front of him.

Bombs that fall close by whistle as they descend. Just a long single note that increases in pitch as it draws closer. I heard the thump of successive strikes stomping towards our house. Then the rising whistling sound rushing down. We'd come to call it the death whistle. I felt my dad grab me and throw me hard towards the entrance of the soil covered corrugated tin shelter. It wasn't strong enough to survive a direct hit but was, so the Government claimed, able to withstand most shrapnel and a blast that was not too close.

It was a hard determined throw. My dad was a strong man from years of building site labouring. He was a powerful individual who'd survived the trenches of the first war and he wasn't about to give in. As I flew through the air I saw the house about three doors down just implode. It was unreal and fascinating at the same time. The blast turned me in the air just a bit so that I now flew backwards about four feet off the ground and parallel to it. I saw the same blast lift my dad and throw him forwards. I thought the blast did not throw him as hard as he'd thrown me.

During the Blitz I heard tales of how one person might be torn to pieces by a blast while the person next to them was just knocked off their feet. The blast is a strange and unpredictable thing. That's how it was now. The air itself seemed to cradle me it its arms and place me gently on the dirt floor just inside the shelter. I couldn't see my dad now but later learned he had crashed into the small apple tree we had in our garden. It never did provide much fruit and managed to survive the whole long onslaught untouched. It was small but sturdy and didn't give an inch as my dad slammed into it.

I couldn't hear anything for a few seconds and the world seemed quiet and peaceful. As the regular thump of the brutal battering of our city wormed its way back into my consciousness I heard, or rather sensed, my grandmother shouting at me to look after Joe. She stepped over me and out into the deadly shower. I slowly climbed my way back onto my feet and then picked up my brother from the small wooden cot like bed left for him in the shelter. I moved back to the door opening, oblivious to the danger.

My grandmother was kneeling by my dad. He was groaning and writhing. From the garden next door, I heard a man shouting, 'Speedy, get to Jack, we'll do what we can at the house.'

Our neighbour was called Speedy. That of course was a nickname but that's how I knew him and what I called him, I don't know his real name. He was a docker and every bit as powerful as my dad. A huge man with a scarred face and one eye smaller than the other. I always thought he was sad inside.

In the summer they used to fish and drink and sometimes wrestle each other for fun. My gran said they'd been in the same battles and used each other to keep their demons at bay, I didn't really understand that at the time.

'Not this time, Jack. No stinking Hunpig gets to end you, my son. Up you come.' I saw the massive Speedy pick up my dad and place him across the back of both his shoulders. He told my gran to get back in the shelter and then he just smashed through the wooden garden fence that led to the back alley. Then he was off at a run and I knew that no power on earth was going to stand in his way on this night. My gran told me that he'd become a soldier again, just for tonight in order to save my dad. She said they'd fought the Germans in France when they were young and probably owed each other their lives several times over.

My dad came back the following morning, the raid was over and we likely had a few hours before the next one. The streets were full of people, old men and women and children, clearing the rubble and searching for the dead. The wounded were pretty much on their own if they could walk or waited for the overworked ambulances if they couldn't. Dad's ribs had been broken and he was strapped up with bandages wrapped around his torso, that's what they did in those days whereas now they just leave them to heal on their own.

The sharp broken ribs had caused internal lacerations and he developed an infection that killed him a few weeks later. Probably just some stupid bacterial infection that would now be cleared by anti-biotics and a bit of rest, that's how it was then. You know I survived TB in 1947, one of the earliest trials of anti-biotics, I think.

I've already told you about the rest of my life, how my mum died of stress and distress and poor nutrition just after Joe was born. That was just before the war but for people where we were, peacetime was scarcely less painful than wartime; get born, work hard, die young and be hungry and insecure in between.

You know how Joe and I were taken in by the Bernardo network after dad died and how I met your father just before the war and how I grew into adulthood. Eventually Joe and I lived with my maternal gran. She was old then and it was hard for her. You met my gran, she lived to a ripe old age in a cottage at Ware and she was over 100 when you met her, you were only about three or four so might not remember her.

There is one thing I can't tell you but it is something you have the right to know.

I promised my dad I'd never reveal the secret. I suppose it's really the family secret although it's probably not as big a deal now as it was then. My mum never mentioned it although it's about her, really. I can't and I won't break the promise I made to my dad but I wish I'd thought to get him to agree to me telling my children when they grew up. Still, I didn't and so I can't tell you.

I can tell you that my dad wrote a journal and in it he tells the secret. I could never bring myself to read it but he told me the secret's in there.

I hid the journal at number thirteen many years ago. It should still be there if the house is still standing. It's in a hidden space in the front chimney stack up in the loft. It's a good quality notebook that my dad used throughout the first war to write about his experiences. The secret's in there. Go and get it.

Thank you for being my son. Goodbye.

∞ ∞ ∞ ∞

An interesting letter, I thought. My mum could never speak like that but she could write well. I found it interesting that at times she seemed to fall into story telling, complete with dialogue and quoted speech. I considered phoning Dave but decided against it. I would take his advice and revisit my childhood haunts. The funeral was in just a few days and that would place me in the area. If I felt up to it afterwards I'd do the grand tour.

The family gathered at my dad's flat. A small block behind the Saxon church of All Saints near Stratford Portway. Hardly really Saxon any more. A millennium and a half of additions and rebuilds had left it in that common mix of styles and periods that characterises most old churches. It was pretty much falling into disrepair now.

Although I was very close to my parents that never really extended to my sole sibling. A hundred issues caused my sister and me to become distant and almost estranged. She left home young and took to a lifestyle with which my mother profoundly disagreed. I see no reason to expand on that other than to say it broke my mum's heart and although I now act civilly towards her, I do not consider her my sister, just my parent's daughter. Neither she nor I have any real interest in reigniting our sibling bond and it causes me no distress.

Her four children grew up very well. They were now all adults with good careers and although some were estranged from my parents' daughter they all attended the funeral. Families, eh?

My own daughter did not attend. Now that looming exams demanded her full attention, we agreed she would simply send flowers. I knew she'd cope well, no guilt at her absence. Funerals are not really for the dead; they are for the living to find closure. If one is of the mindset that provides natural closure, then funerals are less important than memories and pressing on in order to take the deceased's influence forward. It shows respect to attend but does not in any way imply disrespect or lack of love among those unable to attend.

Dawn was with me. In total there were about twelve of us attending the funeral. I knew some of them well and some of them casually. Everybody remained polite. A mixture of siblings, cousins and offspring, not close but not entirely alienated either. There was nobody from my mum's side of the family. Her brother, Joe, had died decades ago and although he had children nobody knew them. I don't know why that happened, I barely met any of my relatives when I was young and there was never any explanation for that.

A hearse carrying my mother's coffin followed by a passenger limo arrived. Just me, dad and my sister got in the limo. The others would follow in their own cars. Chief burying bod, Jay, introduced himself. He exuded the professional serious caring friendliness of his occupation. He explained that he would also conduct the service at the cemetery chapel.

The lawn in front of the flats was strewn with flowers from us and other people. Floral tributes and people loaded, the cortege set off on its slow respectful four-mile ride to the cemetery. Traffic invariably gave way to it and waited politely for it to pass; then promptly returned to typical aggressive and unforgiving London driving.

Dave was at the chapel. I was surprised to see him in a well pressed suit and tie instead of his usual crumpled priest uniform.

"Mufti today then?" I said to him.

"I don't want to distract from the service," he explained. I thanked him for coming and he said he'd stay at the back and not interfere.

As we entered the chapel the wartime song 'We'll Meet Again' was playing from speakers. I thought it excruciatingly sad.

Jay conducted a half secular half Christian service. I thought this was appropriate for mum's half Christian half agnostic life and views.

Then Jay introduced hymns. "Margaret asked for two hymns," he said. We all knocked out a terrible rendition of 'Abide With Me'. While we outrageously tortured this wonderful piece of music my mum's coffin was carried down the aisle to the front. It was probably the sight of it that made it real for me, at that point the switch turned off and the dam broke.

Even here I was embarrassed at my own bawling. It took me a few seconds to get myself under control by which time I was blind from my tears and choking on mucus. I felt Dawn's hand on my arm but gently shook it off.

Jay introduced the second hymn. "Just a bit of fun, at Margaret's request," he said in a voice revealing that even he found it inappropriate. "All Things Bright and Beautiful." My mum always said she loved singing it as a child but I'm fairly sure she didn't really understand it.

"...All creatures great and small..." we all mumbled tunelessly. Then the bit that really annoys me, "... the rich man in his castle, the poor man at his gate. God made them high or lowly and ordered their estate..."

Fuck this, I thought. I glanced back at Dave and he was grinning at me, he knew that this was provocation for me. He shook his head at me. I held Dawn's hand and think I may have hurt her a little by squeezing too hard. She knew my feelings about this hymn, nothing more than propaganda for children to sing and learn their place early in life. Education always includes propaganda, even now.

When I was seven I had to run around a playground with a wooden rifle before doing drill. This was because we were being groomed to die courageously for the Empire when we grew up, even though the Empire was already gone by then.

They say that when the Roman Empire ended it was fifty years before anybody noticed. Similarly, the British Empire. The institutions of successful Empires continue to function after the demise of the imperial body. It's not until later that everybody realises that the crown has fallen because there is no dramatically obvious total conquest by outside forces.

Today the propaganda in education is about other things but I won't try to identify what, I'm not that brave. I bet any two people, choosing independently, would spot the same propaganda in modern education. It's always there. In my childhood the School Board supervised to ensure the correct political message was delivered.

Today, Ofsted have a political policing component to them when they grade schools. Just take a look at exactly which criteria Ofsted use to grade a school or college. Now consider just how essential any criterion is to the pedagogy and which merely propagates behavioural traits or thought required by the existing political flavour. It's not surprising that the criteria change from time to time, the political objective changes with the politicians. You may note that any constant criterion is probably a proper review of the unpoliticised real teaching. Bollocks to it is what I say. Education should just be about learning and we'll all form our own views.

When we left the chapel we made our way to an open grave about half a mile further into the cemetery. Here my mum was lowered into the earth to rest forever, or for at least seventy years because that was the time limit on the land lease. What happens then? I wondered. Will they evict her if she won't leave? Much of my family is in this cemetery and none of them have ever been asked to leave so I suppose it'll be OK.

My dad was a little out of his mind. His distress was enormous and drove him beyond reason. He stood at the graveside leaning forwards. At his age he's a bit unsteady anyway, today he was just likely to tumble in. I stood with him, one arm across him to prevent this. I imagined my mum chastising him: "You silly old fool, take a step back," she said in my head. I struggled with an urge to laugh; that would not have enhanced my reputation. I suddenly realised that Dave was the other side of him and led him away, I hadn't seen the priest approach but as usual he intervened at just the right moment.

The journey back to the flat was without the convoy that attended. The big limo had just the three of us in it, the driver an invisible presence beyond a screen separating us from the front. My sister sat with my dad on the front most rear cabin seats. I sat on the comfortable rear bench seat. I was watching the world from the rear window. We rolled though the part of Forest Gate that is now primarily Muslim. The road leads down toward a disused pub that was allegedly frequented by Dick Turpin. Most of the current locals don't use pubs and probably don't know or care who Dick Turpin was, either.

A few hundred yards before this pub are two mosques. The first and smaller mosque is housed in what used to be a Methodist church. The congregation seems to largely consist of older suited and booted people of Asian origin. The second, about 50 yards away from the first, is a purpose built red bricked modern building with a small minaret at each corner. I've never given them much thought.

As the original white working classes seeped away in the seventies and later, Islamic cultures were among the incoming groups and they slowly imposed the society with which they were comfortable. That there was more than one version of Islam did not surprise me even when I was young. Just look at the various and sometimes bizarre interpretations of Christianity. Humanity seeks to make God in its own perceived parochial image.

The limo was travelling slowly. As we passed the newer mosque a man of about forty walked off the building steps and out into the road behind us. He wore an impressive bushy beard which somehow complemented the clean white Arabic dishdasha thawb clothing and he looked physically fit.

I suppose the limo looked like an official Government vehicle or something. As I watched him he snarled towards us and ran his right forefinger across his own throat. The cut-throat gesture took me aback a little. Even at our slow speed we would be gone from him soon. "Fuck off," I mouthed at him and gave him the finger. Well, that was my useful input to intercultural relations in Newham.

This was new to me, in the past all cultures and races have rubbed along together reasonably well in this area. Most of the minority groups normally complained about the police but in fairness so did most of the original whites. Conflict with the police in the East End was not a new phenomenon. The middle class socialist agitators who sometimes play their political games in the area don't recognise this and often pointlessly seek to make political capital out of minority grievances.

Later that day I told my dad about this strange incident because he hadn't noticed it.

"Oh, yeah," he said. "Since the wars that followed nine eleven, we've had a few tossers trying to stir up trouble around here. They don't get anywhere, the older Muslims try to stamp it out and keep a grip on their stupid young men. Our stupid young men sometimes try to provoke them as well. As long as we all keep talking it'll be fine." Peace prize for my dad. He's a violent old sod but it's always the violent old sods who keep the peace in the end, which is one of life's little ironies.

Dawn left for home because she had to prepare for another work trip to another county prepared to pay too much for its early years educational services to be assessed. I spent some time in dad's flat. He didn't know much about mum's parents. Sarah and Jack shared a grave in the East London Cemetery and that was all he knew. He suspected the lease had expired because he and mum looked for it some years ago and couldn't find it. London has lots of dead and once you've been dead for long enough they nick your space and trash your headstone, charming.

I told my dad I was going home. I wasn't but I didn't want to complicate things. I'd told Dawn that I'd put up in a hotel and tour the area in the morning. The 2012 Olympics had left plenty of hotel space behind it. Surprisingly, most of the hotels still operated these few years afterwards. I suppose the nearby international railway station, City airport and the sports facilities helped. I had paid ridiculous London prices for a room for one night. A complete rip off but I just didn't feel like crashing at my dad's. He needed to be alone with his thoughts. He had my mobile number if he needed me.

That night I stayed in a hotel in the Romford Road. I'd decided to eschew the more modern post-games hotels for one that had been there a long time. Romford Road is a main artery that connects the east of London to the old market town of Romford. In today's world it's not as impressive as it probably once was. Now it is overshadowed by more recent motorway standard roads. To walk the Romford Road is to stroll a part of forgotten history. I imagine that all ancient cities are like this. The old main drags of London still carry thousands of vehicles but can now appear narrow and not very important.

For some reason the hotel boasted a sign declaring itself to be a 'motel'. I remember when it opened in the early sixties. It was then probably just trying to emulate the increasingly popular American way of things and perhaps somebody thought this made it look modern.

I once read an article which suggested that we lost the war but were occupied by our friends instead of our enemies. The thrust of post-war history has certainly drawn us towards the United States of Amortization in a big way but I'm not convinced that we've completely bought the American way.

Within this country there are still plenty of signs of good old fashioned pluralism. Here we swing somewhere between left and right and mix and match the two as we think necessary. I suspect that a thousand years of class based bickering does not simply dissolve. Maybe that's why we speak respectfully of both Karl Marx and Adam Smith.

Opposite the hotel/motel sits a leisure centre that was once just Romford Road baths. It was previously both a public bath house and a couple of Olympic size swimming pools that were drained and used to hold some of the dead during the blitz. Every Sunday when I was small, my dad would bring me here to swim. Swimming was considered an essential skill because of the proximity of the Royal docks. He mentioned the wartime use on more than one occasion, probably because as a lad he'd visited it on an errand when it was full of victims. Protecting the sensibilities of the young had low priority in the explosive deluge.

The area of my young life was huge. I considered the Ilford borders all the way to Bow flyover as my demesne. To the south the Thames and the docks created a natural border despite the semi-secret pedestrian tunnels under the river. That's a lot of land and I'd never cover it all on foot in one day.

It was a safer world then, or maybe just a less overtly threatening world, young me had covered this area by foot and bus without a single thought for danger. The hunting predatory paedophile or the roaming street gang were unheard of. Well, not exactly unheard of, I had a couple of weird teachers and in the sixth form we all knew of one teacher who was in a sexual relationship with one of our classmates. We all considered it consensual and nobody informed any authority.

This was a school and area where it was not unusual for we sixth formers to visit the local pub with our teachers. I had more than one lesson accompanied by a pint of beer. It's probably not worth mentioning smoking in the classroom. A different world.

The streets felt safe whether they were or not. I think that maybe we just accepted some incidents and situations that today would make excited prurient news.

The world has become much more ostentatiously mawkish in general with roadside shrines, ersatz morality about other people's foibles and crowds of noisily distressed strangers and emotional displays common as hordes of strangers arrive to enjoy the grief at any scene of disaster or murder.

I considered crowd behaviour at the funeral of Diana to be disrespectful and undignified but maybe that's just me being old and reserved. Nonetheless, it was that event that first made public the changed response to disaster; traditional reserve had been replaced by, or drowned out by, a noisier more demonstrative demand to be heard.

Those of us who disagree with such behaviour are vilified not for our more traditional view but because we dare challenge the self sanctioned right of others to impose their unrelated snivelling on other people's grief. Respectful silence says much more.

I know of at least one instance of a horrible child murder where the crowds, unconnected rubber necking gushers relishing the exaggerated blubbing, ignored police requests to disperse and as a result trampled some important evidence.

I decided to start at the Ilford end, just where the Romford Road touches the new north circular ring road, one of the modern fast roads that replaced the old routes. These major motorways act as effective borders and the local cultures change noticeably as they are crossed. The large Ilford area retains a significant Jewish/Anglo/Black/Asian mix that rumbles along more or less comfortably.

The other side, moving deeper into my old lands, quickly develops into a large Asian Hindu/Muslim culture tacked onto the remains of the original white working class and black communities that still continue in pockets. The general area is growing whiter now with significant but isolationist eastern European communities.

A confusing variety of languages touch one's ear in this place. This mix hides a score of petty conflicts between cultures but somehow manages to maintain an underlying acceptance of diversity that enables it to function. What trouble there is tends to be internal to the hundreds of discrete cultures that make up the area.

Each of them tries to maintain its own integrity and this can cause conflict within them as children seek to grow into a greater mixed culture.

This end of the tour had a larger number of older buildings than there are as one moves closer to the old dockland and industrial zones of Stratford and Plaistow. Those areas were more heavily bombed in the second world war and now sport labyrinths of sixties concrete replacement housing blocks, now slowly being replaced themselves by modern rickety mass housing.

I've met people who have expressed surprise that rebuilding took place so long after the destruction. The fact is that rebuilding London continued into the seventies and some in the eighties.

The war damage was immense; I was basically brought up in the shattered shell of the old London with bomb sites and shored up buildings everywhere. As I grew, the new world grew up around me. I was raised in a culture that was moving on, the new towns and suburbs provided new places that bled the occupants from this part of London. Nowadays, Romford, Basildon, Crawley and Harlow are closer to the culture that I knew than the area I was now in. The London working class diaspora spread across the south east and further.

As I began my tour I tried to imagine the missing, Dave's twenty five million. More, really, if you include the losses from all wars in which this bellicose land has involved itself. I expect all of them seemed necessary and proper at the time; protect trade, impose influence on distant regions, defend the proper values etc. Wars are the way of humanity, it seems. Every search for peace or disarmament appears to have resulted in war. As we became capable of indulging this frightening instinct with industrial grade weapons, the fighting defeated our attempts to explain and justify it and horrified even us.

Millennia ago isolated human families came into conflict and alliances with other families. As time passed the families amalgamated and merged cultures and thus became clans.

The clans came into conflict and alliances with other clans. As time passed the clans amalgamated and merged cultures and thus became tribes.

The tribes came into conflict and alliances with other tribes. As time passed the tribes amalgamated and merged cultures and thus became nations.

The nations came into conflict and alliances with other nations. As time passed the nations amalgamated and merged cultures and thus became continental blocs.

The continental blocs will also come into conflict before amalgamating and merging into a unified global governance. We'll probably still find something to fight about even then. So many ghosts, an incalculable number overall. I dare not even count the losses from plagues provoked by human activity, the post first war flu killed thirty million all on its own.

On that cheery thought I decided that at this point I was unable to see the ghosts. I'd half expected to see the nebulous forms of people in places where they should have been. I saw nothing of the sort but that did not detract from the idea. Maybe as I strolled I'd see them but I've never been particularly prone to ghostly and creepy imaginings. This would be a long arduous day, I made regular stops for water and snacks.

From this end of Romford Road I could see the edge of the cemetery where my mother's funeral took place. Her place of rest is just the other side of the railway line that runs parallel with the road at this point. I could just make out some grave stones. This was the only point of note on the long hike toward East Ham.

About half way along, I changed my route onto the Wanstead Flats. This ancient common land has endless football fields and is used by dog walkers, runners, hikers, flashers and anybody else. The ponds on this large piece of green space are where I used to net sticklebacks as a kid, when I wasn't adventuring on the many bomb sites. I'm told that at night the land is given over to doggers and other miscreants. I think this might not be true, the local population of white nominal Christians, black actual Christians and any colour devout Muslims is unlikely to put up with that. The occasional murder victim crops up on them, too; that must spoil their leisure pursuits.

I didn't spend long on the flats, instead I started to walk down to the Forest Gate area, in particular a crossroads called Manor House although if there ever was a real manor house it's long since gone. From there I could walk down to West Ham park.

The road down to the crossroad takes one past a sixties built church. I think it's Methodist and the congregation is largely older black people. I'm not aware of anything interesting about it except the statue of a man on the wall. I mean quiet literally on the wall, feet planted on the brick and body leaning far forward defying every sensible physical and gravitational law. The arms are held out wildly as if waving, there is a bible in one hand. This figure intimidated me when I was young, I always feared it would leap off and chase me. I'm surprised it hasn't fallen off.

The site on which the church sits was once a bomb site and before that a pub. The blitz had a curious tendency to destroy the pubs, maybe the Nazis were financed by German brewers looking to take the trade. That's a bit unfair on German brewers but it makes as much sense as any other explanation or excuse for the war. It's been suggested that the early Nazis were in fact financed by loans from the Rothschild's banks. If that's true it must be one of the nastier historic business errors. I doubt that they were ever repaid but I don't imagine the Nazis were much worried about their credit score.

The other side of the crossroads is a Victorian church, Anglican I think. It's almost always locked and barred and I've never seen anybody going into it. As kids we considered it creepy.

A little further on are the mosques that we drove past in the funeral car. The time of day that I walked towards them must have been outside of the normal prayer times, there was nobody about except standard pedestrians plodding about their everyday business.

Remembering the incident of the cut-throat gesture I lingered in front of the steps when I reached the more modern mosque. I slowly climbed the steps and peered inside through the glass doors. It just looked like any office block foyer boasting light not quite white plaster board walls, except the posters were in Arabic.

"Hello sir, can I help you?" I was a little embarrassed at jumping visibly as the small Asian man spoke. I don't know how he'd suddenly appeared beside me without me noticing. He was about fifty and dressed in casual western clothing, a tweed jacket and mole skin trousers but wore an incongruous tall red woollen cap. He spoke with a London accent revealing a slight Pakistani lilt.

"No, not really," I replied. "I'm just curious that's all. If I'm in the way I'll go."

"You're not, you are welcome. Are you curious about Islam, the architecture or something else?"

"I'm Christian," I don't think I've ever before defined myself by religion. "Well, sort of Christian, C of E." We both chuckled softly. "It's just a casual general curiosity, really." I told him about the cut throat incident. In reply to his concerns I assured him I wasn't there looking for anybody to cause trouble with, I was just passing and curiosity got the better of me. I'm a big and heavy guy and this small man apparently remonstrating with me must have looked comical to any observer.

The man told me his name was Charlie, which I considered an unlikely name for him but that's just my own prejudice; I'd expected a Pakistani name or Arabic sounding at the very least. He pushed the door open and invited me in. As we entered I heard a door open further down along the foyer.

"Hey, Charlie," said a vaguely familiar voice. "Oh, it's Mr Aitchsmith, isn't it?" Walking towards us was Taz

Khan, the young man from my dad's awkward pension interview.

Charlie looked pleased to see him. "I didn't realise you were here. This chap had an unfortunate encounter with mad Shafi a few days ago." Charlie explained that Shafi, no other names and this one appeared to be just an abbreviation of something, was a man sometimes subject to paranoid schizophrenic episodes who frequented the mosque. I was a bit taken aback by the lack of political correctness in their description of *mad* Shafi. I kind of sympathised with him but still, cut-throat gestures to funeral goers is a bit much. Charlie explained that Shafi was harmless and anyway at the moment he was hospitalised for his own and others safety. I chose not to juxtapose 'harmless' with 'hospitalised for safety'. Let it go, it's not important.

"I remember you and your dad," Taz explained. "He made me laugh so he stands out a bit. I am surprised to see you here, though. I'm sorry about Shafi, when he's up to it I'll advise him not to make death gestures to strangers, it's not good for public relations especially the way things are now."

It turned out that Taz was on the board of trustees for the mosque and he and Charlie basically ran the place between them. Charlie seemed to be the theologian of the team, he led payers and generally did all the cleric stuff, Taz dealt with the finances and kept the administration running smoothly.

I explained what I was doing that day. They both offered condolence for my mother and invited me to tour the mosque. I declined with thanks, I was grateful and interested but today was not the day for me to explore comparative religions; I was looking for ghosts.

The thought struck me that they have their ghosts here, too. Hundreds of thousands, maybe millions, of Muslims died fighting in Europe and Asia. At that point they were not part of European or Brit home culture but the effects are the same, lots of non people not existing. There are people not in this mosque who should be. It's the same worldwide, kill one person and the spreading tentacles of their line just stops; we never get to see the growth that should have been.

On the South Downs, near where I now reside in my retreat, there is a monument to the Indian fallen. It's hidden away from population centres just as the Indian troops were; Indian army groups waiting for deployment into Europe were, in both wars, camped on the South Downs away from the local people. It was felt at the time that large numbers of Indians, Empire subjects, would be too much for the local population's sensitivities.

I thanked them both, shook hands and promised I'd visit again for the tour. They were both fascinated by and supportive of what I was doing on my tour. Charlie particularly loved the idea of Dave's missing millions, I suggested he contact Dave and discuss it. I'm not fool enough to think that all mosques would be this welcoming to me but I think most of them would be. They need to sort out their nutters and they know it. They will, I'm sure of that. In fairness, we need to sort out a few nutters as well and I'm not quite as convinced we'll do it.

When I left the mosque I wandered through a couple

of back streets. I was looking to pass a red brick hall known as the Cornwell Centre. It was named after John, or Jack, Cornwell who died heroically and pointlessly in the battle of Jutland, at sixteen years of age he continued to man his ship's gun even after being badly wounded. The gun itself is in the Imperial War Museum. Legless and dazed he kept firing and drove the enemy away. Stunningly brave, I can't deny that, but because he died there were no little John Cornwells to carry on. By Dave's formula there are about fifty or so people who have never existed because of his courage and that's without counting anybody he killed in the action. A fine genome extinguished.

About forty years ago, as the original population was beginning the process of removing itself and the new population establishing itself, there was a move to change the name to some Indian or Pakistani philosopher. It's one of only two occasions that I've seen the originals take real offence. I don't mean the individual racists acts of idiots, there are plenty of them, I mean a whole community up in arms. When the reason was explained to them the new group in possession of the hall, Hindu I think, agreed that the Cornwell name would stay in perpetuity. Each November they laid a wreath of poppies under the name plaque.

The hall is now council offices, a one stop shop for the locals to turn to. The wreath no longer appears and poor young Master Cornwell seems to have been forgotten again in the streets where he lived, played and worked. I heard somewhere that the name of the hall can never be changed because the Hindus placed a covenant on the deeds to prevent the problem ever arising again. Truth or rumour? I don't know.

The other occasion really engages the challenges inherent in diverse cultures, in spades. It was way back when I was policing. I was part of a team tasked with solving the problems faced by a new large mosque recently built in inner east London. Smashed windows and pig's heads were a regular occurrence. No matter how many people were arrested in operations to protect the building, it kept happening. As loudspeakers broadcast to call the faithful to prayer, the cars in the street would all sound their horns and fights would break out.

A meeting was called. Those involved included me, the Imam (Bangladeshi), the local police area commander (Scots), the local borough commander (Welsh), the local policing team leader (Geordie) and the local intelligence officer (Scouse). As the meeting progressed it became clear that none of them really knew what was behind this.

"Am I the only one here who knows why this is happening?" They all looked at me, surprised by my exasperated tone.

"Go on then," growled the area commander, "enlighten us." The others chuckled. Everyone except the Imam, that is. He recognised the local boy and wanted to hear what I had to say.

"OK," I said, never one to suffer from obsequious reticence. "Under that building were about five hundred bodies and some of them are still there." Mouths dropped, eyes widened. "That site was originally a huge rubber warehouse with several sub-basements.

When it was bombed out the resulting pit was used to place blitz victims. Most, but not all, were eventually relocated to the City of London cemetery, fog of war and the exigencies of the emergency and all that. The locals are incensed because their dead are being disrespected by not acknowledging this. If any of you knew anything about this area, you'd have known that." General silence.

The shocked Imam put his head in his hands, the others looked at me in that 'you know it all bastard' way that you get used to if you're an inner city Londoner in London's police, most are from elsewhere in the country and many from outer London. Inner Londoners are a minority. It's probably why I never achieved high rank; that and a tendency to piss people off.

The mosque paid for a small Christian chapel at the side, nobody ever visited it and the mosque keeps it in good repair. The local vicar led a service to the lost, and the local Muslim community leaders paid for a plaque to commemorate the dead. The pig's heads stopped appearing, the car horns fell silent, the windows remained intact. Job done.

After the Cornwell centre, which was closed and lonely looking, I returned to the main road. Now on a winding road that leads to West Ham park, which was once the grounds of Elizabeth Fry's home and dedicated to the public on her demise, as we were always told at school in attempts to elicit our gratitude for the largesse of our betters.

On the sharpest bend sits the Spotted Dog pub. Now boarded up and sorry looking, this dilapidated old building dates back centuries in parts. Local legend says it was used by Dick Turpin as his base and from here he first urged Black Bess towards York. I don't know about that, I do remember seeing my dad and my uncle Tam get drunk there from time to time.

Tam, real name Alistair but he preferred to be called Tam, was a friendly and amusing man but liked a drink or several. He died in his sixties after years of alcohol abuse. I liked the man and I don't intend to wax moral over his love of drink. Each to his own, hem's own, and who am I to say who should do what? He was happy and fun. Nobody likes a serious morose puritan.

He wasn't a blood relative, he had married one of my dad's sisters, dad says that his father was delighted that she'd married a Scotsman. Dad is about third generation London Scots which makes me part Scot, I guess. Then again, I'm roughly part anything, the family tree on that side even includes one chap by the name Goldberg, not a very Anglo or Celt name.

I stopped just to look for a few moments. For the first time I imagined happy and social translucent shadows enjoying a beverage in and around the pub. Shadows of people who are no longer here or have never existed. Why now? Why here? Maybe the long walk on a warmish day had left me light headed but I felt fine. Maybe this small area, now so different from my memories, highlighted the change brought on by the losses. Maybe the historic associations of the building, maybe my meet with Charlie and Taz, who knows? For whatever reason, I could now see the missing millions, or at least some of them.

Enoch Powell, an intelligent though controversial

man, would have called this part of Forest Gate one of the swathes no longer recognisably British. He was right in so far as the changes and his view of 'British' go, his concept of British culture being very much informed by the pre-war paradigm. He was very wrong if he believed that British means unchanging and fixed as a culture.

I may have mentioned that the lost traditional working class culture, often mourned by some, was in my opinion shit. I don't mourn its passing; I hope it died suffering. I don't think he really considered the consequences of losing two generations in wars, the inevitable diversity when lost generations leave a gap to be filled. I'm not one who struggles with diversity, I enjoy it because it's interesting and it's not the crap cloth cap world where I never knew my place.

I sat for a while on a remaining wooden bench. Possibly the same one I used to wait on as a child while dad and Tam imbibed the evening away. There was plenty of junk on the floor. This detritus included sweet and crisp packets and empty glue tins. Over by the base of a low wall I could just see the plunger end of a syringe covered by moss. I didn't stay there for long. The shadowy ghosts faded and that was the first and last time I actually saw them.

However, I now felt their presence, I always had but now I knew what that constant underlying subtle sense of loss and regret was. I'd always put it down to being brought up in the aftermath of the war with the ruptured buildings and traumatised adults. Now I knew, as I'd always felt, that it was real. The future that didn't and couldn't occur called out its distress at not being allowed to happen.

The park is seventy-seven acres of grassland and small copses, a huge area in inner city London. I entered it by what I always thought of as the back gates although they are probably the front gates for people who live at this side. Part of the park is given over to an army reserve depot and so the military keeps touch with a place that was once a prime source of recruits. I suspect that it's not so prime now but the base remains. The regular Sunday military parades along the local roads ceased many years ago.

This 'rear' set of double iron gates are near a fenced off playground. My dad says that in his childhood it was a shallow pond. In mine it was an adventurous place of swings, slides and a thing we called The Horse. This was basically a huge RSJ built structure that swung end to end, always staying parallel to the ground by some cantilevered artifice, it could accommodate about fifty or more kids. It was nowhere near safe and often children were thrown off, smashed up a bit on the concrete floor and escorted to hospital. I suppose that this level of excitement was required when the same kids could just as easily go off to explore some fascinating bombsite, of which there were hundreds. Now, of course, it is long gone, the swings are low and the slides have safety sides. No risk allowed.

The park really acts as a buffer between Forest Gate on the 'rear' side and West Ham on the other. When I was little, Forest Gate had a predominately black population mainly of West Indian origin. West Ham was largely traditional white. As more people of Asian descent moved into the area and the whites slowly took advantage of increased income and left, both areas started to develop their own micro cultures.

There'd been more people movement since and Forest Gate was now largely black and Asian Muslim and West Ham black, Hindu and Sikh. Both sides, of course, retain vestiges of the original white groups. More white faces appear everyday now as the Eastern European presence increases. The park buffer accommodates the leisure needs of everybody.

The resident park keepers disappeared long ago, the houses supplied to them as part of their employment are now expensive private residences and the park is patrolled and maintained by mobile council patrols. Forgive the suspicious nature I'm about to display but... the park was maintained by a trust fund and grant set up by the late Ms Fry. Now that this function is absorbed by local authority services, what happened to the money that was set aside to administer the land?

I enjoyed strolling through the parkland lost in a personal nostalgia; here was where I played golf, here I played football, here we picnicked and here my friends and I built our hidden den. After about twenty five minutes I emerged through the West Ham gates into a similar but slightly different community. I'm told there is some conflict between the two park sides but it all seemed peaceful to me.

The only concerning thing I saw was an obviously homeless and mentally ill man carrying his world in his arms. His world consisted of a dirty sleeping bag and a bulging and tatty Tesco carrier bag. He was walking in small circles and muttering loudly to himself. I never saw anything like this when I was small, this stuff is fairly new. There were always tramps but the modern homeless, the ignored mentally ill, they started to appear in the eighties as the country discovered selfishness and profit based services. Profit based services? That's an oxymoron if ever I heard one.

A short walk took me to Richford Road. I planned to head towards Stratford Broadway and if I veered round to the parish church near my dad's flat I could still first walk down the road of my childhood. I paused at number one, I lived here until I was one but I don't remember it. I paused again at number thirteen, this house I remembered. It was a bog standard terraced house. The Victorian front bay window had been replaced with one huge flat window, the same above it, it just looked wrong. The front low brick wall that my dad built was still in place. The house appeared empty and there was a sales board tacked onto a wooden pole. I entered the estate agent's number into my phone. I'd call them later; probably still secreted in the house was the journal.

I tabbed down to the sixties flats at the bottom of the road. This estate is built on one of the primary bomb sites/playgrounds I remember. An alley led down to the church and past my dad's place. I continued straight past and onto the main road that took me past my old school, now a training centre, and the police station, built on the bombed out pit of what was once another church, about four hundred yards from the original police station, now offices.

The churches didn't fare well in the blitz, most of them were very old and did not withstand blast well.

That's true of the pubs as well which explains the strange fact that they were the two most commonly destroyed major buildings.

This church had been opened up all the way to the crypt and I recall playing in the destruction where it wasn't unusual to find old bones and coffins. Things that would be considered horrific now were just my normal world. Mind you, even then there were limits, this we learned when a friend and I suffered two strokes of the cane at school because we were seen fencing with two femurs. Most unreasonable in my view.

About half way from this spot to my dad's flat is St Lucia Drive. It's part of a nineties build and the council probably named it to reflect the more cosmopolitan nature of the place. Historical ignorance once again provoked a response.

Sade Morgenthau was a little Jewish girl of German extraction. She and her family escaped the Teutonic insanity of the nineteen thirties and resettled in this area, she must have been a baby at the time. They were not wealthy and her father worked in the docks to make a living. They were almost interned at the outbreak of war but somehow convinced the authorities that the family was now British and posed no threat.

Morgenthau is a beautiful name; it means morning dew. Sade was a beautiful little girl and everybody loved her and her amiable family.

The place where St Lucia Drive now stands was at that time a public bath house. It was flattened early in the blitz and the rubble cleared. Later in the war it had grassed over and was an empty area where the kids played. Sade's father had gone to war with one of the Guards regiments. She, like many others, had returned to her mother from evacuation. She often played in the bombed out clearing.

In the latter part of the war V2 rockets, launched because the Nazis were having a murderous tantrum at the prospect of losing, fell often in London. They were the brainchild of Wernher von Braun, later the architect of the US Moon shots. My dad says they were the least frightening of all the weapons used against this city and had no tactical value. He said that bombs and V1 doodlebugs create anticipatory fear, they announce their deadly intention and then follow through. The V2 just happened, one moment nothing then the next an explosion. The V2 didn't create fear the way the other attacks could.

As Sade played in the grass a V2 struck. The rockets were fast but one could just about see them a moment before they struck, a vengeful streak from the sky. This V2 crashed down and hit Sade directly. She was vaporised. Nothing of her was found. One second a happy little girl, the next she was molecules floating in the air. People wept and comforted themselves with the knowledge that at least it was quick and she was happy beforehand.

Her father died a few months later while fighting in France. He rushed at a fortified position on some bridge and won a medal. Eyewitnesses said he'd been out of his mind at the time and they'd never seen such an enraged charge at the enemy.

Since the new road started at the location of the V2 strike, my dad decided it should be called Morgenthau Drive. He launched a one man campaign and started to call door to door explaining he didn't want it called St Lucia Drive. Typically, it didn't occur to him to explain why and he was a little upset by the indifference he encountered. The fact is that most people now in the area didn't know about Sade but my dad assumed everybody did. Demographic changes hadn't exactly passed him by but for some reason he thought it was the same culture but with different people.

While dad was on his rounds to garner support an elderly Jamaican man decided to confront the door to door racist he'd heard about. Two old men arguing must be a funny sight. It could have ended in some kind of embarrassing incident with both injured and probably arrested. Fortunately, both men were similar in that neither of them would strike the first blow. Neither of them would retreat either and so the neighbourhood was entertained for a few minutes while they shouted incoherently at each other.

Eventually they understood that the Jamaican had mistaken my dad for a racist activist and my dad had mistaken him for an uncaring nihilist. Then they quieted down and explained themselves to each other. When the Jamaican heard the story he shook my dad's hand and joined him, dad's first and only convert to the cause. I'm told that these two caused much local amusement with passionate but inept attempts to explain their position to people.

Eventually a kindly Sikh retired teacher living

nearby listened to their story and wrote to the council on their behalf. The council was sympathetic but felt that the naming process was complete and didn't want to spend more time and money on altering it. My dad is still furious with them but is happy that Sade's name is known again.

I headed on up to Stratford Broadway. There's another small park just off of this route but I chose not to go through it. On the corner by the lane at the side of this park there used to be a red telephone box. In the early sixties a suspect in the nearby old police station produced a hand gun and killed two officers. As he fled he killed another who tried to stop him. His short flight ended in this phone box where he shot himself dead.

The local rumour was that the police executed him with his own gun. Maybe, maybe not. I remember that nobody much cared if they had. The world of my childhood was more accepting and understanding. Several years later a small parcel bomb exploded at the new police station. Strangely, it was only the locals, not the police, who recognised that it was the anniversary of the killings.

The area was full of rumours of one sort and another. Like the belief that Jack 'the hat' McVitie, an undiscovered victim of the Kray gang, was planted in one of the pillars on Bow flyover. Lots of rumours based on no evidence except hearsay. The Krays loomed large in the lore of the people then in the area, a pair of thugs in danger of drifting into the noble villain category. A childhood friend of mine claimed to be a cousin of the twins, nobody challenged the claim because it's very likely. The area had many large extended families and a lot of interrelatedness.

I was still feeling the ghosts but considered I might just be sinking into nostalgic whimsy. Perhaps they were the same thing. The approach to the Broadway passes an office block that I remembered as the site of Bill Steven's gym. Bill was well known locally for his muscles and his commitment to helping youngsters stay out of trouble. A young Arnold Schwarzenegger was a common sight in the area since he trained there, the massive and tall young man was referred to locally as Tarzan. He was known for his easy going friendly manner. It says much for the people of the area that an accent as strongly Germanic as his was so readily welcomed in the area the Luftwaffe pounded for months on end.

Not always so accepting, though. As I moved into the Broadway I passed a pub, the Edward Vll. In the first war a Zeppelin floated over the Stratford railway junction, a prime target in both world wars, and hand dropped a few small bombs. I've seen a photograph of two soldiers on leave shooting at it, it seems that first war soldiers took their weapons home with them when on leave.

A furious crowd attacked the pub, at that time called The King of Prussia, and as a result the name was changed. A mob has no intelligence and does some stupid stuff, this was an example. As a young man I used that pub many times. The rumour was that behind the portrait of King Edward was one of the Kaiser, still hidden after all these years. It's probably wise not to trust rumours that circulate in pubs.

Opposite the Edward, in the grounds of St John's church there is a monument to the peasants who died in the famous revolt of 1381. It has been suggested they were executed and tipped into a mass grave just here. Probably they were trying to retreat back to Jack Straw's Essex at the time and hence died locally.

The 2012 Olympics changed the physical area almost beyond recognition. The Stratford station I recall had a small entrance accessed through a gap between the sooty drab houses and a steep set of steps leading down to a surprisingly large railway station. It hasn't got much larger, it's just now very open and declares its presence loudly. Beyond it is most of the Olympic site and posh new shopping zones.

The 2012 Olympic summer games opened with a well choreographed though very slightly eccentric ceremony. Lots of drums, noise and celebrations of things British. Many people who saw it were very impressed. The locals were less than impressed. The building of the stadium and other venues displaced a lot of reluctant and resentful locals. Many considered it the final nail in the coffin of the old culture. That's probably a bit if an exaggeration since many of the people are still quite local, having been pushed to Leytonstone and similar places, but the fact is that many people were angry about the Olympics.

While the opening ceremony did its thing, outside the stadium six hundred or more protesters were detained in that corralling and legally questionable people trap the police call kettling. Over one hundred and eighty were formally arrested. That got very little press coverage and locals have, and do, compare it to the Chinese treatment of people and news control. I would not advise Lord Coe to try jogging in some parts of the East End. Memories are long, it's difficult to earn real enmity among these people but once that's achieved it doesn't disappear easily.

In need of a little rest, I jumped on a train and trundled down to North Woolwich. This is a curious area, the Royal docks effectively make it an island and the culture here is more traditional. Being trapped between the docks and the river creates a sense of camaraderie lacking in many parts of London. The population is mainly white with some middle class black and Asian families. As islanders they all rub along together well.

This area was almost completely flattened in the second war although a small pocket of pre-war housing close to the docks somehow survived. The docks were a major target and even today ordnance is still pulled from the river or dug up during building. It used to be that the local gas containers, huge structures like giant buckets upturned in water and filled with gas fuel feeding to the houses, were painted either black or white. The black ones indicated that a bomb had pierced the container and was probably still there. It didn't much worry anybody. I think the last one was removed in the eighties.

In the first war there was a large shell manufacturing centre here. One day it exploded, killing scores of people and injuring hundreds.. One of the dead was the local policeman who, it is said, died trying to rescue some workers. The local police station uses a brass shell tip as a paperweight and it's claimed the shell tip comes from the explosion. Nearly a thousand houses were destroyed or badly damaged. The blast crossed the river and caused more damage south of the Thames.

Wounded soldiers in local hospitals made their way to the scene, if they could, and helped the rescue effort. The War Office, on hearing this, decided they must be fit for duty and returned them to the front. There's a lesson in Government compassion for you.

Another daft local rumour is that the Tate and Lyle sugar factory, fast by the river, was swastika shaped from the air and therefore attacking bombers ignored it. Certainly it survived the blitz that demolished almost everything else. As a boy my dad was a spotter for a search light on top of the factory. I think the planes were probably avoiding the light rather that the factory. Nobody likes to be lit up and then battered with hundreds of air burst shells, it's just human nature.

The same collector who years ago showed me the Stratford Broadway Zeppelin photograph also showed me another of two German airmen in the North Woolwich Road. Obviously shot down and safely bailed out, they walked towards the police station but held Lugers firmly pointed at some surly looking workmen watching them in the street. The police station also survived more or less intact, I wonder if it's fanciful to suspect that the bombers left it alone in order to allow the crews somewhere safe to go for surrender if shot down.

I wandered around for a while feeling but not seeing the ghosts. I spent some time just staring at the indestructible gas works. This stunningly sturdy structure survived a county load of direct hit bombs and still stood proud. Attempts to demolish it in the eighties failed miserably when the explosives just shifted the walls a bit. I have no idea what it was built with, it looked like concrete but was obviously particularly strong concrete.

After the eighties' attempt failed the site was rented out to make some scenes for the film *Full Metal Jacket*. I saw it when it was faked up to look like Saigon, it was a strange sight. This time I noticed that some of it was gone, I have no idea how, and some of it still stood. The long departed builder of this place should be proud, this was one impressive piece of work.

I gave some thought to just how many 'communities' I'd walked through that day. Probably all sorts and then some more. London is really just a series of small villages all crushed up against each other. It's always been that way but it's more recently that we talk about 'communities'. I have a slight problem with it. Dave, as often is the case, gave me the idea and that caused the difficulty.

I'm OK with the somewhat definition-stretching idea that a community can have geographic location, religious affiliation, orientation positions, physical attributes, whatever. It all sounds cosy but the problem with the declaration of 'community' is that it immediately excludes others. It creates the sense of 'other' and 'us' that can have more serious implications.

Many years ago I entered a pub in central London. I was tired and hot, shopping for something I can't now remember, and just needed a sit down and a drink. I'd walked down from Oxford Street into the narrow and older streets around Soho Square. In my youth this was considered a debauched and fun area filled with dodgy girly clubs and naughty film shows. The pub doorman asked me if I was gay.

"No, does it matter?"

"This is a gay bar, friend," as if that explained everything.

"Does that mean I can't go in for a quick drink?"

"No, of course not. I just thought you should be aware. You might not be comfortable and the regulars might find it awkward."

"I'm sure they won't and I won't. I just need a drink, I promise not to offend anybody with my blatant straightness." He looked a bit annoyed by that.

I did get the drink and moved on. Everything was fine, I could see no reason why it should be otherwise. I wasn't exactly prevented from entering the place and I understand the doorman's reasoning. Nonetheless, the idea of 'community' had labelled me 'other' and I didn't care for it.

I was pretty much worn out and decided to take a cab back to the hotel/motel and rent an extra night or two there. The place wasn't busy and it was no problem to just rent night after night without making a firm reservation. After a meal and a few drinks I retired to the room and phoned Dave. I had a plan for Richford Road and wanted to run it past him.

"OK," is all he said.

"Dave, I've just told you that I plan to commit a crime and you just say OK?"

"Nah, that's no crime. The courts might not agree so

don't get caught, it might be a bit embarrassing for you if you are. What's the worst that could happen if you are?"

"Well," I said, "the worst would be that I get convicted of a crime and lose my police pension and become homeless and starving."

"Well, if that happens, come and see me, I know some half decent homeless shelters you could use. Seriously, Steve, do be careful but get the journal. I've got a feeling it'll be fascinating. Call me if you need anything, anything other than a dishonest alibi, that is."

"Piss off. Thanks, Dave. I'll call when it's done and when I've read it."

"Call me anytime," he said. "I can be down to Brighton in a couple of hours if I need to. This is an overall difficult time for you, you're doing well. Never stop doing things, never stop pushing on, never give in. If this turns out to be something you need me for, call me, please."

He was a good man. "If I need a dodgy drinking, fighting, ex-fornicator of a priest, you mean." He laughed. We exchanged a few pleasantries and the call ended. I'd still have the army and teaching pensions. Between them they're nearly a third as large as the police pension.

The following morning I phoned the estate agent and feigned interest in the house. I'd taken care to call from a hotel pay phone so that I didn't send my mobile number. I arranged to meet an agent at the address at ten. I took another walk through the park and down to Richford Road. I waited outside the house for about twenty minutes when they arrived in a not very new tarnished silver BMW.

There were two agents, the first, a woman of about forty who was power dressed in a snazzy greyish suit with pleated skirt and flowery blouse. Her peroxide bouffant was Dynasty Dallas big hair style and her jacket sported shoulder pads, really, and for a second I imagined I'd time warped back thirty years.

The second agent was a man of about twenty with stupid stand up short bright red gelled hair. Tieless and in a rumpled brown suit, he looked like a spiv. Typical estate agents in my view; moderately educated and ambitiously avaricious. In my head I saw the lad as a mouthy, self centred quasi sociopathic prat. I had no qualms about playing my part for them.

I explained that I was a lawyer who had just found work in the area. I had significant funds available and really liked the look of this grotty age worn terrace and would like to see the house. They led me around the house. Every inch was filled with memories for me but I could not let on about that. They explained how the house had been wonderfully maintained by a caring long term owner who now had to reluctantly sell.

I noticed that the original stair bannister was still in place and couldn't resist resting my hand on the bottom end of the hand rail on which there was a carved wooden rose. When I was fifteen I decided that bannisters were for leaping over, I misjudged the leap and broke the rose off at its base. Dad glued it back in place but ever after the slightest amount of pressure would dislodge it. I leaned my weight on it and off it duly popped.

"Oh, that's recent damage. The vendor told us about that and we'll fix it. We'll have a specialist joiner in to do the job and by the time you move in it'll be done."

Bollocks, I thought. "Oh, that's good, no problem," I said. This really was a moment of universal disingenuous discourse. You lie, I lie, I win, fuck you. I acted my part of cash flow advantaged dumb potential buyer as they led me through my old bedroom, my parent's bedroom, my sister's and the spare. They were especially complimentary about the well decorated front room. I knew that if you peeled back the wallpaper by the chimney stack you'd find the graffiti 'Steve Aitchsmith....1964...9 yrs old" in indelible ink on the plaster.

During this dishonest charade I expressed interest in the tiny back garden. I was promptly led to it through the kitchen back door. I exclaimed wonder and desire for the tiny crummy poor soiled lot. I also took a previously tightly packed wad of paper from my pocket and surreptitiously pressed it into the dead lock receiver of the rear door. When we re-entered I was gratified to note that they did not set the inside door bolts. My paper would prevent the dead lock fully entering the receiver and I'd be able to open it with pressure. I've picked up a lot of dodgy skills in my time.

At the end of the sales pitch I told them that I'd almost certainly get back to them with an offer. I loved the house, which was true, and would love to live in the area, which was not true. They tried to get my details so I gave them a false mobile number and e-mail address and promised I'd contact them in the morning. I returned to the hotel/motel for a good meal and a nap.

My fraudulent playacting had achieved three things for me: I obtained a reconnaissance and preview of my target location, compromised the rear lock and created a valid reason for the presence of my DNA at the location should it become necessary to have one.

This is now a much more twenty-four-hour society than the London I knew. In the seventies you'd rarely see anybody on the streets after midnight. The night economy started to expand in the mid-eighties and quickly developed into the all-day city we now see.

Continuous nocturnal enterprise or not, in residential areas of London the night is still quiet most of the time. Normal, working, sensible people are in bed asleep at four in the morning. The police like this time of day, the nuisance public have mainly buggered of and it's just the goodies and the baddies taking each other on. Of course, the occasional proper person returning from some legitimate activity gets caught up in it but most of the time it's true.

At this quiet and peaceful time, I stood in the courtyard of the disused garages in the road that backs onto Richford Road. I had with me a three cell Maglite, the heavy metal torch useful both for light and bashing. I didn't anticipate trouble with anybody but it was four in the morning and I was in a deserted crappy zone that might house drunks, druggies, lovers or anything. It was empty of anybody.

I knew that if I clambered up the rear wall, dropped down into the garden behind it and then scaled the small fence, I'd be in the garden of number thirteen. I'd done it many times when I was a teenager, after the bombed out buildings of this street were replaced with the houses now there, and this useless garage area was supplied for the people who didn't have cars. Sixties planning getting it wrong again, well done dippy middle class architect with your incorrect assumptions and prejudices.

This little journey used to take me seconds. My first attempt failed because I forgot that I'm now sixty something and the grace of movement I had forty-five years ago has deserted me, not that I was ever exactly balletic. With some effort I made it to the rear garden of number thirteen in about fifteen painful struggling minutes. I'd made enough noise to wake an ancient corpse but nobody seemed to hear me. At this rate I might not have enough time to do this.

I pressured the rear door. Pressure is cumulative. If you push against, say, a ship at a quayside, it won't initially move but if you maintain that pressure then eventually the whole ship will move and all with just little old you pushing it. The same applies to pressuring a lock. Just put your flat hands by the lock and push. Don't jerk, just keep the pressure on and eventually the lock will give way. Since I'd prevented the lock going fully home, it didn't take long and the door just clicked open. This still would have worked without the preparation but it would have given with a loud crack as the lock or door jamb broke and would have taken longer. The objective with locks is to set them so that they don't give in to pressure for a long time, the burglar then gets bored and goes away.

I was in. I have good night vision and could manage

without artificial light at the moment. I was imagining ghosts. Not real ghosts, even though the upstairs rear bedroom floor boards are disfigured with burn marks from where, sometime in the nineteen twenties, a small girl died after her clothing was ignited by the old copper boiler that was there at the time. As a child I worried that her spirit might haunt me. The ghosts I felt were of my family, my young self, the world now gone. They say that as we age we are condemned to live in a foreign land. It's true, the world of one's childhood, so apparently secure and enduring, gives way to a new social structure just as the one before it gave way. Nothing is constant but many of us find change unsettling.

The world we live in now will also give way. It's called a Kondratieff, The Russian social scientist Nikolai Kondratieff identified and described this period of change. About every fifty years or so, technology and social norms slowly morph into differentness as societal and scientific advances influence our world.

The phone zombies of today, so ridiculous to people like me, will in their turn stare and despair at the attitudes and behaviour of their young, if they can leave the phones and social media long enough to actually produce any.

In 1968 the visionary Arthur C Clarke published a short novel; *The Lion of Comarre*. He didn't foresee the modern microtech but he did imagine a large all knowing computerised information centre, a kind of large physical internet. He saw around it a static human society where many people spent their lives wired up to virtual worlds within the machine. I think of that every time I have to dodge a mindless phone slave walking into everybody. Wake up, phone zombies, you have nothing to lose but your brains.

I blame the blasted priest for provoking my growing obsession with ghosts and social disaster. I thought he had an interesting observation but trying to visualise the missing, departed and the never existed becomes a bit of a mugging of the mind. Multiverse options begin to creep in and I started to imagine all kinds of alternative timelines. What if this person lived instead of died or this other died instead of lived?

My life has taught me to accept and adapt, to face facts stoically and work with what is, not what might have been or what I would have preferred. It can appear cold at times but if the alternative is this constant review of possibilities, well then, bring on the chill. How far do we go with this? If the first multicelled organism had floated up instead of down, would the dinosaurs still rule the Earth? You see, it's nonsense but at the same time I kept finding myself looking for the missing.

I decided that since I'd now joined the burglar community I should focus on committing my crime and buggering off as soon as possible.

Displaying an embarrassing practical knowledge of housebreaking protocol, I went to the front door and pushed home the bolts. This would slow any owner or other legitimate caller at that point and give me more time to escape through the back garden. I made sure the rear door was open so that I could flee whippet-like, or more correctly lumbering bear-like, back to the garages. I closed the kitchen door to the downstairs corridor so that anybody entering from the rear would warn me by opening it.

I made my way upstairs. I could not resist knocking off the wooden rose again, I don't know why. Perhaps I just wanted to make some proprietary like gesture, the house still felt like home to me and I very slightly resented the fact that it now belonged to somebody else. I went up to what used to be my bedroom where there should have been a small hatch leading into the loft. It was not there; I hadn't noticed that during the estate agent visit.

I felt the ceiling at the place it should have been and realised it was plaster board. It was flush with the rest of the ceiling but when I felt elsewhere I could feel the more expected plaster and lathe. I just punched the plaster board and it made a hole. I shone the torch and could see the wooden hatch just behind it. I cleared the board and pushed the hatch open slightly. It was at this point I realised I didn't have a ladder and hadn't even considered how I would get into the loft, I wasn't exactly sprightly.

I searched around the house, and in the small cellar found an old high backed wooden dining chair, that would have to do. I wondered where it had come from, probably some owner between us and now had just dumped it there and forgotten about it. Standing on it I was able to push the hatch fully open. I'd expected the hatch to fall backwards the way it always used to. Instead it clicked onto some clever little catch that had been fitted after we left.

By standing on the chair back I was able to ease

myself fully into the loft. I then realised I'd left the torch on the floor by the chair and had to climb out again to retrieve it. Climbing in for the second time I knocked the chair over. Lithe cat burglar I wasn't. I hoped the noise didn't disturb anybody or make them realise somebody was in the empty house. I could get down again just by lowering myself; being tall and having respectable upper body strength can be an advantage sometimes, especially when lowering oneself through small hatches during a burglary.

In the torchlight I could see that there were far fewer cobwebs than I'd expected. The space smelled clean and dry though unaired. It was empty and the grey slates of the roof were visible, all of the insulation was between the rafters at my feet and this place was built with the slates directly onto battens on an open roof. Slate is an excellent roofing material and I couldn't see any dislodged in any place. Considering I might be the first person in here for many years, that was quite impressive.

Mum's letter said the journal was hidden in the front chimney stack. I'd expected to search around it for hidden compartments or loose bricks. That was not necessary, on a small brick shelf half way up the stack was a greasy looking cloth covering something book shaped. A quick glance inside revealed it was the journal. I was surprised that it had managed to just sit there undiscovered for so long. It was hard covered and appeared to have a sewn and muslin backed paper block. It was good quality and must have been very expensive. The paper was heavy sheeted and small print on the back cover promised it was long lasting 'neutralised' paper, made in the USA. I assume that meant acid free. The gold inlaid small print beneath that boast was in German, just the Berlin address of the shop selling it. Why German? Maybe grandad Jack found time to go shopping in the enemy city during the war to end all wars.

I managed to extract myself from the loft, retreat to the rear door, recover my wad of paper from the lock and make a not exactly athletic return to the garages. I noticed an upstairs light was on in the house next door, I just hoped that the area retained its reluctance to call the police. Since the light went out as I watched and no police arrived, I assumed it did.

It was now almost fully light and I would walk back to the hotel, get my things and return home. Steve Aitchsmith, master burglar and veteran fool chalked up another small success. Special forces missed out by not finding me. "Who dares whines," I mumbled to myself as I walked, trying to rub the pain out of the small of my back.

On the train back to the south coast I received a text from Dave.

< Position > it stated.
< Sitting > I replied.
< Dick. Me trying to be circumcised >
< Really? >
< Circumspect. stupid spell cheque… how wented it >
< Done … got it …… will fone when read >
< Okee dokee m8tee. Cu soon Sassoon platoon>

"What?" I muttered to myself. He needs training in modern tech, for sure.

< Don't try txt speak... you useless at it ... both too old ... speak soon >

< I look forwardly.... wellies done >.

I'd so far resisted the temptation to read the journal. I wanted to be settled and comfortable to read it and so set aside an evening to do so. I completed all of the usual mundane boring household chores then reviewed the ant situation.

You can't keep a good ant down, they seemed to have recovered and were threatening the conservatory once again. Not quite the invasive force they had been but still slipping indoors and the nest, if anything, seemed busier.

Time for genocide as advised by the Roman Catholic Church representative for drinking, swearing and doing things good. I felt the ants deserved a fresh tin, not one just recovered from my shed where it stored old nails for no sensible reason. I fed on some tinned spaghetti and then cleaned and dried the tin. I spent some time removing all of the label. I don't really know why, maybe I didn't want the ants to read it and realise the trap.

I observed the nest for a while and identified several entrances in use. I blocked some of them with stones then placed the upended tin over the entrance I judged to be in the sunniest spot. Now we'd see. It was now late afternoon so I opened a bottle of wine, split a packet of chocolate covered peanuts and settled into an armchair to read.

I removed the greasy cloth that wrapped the book. As I opened it at the first page a flimsy, thin sheet of paper fell out. On it was a typed poem based on the famous *In Flanders Fields*. No name was attached to it but given its location I assumed it was Jack's. I read it slowly then placed it safely onto the coffee table. He must have added this to the book later, there was no date so I could not be sure. I took a pen and added his name below it. That gave me a little thrill, I was doing something with Jack.

The rest of the journal was written by hand. Sometimes in ink and often in pencil. Some was a bit faded but not too much; It had not seen much light since it was left on the brick ledge where incredibly it remained until I recovered it.

∞ ∞ ∞ ∞

The Journal of John 'Jack' Adams

27th May 1916.

I wish I knew the man's name. I could have found it on his identity tags but I was in such a blue funk I just wanted to get out of the shell hole.

I sort of slid into it while we were retreating from another failed attack. If we keep throwing hundreds forward and come back with a mere third of them, I don't know how long this can last. As I passed the huge shell hole I just lost my footing, the muddy side slid away and down I went. At first I was afraid I'd end up in the vile bubbling black liquid mud in the middle of it, horrible stuff that sucks you down like a descent into some terrible airless hell. It even smells of sulphur. The bubbles? That's the men and animals already reposing in that slimy mud grave. They give off gasses as they decompose, sometimes it ignites and a ghostly whooshing blue flame erupts out of the hole. We call it 'Wilhelm-O'-the Wisp'.

I managed not to join the drowned and I just lay there for a few seconds. Then I heard a German voice. He was about forty or so, an officer, short and stout with a silly little moustache. His grimy uniform suggested he'd been in this hole for a while. His pistol was still in its belt holder and he held his hands out in front of him as if to calm me down while he spoke softly.

I couldn't understand him. For some reason I got the idea he was a school master, just the way he crouched slightly and focussed on me. Maybe he was, maybe he saw me as a boy who shouldn't be here. Whatever the truth, he was trying to keep me calm.

I did a terrible thing. My smelly (SMLE or short magazine Lee-Enfield rifle, to you) was still in my hands, the long bayonet muddied and already bloodied from the assault. I stuck it deep into his gut. He made a kind of 'umph' sound and fell to his knees. I pulled it out and stuck it into his chest. He didn't move, just gurgled. Then a tear slid out of his eye and he died in front of me then slumped in a heap as I removed the bayonet by pushing him off with my foot.

I felt like a criminal. Did I really need to do this? What was the tear? Was he weeping for himself or his family? Was he weeping for me? Was he trying to help me? No, I told myself, he's a sodding German pig and not a person. He deserved to die, the pig. Hunpigs exist to die, that is their purpose.

Did he see me as a silly boy playing grown up games? I showed him. I searched him. I was looking for cigarettes, food, money, anything I could use. I don't smoke, mum never let me in spite of the doctor's recommendation that it was good for me, but I can use them to buy things from the other men. I found a small bar of chocolate and this note book, which was blank and unused. I tucked them both in my tunic pocket and scrambled out of the hole. Part of me wanted to cry as I did so but I knew I had to be tougher than that. For Christ's sake, I've killed about twenty men since I got here. I don't know why this one bothered me more than the others.

Airbursts were still exploding overhead, splatter plunking the mud and dirt with their nasty twisted shrapnel, and the pop pop pop pop pop from the German machine gun crews as they cut an arc across the ground. I dashed for our trenches. I made sure I was still clutching my smelly; returning without it was a real problem, I'd known even brave men get accused of cowardice for losing their rifle. I knew of one incident where a Canadian had fought hand to hand in enemy trenches to allow his mates to retreat, his last act was to wedge his rifle across the mouth of a dugout to slow the Germans rushing out of it and then fall back himself. He was shot for cowardice because he returned without his weapon.

As I lay panting in our own lines I continued to wonder why this one was affecting me like this. Perhaps because it was close up this time. Up until now I've fired at Germans, I know I've hit a few but you never really know what happens after that. You see them fall or stagger away. You're fairly certain you did it, but you never know. I've stuck my bayonet in a couple as well, I've even smashed a few with trenching tools or stamped on their faces but in the heat and fear of the fight you just move on before somebody does it to you. This time I saw his eyes as his soul left him. This time it was a man not just a German. I can't think like this, it can get me killed.

It's the following day and I've made a decision. I'm going to use this book to write about my life in this war. I've decided not to put dates in it, just write down what I'm thinking. I will be a different person at the end of all this. I'm a different person every day. Part of me knows this is not a normal life and yet another part of me, the part that frightens me, enjoys this bloody nightmare. I have to record all of this in order to remind myself who I am. I need the monster inside to enable me to survive this. I don't want to keep the monster when it's over. I will apologise to the souls of the men I kill when it's safe to do so. I hope that God will forgive me.

Not many of us were religious when we got here. Now even the most devout atheist talks to God. I don't think God's very impressed.

It all went quiet for a while, it always did. It takes a factory at home a full nine hour shift to create about two hundred and fifty shells. With double shifts that's about five hundred a day for each factory. During an assault we fire them at about seven a minute for each big gun and they are in five blocks of twenty or more guns at this location. We can use the shells a lot quicker than Blighty can make them. We're firing more than a day's output from one factory in less than a minute.

There will now be a few days of sniping, just to make each side keep their heads down, there will be small reconnaissance groups trying to gain information and if possible snatch somebody from the other side's trench, and of course the occasional lone shell thrown over just to remind everybody there's a war on.

Once in a while each side's reconnaissance groups meet up in no man's land, normally in the dead of night. Sometimes they have a nasty little hand to hand fight. More often than most people realise, they just ignore each other. I've heard that once or twice they've traded cigarettes and stuff but nobody would be stupid enough to own up to that.

At night, if there's any unusual noise out in no man's land then some fool will launch a phosphorous flare and light up the place like daylight. Anybody moving about in between the combatants' trenches at that point is in deep trouble. Not too many soldiers get caught up on the wire. If they do get caught up and can't be rescued then at some point in the next few hours somebody will shoot them, often their own side if they're wounded and suffering. Just once in a blue moon somebody is caught on the wire for days because nobody has a clear shot without taking a risk.

When that happens they can moan pathetically for days, it's the most awful and depressing sound.

Normally, we, or the other side, order a few shells, claiming we're trying to cut the wire with the blast, just to end the poor bastard's misery. It's a kind of soldierly gentleman's agreement; anybody on the wire has to be granted a mercy blow to end the suffering. In this part of the line we've fallen into an agreement with the Krauts. If either of us plan to drop a few mercy shells we wave a pair of long johns on a stick just to warn the other side, it avoids misunderstandings. Normally we're in the front trench for about eight or more weeks and various kinds of local agreements are not uncommon.

War activities in the quiet times include delousing as far as possible by using skin burning potash water as well as running candle flame along the seams of clothing to kill the eggs, washing as best we can and trying to find a safe moment to shit. Shitting's not normally a major priority because the rations really constipate you up. The problem is, this means that later you need to find a semi-private spot to squat over the latrine bucket to strain and groan the monster in your bowel out into the world. The laughter and mickey-taking comments of the blokes nearby don't help. Peeing's different but has dangers of its own; the bucket can't be left in one place for too long because the enemy notice its location and try to lob a few small bombs over at the right time, like early morning.

A lot of the men pee on their boots. It helps to keep the leather supple and kill fungus inside. New lads in the trenches often make the mistake of untying their boots and taking them off. This should never be done. Once the feet swell into the boot they should be left alone or it's impossible to get them back on. Of course, wearing them permanently leads to trench foot as the skin rots away. Pissing on them helps reduce that.

Food gets dragged in from the reserve trenches just behind the front. There's an almost constant brew going on so we have lots of tea with as much sugar as we can find.

Ablutions for the men are an ongoing opportunistic affair that doesn't do much to get you clean or tidied. Our smell must be appalling but fortunately we're spared it because of the overpowering stink of rotting flesh. You can get used to anything.

Ablutions for the officers are not much better. I did once see some simple public school idiot of a lieutenant have his driver deliver him a tin bath. The fool placed it on the rear parapet, stole the brew water to warm it, stripped off and jumped in. He was warned but other than that we stayed silent; it's best not to mock the backward sons of the elite.

The Germans, who could clearly see him, were not so reticent. How they jeered, often in English. They howled with laughter when one of their snipers blew his head open. About a hundred of us replied with rapid rifle fire just to stop their filthy cackling.

Remembering that particular murder made me feel slightly less evil about the shell-hole killing. This really was a war where anything goes and there are no rules, chivalric, moral or any other kind.

The most horrible part was that it was too dangerous to recover the dead officer from the exposed parapet. He sat in that bath for nearly a week growing bloated and putrid, then a shell landed near him and he was pounded into the trench rear wall, tin bath as well. He's not the only former comrade we see decorating our trench walls. We were all somewhat annoyed that we got sprayed by his rank innards.

As the quieter period settles in there's time to write letters, chat and think. How did I come to this? I question myself a lot now, this isn't the glory of war I'd expected.

When the country called I was glad to volunteer. Well, I say glad but it was either that or begin a lifetime of manual work at the local abattoir 'cos it was the only job available. Both mum and dad supported me, dad even offered to join up with me but he'd already been turned down because of his bad lungs, he could hardly breathe after decades working in a flour mill.

The war had been going on for over a year but I was too young to enlist and I was worried it might be over by the time I was old enough. I lied about my age to get in, sixteen-year-olds are not supposed to be fighting. I'm a big strong lad and can easily pass for somebody older, I've even been in a pub or two so I must look at least twenty one. The recruiting office didn't put any effort into finding out my real age, they just needed willing fighters.

I was stuck into a London rifle regiment, created just for the war, beasted down at Salisbury training grounds for six weeks and then shipped to France. When we arrived in Calais the locals just ignored us, they'd seen thousands of us arrive by then and we were nothing new. They were friendly enough, though; the young mademoiselles, and quite a few of the older ones, happily returned a cheeky smile. I felt I would like it here. I didn't see any young Frenchmen, they were off to war as well, I imagined. Just the pretty girls and the old left to run the town. I wondered if England looked like this to a visitor.

I have to be honest, I'm not entirely sure where I am at the moment, in a battered trench somewhere in Northern France near Belgium, I think. The first engagement I was in sort of left me not caring where I was anymore, strange that.

When we first got to France they entrained us almost immediately for a place called Neuve Chappelle. Apparently the Germans, not yet having properly fought us, had insulted us by not bothering to position too many men opposite our line. They'd pay for that. The fact that the place was a salient, our trenches into their lines, meant that a decent surprise attack would probably overwhelm them.

A protruding salient is an exciting place to hold, what with fire coming from all directions. However, it's great to attack from because you fan out in all directions and as they adapt firing angles when you get close they have trouble blasting at you without hitting their own trenches further along. They were in place on a ridge so we'd be attacking up hill. The attack would be large, involve thousands of troops and break the German entrenchment in that area.

We were placed in the first reserve trenches, so we would be the second wave. Our briefing was the first indication I had of just how daft this war was. We were told that the first wave would walk toward the enemy (really they would, slowly and intimidatingly so that they looked good, even my, as yet, unbloodied self knew they'd get slaughtered). This lunacy would occur after the Germans had been stunned into inaction by out magnificent shell barrage. As the first wave secured the enemy trenches we, the second wave, would stroll (stroll? Bloody hell) towards and beyond the enemy trenches in order to neutralise the enemy reserve trenches. The third wave, behind us, would run at the charge (great, they get to run after we've done the work at a sodding snail's pace) to mop up and capture survivors, if they had any (if we bloody had any).

"Any questions?" asked the briefing officer.

An older grizzled looking soldier put up his hand.

"Yes…" said the officer.

"I just wondered, sir. In the event that the enemy is not stunned, what should we do, what is our second action contingency if the first plan fails."

"It won't," said the officer cheerfully. "Just bash the Boche, that's all."

Another older soldier vomited.

The battle itself is a bit of a blur now. The barrage started and by the end of it I was half deaf. It culminated in what they called a creeping barrage, the idea being that the wall of shells slowly move forward, ripping up wire, as the troops follow behind the barrage up to the enemy. That didn't work and the barrage stopped while the first wave was only half way across no man's land.

The Germans were not stunned. They piled out of their deep shelters and manned their machine guns. I heard the distinctive staccato sound of the damn things delivering their lethal hail. Thousands were mown down and nobody got anywhere near the enemy trench.

Now, any sensible plan would have cancelled the second wave. Not here, not in this war, the second wave was ordered to go so off we set.

"You may run," instructed an officer. Oh I wanted to run alright but not towards the enemy.

As we moved towards our launch ladders in the front trench, I thought that there were several stupid things about this plan. Not just the stupid plan itself, but the stupid considerations and stupid assumptions behind it; why was it so confidently believed that the Germans would all faint, unable to move as a result of our shelling? Why not shell their trenches directly, instead of using it to slow down our soldiers? Why? Why? Why did I join in this? And there's one other thing but it's subtle and I don't think it's occurred to anybody else. It was known that this would be a dangerous attack (no joking there) so the men in it were chosen especially for it. Not for our soldierly skills or brute toughness, we were all chosen because we are without children, married or unmarried alike.

Now, this is less obvious but just as stupid as the other stupid things; I know that men with children have to get back to work for their kids' upbringing but that's a minority. They should be the ones first put in the danger line to improve the chances of those without children getting home and having some. If the war goes on like this, there'll be empty villages in England in thirty years time.

A not very robust looking officer blew a whistle and we started up the ladders. The scrawny officer observed us climbing and waved his révolver in encouragement.

"Coming with us, boss," grinned an inexplicably cheerful cockney as he climbed. He had a kind of distant look in his eyes. Not drunk but not entirely here with the horror either. He was sort of at peace in the peacelessness.

"Right behind you, men," replied the ashen faced and nervous officer.

"Yes, that's right, you slimy fucker," said the soldier to my shock.

As I emerged over the trench I heard a shot from just behind me. I looked back and to my astonishment the officer had shot a young soldier. The boy, about eighteen years old, lay in a foetal ball and was obviously dead.

"He was a coward who would not attack," explained the officer. He then put the revolver to his own head and shot himself.

"Keep moving mate," this from the same cheerful cockney, his arm on my shoulder. "Don't mind him, he just couldn't face it again. Keep moving and keep low. Don't try to win the bloody war, just try to stay alive, good luck son." With that he was gone.

What was going on? This was my introduction to the sharp end of the Great War. I kept moving forward, aware that around me there were explosions and bullets plunking into the ground, sometimes somebody would twist and fall. I heard shouts of 'Woolly Bear' as overhead explosions created expanding circular black clouds that rained shrapnel down on us. Some of it plinked off my helmet but somehow I was uninjured and kept moving forward.

I found myself at the German trench, already there was close up fighting in it. I stood for a few seconds then a shove in my back sent me tumbling into it. As I said, it's a blur. I remember the funk and the sluggish fight that I was in. My limbs felt heavy and everything I did seemed so slow. I smashed, I hit, I bayoneted, I fired. Then it was quiet. Just us, the Germans gone, we had won, it would appear. The floor felt strange and I looked down to see I was walking on a carpet of bleeding and deformed dead, British and German.

A Scot with a thick Glasgow accent thumped me on the back and grinned at me. "Well done, son. You're a bloody killing demon, that's what you are." Then he was gone as well.

I was not me. I don't remember leaving the enemy trench but somehow I was back in no man's land. I was elated, I was disgusted, I was fearful, I wanted more, I wanted to be dead, I wanted to kill more, I didn't know what I wanted. I didn't know who I was. I didn't know anything. Then I was in our own trenches, I don't know how.

It would appear that in spite of our unexpected success, the staff command decided we couldn't hold it. So after stealing everything we could, damaging what we were able to and planting a few booby traps, we left it for the Germans to reoccupy.

From then on, the Germans never left the lines

facing us undermanned. Now they'd fought us in a large engagement they had a bit more respect. I never saw either the cockney or the Scot again, I hope they both made it.

I started to notice the thousand-yard stare in others, somebody said I had it. It's a look that's constantly searching for danger, trying to maximise both long range and peripheral vision. It's the look of men in war.

We were posted to the front-line trench while replacements were found for the destroyed first wave. It took about seven weeks to relieve us. In that time there was one half-hearted German assault, they dumped a few shells on us, moved some troops about a third of the way into no man's land and then drew back. Not much else happened.

We were sent to a camp just outside Paris for a rest. We were not allowed out of the camp although a few locals came to the camp with bread, cheese and wine for us. We licked our wounds and then moved to the location we're in now. Here we've been, on and off, for over a year. So now, whoever you are reading this, you are right up to date, unless of course you're reading this in a hundred years from now in which case I'm still right up to date and you will have to imagine you are. I'll try to keep it as a journal and hope it's not too confusing.

My survival strategy now is not to worry about where the army send me, just use the creature I've found inside me to permit the real me to reach the end of this. I tried informing the army that I'm below the legal age to fight but the officer told me it didn't matter. Besides, he said,

I'd agreed to be the proper age when I enlisted, the army has a very idiosyncratic logic. He said I would reach the actual legal age, as oppose to the age I'd agreed, while I'm here so I might as well stay, thanks very much.

Since I killed the schoolmaster, that's how I think of him, we haven't moved from this spot. The rumour is that we'll be relieved soon, it's been a long time now. We've started singing to the Germans at night and they reply in kind. A couple of them have good voices.

They were singing last night and it went on for longer than usual, a suspicious sergeant told us to put up a flare. The flare lit up the no man's land and there, close to our wire, were three Germans standing as if posing for a photograph.

One of our men shouted at them to run back to their trenches. He was clumped around the head, not very hard, by the sergeant who gave the order to fire. I didn't feel able to murder a sitting duck in cold blood; my inner blood thirsty lunatic needs the excitement of battle.

Another lad had fewer qualms and shot the middle one. I saw his chest burst open but he just stood there for a while, turned and staggered a few steps before dropping down dead. The man to his left dived to the floor and seemed to be swallowed up by the dirt as he crawled quickly away. A few shots went his way but I don't think he was hit.

The third one must have been out of his mind with fear, or just stunningly brave which may well be the same thing. He lowered his rifle towards us, bayonet already fitted, and charged screaming. They'd obviously cut some of the wire because it didn't slow him. Those of us not already firing brought up our rifles and frantically worked the bolts, he'd be here in seconds. Our own men a bit further along the line, observing but not involved, cheered and applauded him as he dashed at us. A fusillade of shots hit him when he was about ten feet from the edge of our trench. He just dropped face down, jerked about a bit and then stopped moving. Somebody put another round into his head.

We discussed this lad and decided we didn't want him bloating up and stinking, maybe even popping as they sometimes do, this close to our living (dying?) space. It's not unusual for bits of soldiers to crop up out of the dirt, even from the trench side, but they'd normally already completed the most disgusting part of taking the dust to dust trip. We had to move or bury this lad. It had been bad enough living with daft-bath-bugger for a week, we didn't want another malodourous trench mate.

Somebody made contact with the Germans and invited them to come and get him. They decided this was just a bit too close to us and said we should take him to them, not on your nelly. We agreed a short local cease fire and two boys went up to him, while the rest of us kept our guns firmly pointed at the enemy lines. I could see the German guns pointing back. Then a strange thing; before dragging the lad to the trench for disposal, the boys stood to attention and saluted the corpse. As they did so I saw the German guns lower and I knew there would be no fight today.

A few hours later a tin came crashing into our trench, goodness knows how they managed that, and we all dived for whatever cover we could find. Nothing happened so somebody opened the tin. In it was cake, a lovely sweet but slightly crunchy sponge type thing, an icing covered taste sensation. With it was a note with just one word written on it; 'Danke'.

Great. We have just been briefed by a visiting staff officer, they only visit when it's quiet. We are to be relocated further north. He has briefed us about another hard push to recover some useless little Belgium town that has been destroyed anyway and has swapped hands a few time. The idea was that we would occupy a ridge in front of the town while others took ridges on other sides. Then a hard push from another regiment would take the town itself. Nobody seemed to know why we needed this town, apparently it's important.

"This is it, men. Here we end the Hun once and for all." The annoying prat sported a huge bushy moustache, tobacco stained and greying. He looked like he'd stepped out of the 'needs you' poster. He went on to tell us that he was sorry, we couldn't be replaced yet because our experience was required. He promised that as soon as we'd won we'd be relieved and be given time to read, write, study and reflect.

"Time to sleep, drink, shit and fuck," somebody whispered behind me. It made me giggle. Then he continued, "if there's any of us left."

They've just issued our extra ammunition and battle pack. It includes a tin of corned beef, a small metal flask of whiskey and a French letter. What do they think we intend to do to the Germans? Come here, Fritz my

224

sweetie, have a nice drink with your meal and brace yourself for a hard British push.

That last entry was about two weeks ago. That was one terrible and, as usual, pointless carnage field.

We were told to wait at the trench ladders for the whistle to go over the top. We were instructed to walk line abreast because the creeping shell barrage would protect us. I've seen how well that works before.

Then a surprise. I knew there had been mine works under no man's land towards the enemy lines. I thought it was to undermine their trenches and maybe get at their dugouts. The Germans sometimes infiltrate the mines and there's blind claustrophobic hand to hand, thank God I'm not down there. Now we found out what they'd been doing as unbelievably monstrous explosions erupted under the German lines. It was incredible, volcano like blasts flew upwards, millions of tons of soil. The blast, even for those of us sheltered in this trench, burst some ear drums and shook sense out of everybody. There followed a few seconds silence.

Then our shelling started, about thirty feet in front of our trench. Our wire had been cut last night, the enemy wire would be cut by the shells. That's the plan anyway. I glanced at our officer. He held a whistle to his mouth and looked at a wrist watch. It's funny, before the war wristwatches were only for women, really. Now it's considered manly to wear one, it suggests tough trench fighting.

The officer, I didn't know him, looked a bit young but determined. He blew his whistle and up we went. I was about the fourth up. We formed line abreast and started to walk. At this point the dirt from the huge explosions started to rain down on us, I saw one lad felled by a large rock. The shell barrage crept effectively, unusually, but a couple of our men were taken down by shrapnel. That's the problem with shells; they just don't know who they belong to.

We trudged forward, rifles with bayonets held at port arms. To my left was the young brown haired officer. He actually grinned at me. To my right was a man I knew by sight, a big chap who I know lives not far from me. He winked at me and mouthed something, I couldn't hear what. We trudged on for what seemed like hours but could only have been a minute or so. Then the creeping barrage stopped. Most of the attacking line was still standing. There'd been no enemy fire and only a few dozen of us had been hurt by our own shells or the falling dirt and rocks.

I couldn't really understand what I saw. The German trench was gone and in its place was this huge hole, a deep gouge into the land with smoke still issuing from the bottom.

"Go around the mine crater, boys," yelled the officer. We worked our way around it and found ourselves in the German rear reserve trenches. They seemed to be deserted. In small groups we started to explore them. I was with the officer, the familiar chap and two young lads who just looked ashen and frightened, possibly this was their first attack.

As we approached the steep stepped entrance to a dugout shelter the two lads dashed in. The rest of us, all three in unison, called for them to stop but they paid no heed. Within seconds there was shooting from inside. Every firearm has its own distinctive pop and this was not the sound of smellies being fired. We heard groans and thudding sounds. Then German voices chattering urgently to each other.

I dropped a Mill's bomb into the dugout. Then the other chap threw one in as well. Two explosions later the officer listened then we all threw in another one each. When the dust that billowed out cleared a bit, the officer called into the dugout, there was no reply. We went in, it was really deep and looked as if it was brick lined. Among the smoke and throat searing cordite fumes we could find not a single whole body. Bits and guts were splattered about and items of equipment lay twisted and torn. It was impossible to tell friend from foe and even difficult to tell human remains from other detritus. We didn't linger.

As we re-emerged into the trench there was a leg, from the knee down, laying on the floor. No trouser, just a boot, a British boot.

"What's that?" said the officer, I bit stupidly I thought.

"It's a leg, sir," said the familiar chap. "A good British leg carelessly left behind in the urgency of the attack."

"Well, whoever owns it has hopped it by now," said the officer. We all looked at each other and just giggled like schoolboys.

We couldn't see anybody else. The officer checked his watch and exclaimed we'd been in the dugout for fifteen minutes. It had only seemed like seconds. Chronological awareness is always an early casualty of battle.

The trench, like all trenches, zig zags because the

crenelated profile avoids long straight lines in order to limit blast. From around the corner we heard German voices. The officer raised his revolver and we worked our bolts.

An old man wearing German uniform, who looked like he belonged in a sanatorium of some kind, shuffled around the corner. He stopped in surprise at the sight of us. The officer shot him in the chest. He just stood there for a second and then crumpled straight down. There was urgent shouting from around the corner and a Mill's type bomb on a short stick was thrown round it towards us.

We darted round the corner behind us to avoid the blast. We only had two Mill's bombs between us and threw them back to where we had been. By chance two other Germans, younger this time, were just coming round the corner to check the effect of their bomb. They took the full blast.

Taking a serious risk, we hoisted the officer in the air so that he could get a view of whatever was happening. We only kept him sticking up for couple of seconds.

"Oh, dear," he said. "Our men seem to have pushed further on into German lines. But the Germans are back in this trench and manning some quick fire guns on our second wave out in no man's land."

"What do we do?" I asked.

"Buggered if I know, what do you think?" he asked back at me.

This was new, an officer asking me what I thought. I said, "If we push on we'll catch up with our men but be trapped with them behind German lines. The Germans here will decimate our second wave. I think we should attack the machine guns and try to save our second wave 'cos they're getting slaughtered at the moment. If we silence the guns we save our second wave and stop our first wave getting trapped."

He looked at me almost caringly. "Good lad. Yes. We three take on the whole German regiment. Not bad odds." Then he touched each of us and said, "Lads, if we don't make it know that it's been an honour to fight alongside you."

"Save it for the angels," said the familiar chap. "Let's kill some Hun."

The rest is like some monstrous hazy dream. All three of us in full unrestrained bloodlust. We shot, we bayoneted, we stamped, bit, kicked, tore, screamed, gouged and gorged on a feast of insane violence.

"Lads, you've done it. I don't bloody know how but you three just won the battle, this bit anyway, all on your bloody own. Calm down, we're here now." It was an officer from the second wave. We were all of us crazed. We must have looked horrific, all of us splattered in gore. I swear our own officer had a chunk of flesh hanging out of his mouth. Somehow we'd silenced three machine guns and allowed the second wave to reach here.

The officer in charge of the second wave ordered us to return to our own trenches. "You are all wounded," he said. "Head back for treatment." He gave us a hastily written note to confirm his order. The second wave moved on. The third wave was strolling casually across no man's land.

I was bleeding from what appeared to be a gunshot wound to the right side of my gut, I don't remember this happening. The officer had several ugly looking slashes across his face and blood running from his leg into his puttees. The familiar chap had a few teeth missing and one eye closed. We were all limping. We happily clambered over the top and started back to our lines. The men in the third wave looked at us inquisitively and voiced encouragement.

"Gas, gas, gas." That fearful shout from somewhere. I glanced about and saw the awful yellow cloud slowly rolling across no man's land towards the German trench. Oh, shit. It was our gas. Some bloody fool was releasing gas onto our own men. War progresses through a series of cock ups. Battles are won by the side that makes the least mistakes.

"There's a clear spot," shouted the familiar chap. The officer was barely conscious as he walked. I could move only slowly because of the wound. The big man picked the officer up onto his shoulders and then lifted me off my feet in a kind of side hug. He started to run and I've never seen anything like it. He was fast and agile as if he was at an athletics meet. Our weight didn't seem to slow him at all. He ran us at speed to a clear portion of our trench where he unceremoniously threw us in. He then sat down by us and said, "I suppose I've got to get the tea now, have I?"

"Speedy," said the officer slowly. "That's you now, lad. Speedy the brave, Speedy the valiant, Speedy the saviour, Speedy the char wallah. Two sugars, my fine bold fast friend."

We're all in the forward casualty pen now. I learned Speedy's real name, Maurice Van Duke, but everybody just calls him Speedy now. He thinks his family were probably from Holland a few hundred years ago but he doesn't really know. The officer's name is Lieutenant Simon Penn, he says he has asked for us to be posted to his command when we're better. When he's better, more like. Since he's an officer he's already been shipped off to a care home in Scotland. Rumour has it that the OIC third wave has written us all up for medals. He thinks we saved the day. I think we were lucky to save ourselves.

We're on a ship now, me and Maurice. We're being shipped home to fully recover before being reposted. We'd first been moved to a hospital in Boulogne, there I got a letter for both of us from Simon. Yep, I'm now on first name terms with an officer, this war will completely mess up the class system before it's over. Simon gave us his address and invited us to visit.

"Not me," insisted the grave Maurice, now and for always nicknamed Speedy. "I'm not going to try to mix with people like that. Simon will be alright, he's our mate now. His family will still be snooty posh and won't know how to talk to us without being patronising. They've probably got food we won't even know how to cut let alone eat." That made me laugh.

New Penn Court Manor, Ware, Herts. Yes, maybe. I might visit.

∞ ∞ ∞ ∞

I put down the journal and rubbed my eyes, I was tired and a little emotional. This was my maternal grandfather talking to me. Strangely, I recognised him; He wrote in the changing tense and included quoted speech, a style that I thought made my mother's letter unusual. He was writing a journal but also telling a story.

John, Jack? Speedy? His was a time that nicknames were common. So much so that some names came with a nickname already attached. All Johns were Jack just as anybody surnamed Clarke got called Nobby, heaven knows why. Nicknames were the common currency and used like pronouns. Nowadays I've met people named Jack on their birth certificate, I think that's a modern practice since we no longer much apply nicknames. Maybe we're all too self-centred to bother thinking up a name for somebody else.

I hadn't read any dark family secret yet. I decided to take a nap and then continue through the night. I slept on the sofa and dreamed that Jack was talking to me except I couldn't hear what he was saying. He was smiling and tried to hand me a Mill's bomb but I refused it. He stuck it in his jacket pocket, he was dressed like a typical working man of his time in rough trousers, cheap jacket, white neckerchief and cloth cap. I tried to ask him what he wanted but he morphed into a uniformed soldier and marched away whistling. The tune was 'Brother Bertie Went Away…'

I awoke, a tad amused by the dream. I went to the bathroom and washed my face. I then went back, made a cup of tea, grabbed a box of coconut cakes and returned to the journal.

∞ ∞ ∞ ∞

We landed in port at Folkestone two days ago. On the quayside a busy team of doctors and nurses assessed every casualty. Some lads could walk and others were on stretchers, some were already dead. A doctor decided that Speedy would need to go straight to Guys in London if his sight in one eye were to be saved.

As he was led away he turned back to me and called, "Jack, meet me in the Cumberland." The Duke of Cumberland was a pub near to where we both lived.

"Every Friday, Speedy." That reply told him that if we both checked the pub on Friday nights then eventually we'd meet up there.

It was decided that I would probably be further harmed by travelling so would stay in the local hospital. That turned out to be a field hospital just outside the town. Not exactly a fine modern hospital but compared to where I'd come from it was luxury.

I was told the bullet was still inside me. The doctor said I was lucky because it was just sitting in some fatty tissue and not moving. Had it been elsewhere then the trip back to England would have killed me. I told him that the guns in use at the front should normally rip completely through a man but he said that sometimes, if the round had been slowed by hitting something first, or travelling through somebody else, it could come to rest inside somebody. He said we should hope it wasn't a dum-dum, split at the nose to make it disintegrate in the target, but he was fairly sure it wasn't.

They operated the same day. When I returned to

mindfulness I was on a field bed in the field hospital, which was a big tent in a field so both things were aptly named. A very pretty nurse sat on the side of the bed, she was about ten years older than me but that still made her young.

She put her hand on my arm. "You're fine. The bullet was in one piece, nothing vital was hit and it came out smoothly. Lucky you."

"Can I have it as a souvenir?" I asked.

"I'm sorry, no. It has to be sent away to be smelted and made into another bullet."

"Oh, I see. What size was it?"

"Well, there's the thing," she smiled. "It was a .45 calibre Webley round. It was a bullet from a British revolver."

I laughed. She was used to soldier's humour because she laughed with me.

"You are an angel," I said to her.

She smiled. "No, I'm a nurse and you are a wounded hero who thinks he's falling in love but is just relieved to be alive. You are our hero." Then she did something unexpected, she leaned over and kissed me on the forehead, my mother does that. She left and I didn't see her again.

That wasn't the only unexpected thing, I found a purple ribbon tied round my private parts. I roared with laughter when I found it. It must have been put there during the operation.

My guffawing brought the matron. More intimidating than a dozen Hun, this woman.

"What's so funny, my young lad?" She was grinning.

I held up the ribbon. Some of the other patients were leaning up in bed and also grinning. The frightening matron laughed.

"Tell him," called out one of the men.

"You, my boy, have been awarded the Victoria Cross. So have your two friends, I'm told." She just stood there grinning. The tent-come-ward broke out into applause.

I was told that there would only be a short regimental ceremony to present the medal. I was advised that the normal bells and whistles presentation was impossible because the King was busy being King and there was a war on. I was also told that the medal would be sent to my home at a later date because it took time to make and for now I could wear the relevant ribbon if I wanted.

A Staff officer came to confirm the award and reassured me I'd be back at the front as soon as I was better.

"That's reassuring, sir," I told him.

He wanted to know the details of the fight but I didn't know them. I couldn't say we shot and hacked our insane way through men who didn't expect us to be there and we did it all while we were out of our minds with funk and shell concussion.

I made up a suitably noble fictional account of how we stood proudly, bayonets thrust forward, jaws set against a barbaric horde intent on eating British babies if we let them pass. No better way for a man to die and all that bilge.

He puffed up his chest, saluted me and left. I had to resist the urge to shout out rude words after him.

The citation, when it arrived later, said that with no

thought for personal safety we had directly challenged and engaged an overwhelmingly superior enemy force and had thereby neutralised resistance against our third wave and thus prevented an entire battalion being lost to a well equipped and disciplined foe. I was impressed.

"You've got the best medal, mate," said one of the men.

"Yes," I said, "but I've also got the dreams and nerves that go with it." He just nodded at me. A soldier understands. We also understood that I had to keep that to myself and hope it didn't show. I didn't want some staff office twat deciding the hero was now a coward and shooting him.

I've got a few bob now. As a private pig class, now pig class VC, I get one shilling and thrupence, yes 1/3d, a day. Soon I'll get an extra sixpence for being brave. Even though the army stops a few pennies to pay for the uniforms we so carelessly damage in our battle clumsiness, it adds up. With no other expenses to pay, I've come back to about twenty-five quid in the post office, I'm feeling well heeled.

I was discharged yesterday and given a third class ticket to London, a hard wooden bench was good enough for my heroic backside it would appear. I spent the night waiting by the station with a good view of the sea. Here's a weird thing, when it was very quiet in the night I could hear the guns over the channel. Not the rifles, of course, but the big guns. It made me shiver or maybe it was just a cold night.

I slept most of the journey to London. The train came in to Victoria, not its normal terminus I was told. I didn't have my smelly with me. Normally, the army expects you to be fully battle equipped when on leave, just in case you find a German in the garden. Not so if you're wounded, then you don't even travel in uniform, they don't want the injuries to be too obvious to the civilian population. There's been talk of a badge of some kind so that you can show you're an injured soldier recovering at home. I was informed that when I got back to the war I would get a lemmy to replace the smelly. That's a large magazine rifle, twice as many bullets to end lives with.

I felt just as fit as ever so I walked home from Victoria, it took about three hours or more. The wound ached a lot and seeped just a bit but otherwise everything was fine.

Mum and dad were delighted to see me. I told them about the VC and dad almost wept. He'd fought in South Africa so he had some idea of what I'd experienced. 'Some idea' is about as close as anybody can get. Trying to explain the feelings proved impossible. I've come to the conclusion that's because not only is this war unique in its monstrousness but this kind of thing, the emotion after battle and killing, it is not a simple thing.

I've heard of people who can't come to terms with it but I think I can. I have dreams and I have small angry outbursts. I'm beginning to suspect that the real internal horror comes not from fear, revulsion or shock. I think it comes from shame. I'm ashamed at what I did. I'm ashamed of what I didn't do. I'm ashamed of what I will do when I get back there. I'm ashamed of being a hero and I'm ashamed of killing the school master, who was probably, nay, almost certainly, a good man. You can't explain that. Shame at killing and shame at not killing and shame at being alive. Shame at the two lads who entered the dugout, shame at having to be carried by Speedy, shame at the gore and the mud and the carrion smell that permeates my whole being. Most of all a deep penetrating shame in knowing that in my soul I enjoyed it, my God I enjoyed being free from the restraint and rules of normal life.

I will simply block it out. It's there, of course it's there, but I can place it in a part of my mind where it does no harm and I don't need to react to it. I can turn off my humanity. That's not good but it's better than crying and screaming. When all of this is over maybe I'll take a long break or maybe leave London altogether. I'd enjoy farm work, I think. Maybe I'll hide in the countryside. Maybe I won't need to, how likely is it I'll survive the next engagement or the one after that?

The War Office sent me a letter that said I had three weeks before I was reassessed for fitness to die. I've spent a week at home and it's been great. Mum has fed me up and dad boasts to everybody about his son's VC. I went into a local grocer for some spuds and he wouldn't take the money that I tried to pay with. I told him he'd go bust like that and he laughed and said it's just this once, just to say thanks. What is he thanking me for? I don't know.

On the second Friday I was pleased to discover that Speedy was in the Cumberland. His sight is saved but his eye is a little smaller looking and his face a bit scarred. He's in good spirits and we spent some time talking. He's having dreams too and feels that there are not many people he can talk to about it. He doesn't agree with me about the shame idea. He reckons that what happens is we all have an image of ourselves. That image is based on our everyday personality and we develop an idea of ourselves based on what we would prefer to be like. In extreme circumstances, like the front, we are faced with the reality of how we act when our bodies are driven by the chemicals inside us and we revert to a savage state.

He reckons we can then do one of two things: Either we desperately wish and pretend things were more how we'd like them to be, in which case we break down, or we can just accept and adapt and come to terms with reality. He has some interesting ideas, Speedy. We got drunk and the conversation stopped making sense. The publican knows I'm not twenty one and so does the local copper. Nobody cares about that anymore.

I've just got back from visiting Simon, it was an interesting trip. I took a train out into Hertfordshire. Since I'm good for cash at the moment I travelled second class. That was lucky because I learned that the main Ware station has a short platform. It's one of those places where the scum in third class, always the rear carriages, are not allowed to get off. I've never really thought about that before. Who do these bastards think they are, telling us where we can and can't get off a train?

Hertfordshire is short of motor buses but I managed to find a local horse and trap to hire. The owner was a taciturn uncommunicative curmudgeon but knew his way about and was content to take me. He took me to a place called Cold Christmas just outside Ware, Cold Christmas is so named because when the houses were being built it was a particularly chilly winter and they rushed to complete the build. As a result the bottom half of the houses are brick and the upper floors wood framed and filled with plaster.

He dropped me off near the church and told me how to find Penn Court Manor, about a mile cross country, just follow the track through the iron gates. It was a nice walk. The day was warm and I stopped by a pond to wash down my face and drink a bit. Fear of water borne disease has been pretty much cancelled by the slop I've been drinking in the trenches.

Simon was pleased to see me.

I said "I'm sorry Speedy isn't here. He likes you but he said he'd feel out of place here. He's got a bit of a thing about the class system. I think he might be a closet socialist."

Simon laughed. "It's understandable. I'm drifting that way slightly myself. When it was all on top for us three, class didn't matter a jot, did it?" he said.

"No," I replied. "Who cares how toffee nosed the posh bloke is as long as he can fight." We both laughed and shook hands warmly.

His family was nice. His dad died from a blood infection many years ago. His mum was polite and tried to be friendly but found it awkward to talk to me. I don't have any problem with that; she's spent her whole life as part of a secluded privileged elite and she probably hasn't spent much time socialising with the working class. I think she was pleasantly surprised to find I was house trained and didn't spit on the floor. Both Simon and I found it amusing.

He introduced me to his sister, the seventeen year old Sarah. I was instantly smitten. I had to remind myself I was back in civilisation and had to conform to the rules of civilised society. She was very pretty, graceful and laughed easily and often, about five feet seven, auburn haired, brown eyed and with one of those smiles that melt into your soul.

I spent five days at Penn Court Manor. A lot of that time was with Simon but a lot with Sarah as well. I think I fell in love with her over that time. We spent a lot of time walking and talking. She's very bright and we had plenty to argue about; politics, war, horses and the Empire.

She thinks that the class system works, I don't. She thinks that the war is justified and Britain should rule Europe, I don't and I don't. She thinks horses are noble and beautiful, I think they are stupid and fart a lot, that made her laugh. She thinks the Empire is a good thing. I think its function, to enforce laws over global free trade, should be the role of a benevolent international body. We agreed that the countryside was wonderful and these walks and fun arguments made for a very pleasant few days.

On one of these walks she asked me which school I went to. She was surprised when I told her that I only went to the local church teaching group two or three days a week until I was fourteen.

"But you are so clever and thoughtful," she said, kindly I thought.

"I read a lot, we have a library nearby." She giggled at that for some reason.

When it came time to leave, Simon told me that he'd had me and Speedy permanently posted to his team. We'd all meet up again at Dover for mobilisation back to France. His mum drove me back to Ware, they have a lovely big motor car but I don't know the make.

Sarah and Simon came with us. At the station Simon bought my ticket. I objected at first but then found out that he gets paid 28/-a day, that's right I said twenty eight shillings. I was shocked, remember I get 1/9d and that's after the extra for murdering lots of people. How the better classes live, eh? If he gets that, how much does a member of the proper upper classes get? Simon is a simple middle class struggler.

Sarah was quiet the whole journey to Ware. As I went to enter the station I shook hands with Simon. Sarah came forward and hugged me.

"Thank you, Sarah," I said. "I've enjoyed this time. Have a wonderful life."

She kissed me on the side of the mouth. "Be safe, John. Come back."

Her mother gently pulled her from me. Sarah and Simon returned to the car. Their mum placed her hand on my arm and said, "John, Jack, this war is blurring things. I think Sarah loves you at the moment. You are a fine young man and I can understand that. It can never work, you know this. Your worlds are very different. She will grow up and marry a wealthy man and live a privileged life in comfort. You will also have a good life and I hope you are happy in your future. I like and respect you, Jack, but please never return to Ware. Sarah must forget you. If you feel anything for her, you must ignore it and do what is best for her."

I looked at her for few seconds. "I know. I understand. I'll be back in France soon. I will not contact her again, I give you my word."

She smiled, touched her fingers to her mouth and them touched my cheek with them. "Be safe, Jack. And keep Simon safe as well."

The train journey back supplied its own little event. I was sitting and quietly dozing when I was brought back to full consciousness by a war vigilante.

"Coward, take that." The speaker was a middle aged, well spoken woman in expensive clothing. She had placed a white feather in my lap.

"What?" I exclaimed, confused.

"You should be at the front, young man. Good men are fighting while you idle your time here. You inadequately brought up ne'er-do-well."

"I see, madam. I'll try to improve. I shall enlist as soon as we reach London. Thank you for correcting me."

I could see by her glare that she did understand a sardonic riposte. I placed the white feather in my pocket, I might wear it next to the VC.

I'm back on a ship. We mustered at Dover. Simon, me, Speedy and some others were reissued our uniforms and issued our lemmies. It's a nice rifle, a bit heavier and better balanced than the smelly but fundamentally the same gun, just made a bit better. The bolt is smooth and easy unlike the sticky difficult bolt on the smelly. It takes the same bayonet and holds ten rounds. It takes two speed clips to load since nobody bothered to make a ten round fast loader clip.

Simon turned up with his revolver, I learned it belongs to him. He had to buy it because the army had run out by the time he enlisted. I didn't know that people of Simon's class in fine houses could buy revolvers without any kind of authorisation.

They say we'll be retrained in France. We saw a doctor at Dover in order to assess our fitness. I was a bit suspicious that the medical assessment was at Dover by the foot of the gang plank onto the ship. I wonder how many are failed and returned, I didn't see any.

I'm tempted to start this entry with a rude word, I am not happy. Our retraining consisted of a fifty yard dash in full kit, if we managed it we were considered retrained. One lad couldn't make it and was arrested for malingering. We've been told we're going back to the front, there's going to be a push. Great, this is why I'm here; John Bull needs his faithful sons to throw themselves pointlessly at the enemy guns. That's how wars are won. It isn't really. We have a few nights in camp outside a small town west of Boulogne before we go at it again.

I dreamed about Sarah last night, I think it's best I don't go into detail; 'young men dream of love' is probably the politest way to put it. Speedy and I visited the local brothel. Simon counselled against this but we went anyway. We're going to go back to the front, we need this comfort. The French are very good about this kind of thing. Everybody we passed in the street knew where we were going but nobody was judgemental. I like the French and their easy going attitude to such matters, we could learn from them.

When we returned to camp we had to complete a typed report requesting replacement French letters. It made me laugh, more absurdly the items were issued before we'd even submitted the request. The army can be very silly about this kind of thing. We also had to see a doctor, regulations require it, who made us wash our privates with methylated spirits, it stung. We declined the offer to see the chaplain, it seems our moral health is important and we've been told to see him anyway. Speedy said we don't need to bother, it's just so a staff officer can tick a column in the battalion occurrence book, thereby showing he is an efficient leader.

This entry is about five weeks after the last and it's been a busy time. Not long after the washing of the genitals, Simon invited us to dine with him in the officers' mess tent. Speedy didn't really want to go but I made him. The place was a surprise to both of us. We'd prepared mentally for dinner with the toffs, we expected the middle to lower upper classes to be here. I'm comfortable with them but Speedy dislikes them in a quiet, deliberate and slightly cross way.

Instead we were in the company of very young men which included a lot of obviously working class lads.

"So many of the sons of the ruling and privileged elites are dead, we now prepare the hoi polloi for leadership," explained Simon who was inappropriately jovial.

"So take a butchers at the new Ruperts, matey, then take the weight of yer plates," so spoke one of the new officers, deliberately exaggerated London voice as well.

The serious point about this invitation was that Simon had obtained permission for both me and Speedy to be assessed and then trained for junior officer, after we spent some NCO time. He promptly handed us some stripes and said that after the coming push, oops he wasn't supposed to mention it, we'd head back to England to get some pips soldered onto our bare shoulders, or something like that.

It was something to do with, and near to, a place called Arras or something like. Either we had it or they had and we wanted it or they did and we'd had it or they'd had it and we'd take it back or they would try to. I don't know anymore, all I know is that it's back to the butcher's shop for we three.

Simon marched us all up to the reserve trenches. We passed the usual collection of bloated dead horses and obscenely fat rats that fled as we approached. We knew when we were near because we started to see fallen soldiers. None recent, though. This graveyard was mature and the corpses I saw were beyond the stinky stage. Now desiccated or flesh fallen, they were from both sides of the dispute so there'd been a bit of a long term argy bargy here.

Most were beginning to merge with the land and this made the place look like we were sowing human nutrients into the soil. I'm not sure I'd want to eat food grown here when this is over.

Speedy and I commanded five youngsters each. Simon led us and a few other small groups. I gave my boys the usual 'trust God and your training' speech. I didn't know what else to do or tell them; well done for getting here, you idiots, let's all go and die horribly with a stiff upper lip to show the Hun how Englishmen throw their lives away. I'd like to just clip their ears and send them all back to their mums. I don't think the war office would approve of that.

Simon conducted the briefing, he advised us that just before dawn we would move up to the front trench, which was previously the German reserve trench because our reserve trench used to be the German front trench.

I leaned towards Simon and whispered, "too much information. Just tell them what to do." He took the advice and stopped trying to put some sensible reasonable spin on what he said. When he blows his whistle we go over and follow the shells creeping towards the enemy in their new not quite ready front trenches, that's all they needed to know.

We all stood at ladders in the front trench, one lad wet himself but managed to continue to look steadfast and soldierly. Down came the barrage. Whistle, over we all went. All except one boy who just stood at the bottom looking at the ladder and whimpering. Simon had his revolver in his hand, as per standing orders for attacks, and I hesitated at the top. This had to be resolved fast and I shouted at the boy, he just looked at me, he was weeping.

Simon raised his revolver to the boy's head and shouted at him. Simon looked tortured by the thought of what he should do next according to the standing orders and he too was hesitating. There was no time for this, I slid back down the ladder. As I landed in the dirty mud bottom I raised my rifle and using the stock landed the boy an almighty crack to the side of his face. It certainly broke his cheek bone and probably his jaw as well. He collapsed.

"I saw him fall as we went over, something hit him, I don't know what. Leave him here and the medics will find him wounded. Terrible bad luck, hit before he even got into the attack," I said to Simon. He just nodded, for one disturbing moment he looked as if he might kiss me, then he patted me on the back and up we both went to rejoin the charge.

As we went over I shouted to Simon, "and don't bloody shoot me this time." He laughed at me and we rushed to catch the others.

As always in this mess of a war, the planners got it wrong. The barrage stopped when we were only half way across. To our surprise the Germans stopped firing not long after. It transpired that a detachment of Gurkhas and a mix of Muslim and Sikh infantry had taken the trenches. Meet the Empire, Fritz.

We only lost about half our men, not bad for a first wave. We'd pushed the Germans back at least four hundred yards, I suppose that counts as a major advance these days. Their defensive fire hadn't been very effective, most of the damage to our side was from biplanes overhead dropping vicious weighted darts, small bombs and just plain old rocks. That's handy, I thought, now the boy that I hit won't look as if he has an unusual injury.

"God was with us, this day," cried the chaplain.

"What the bloody hell are you doing here, you damn fool?" Simon replied.

"Too see God's work against the barbarians." He was serious. He had the half bonkers look of the truly pious. A piety that, more often than not, people like him use to control and manipulate other people. Not very Christian then.

"Can I shoot him, Sir?" I called to Simon.

"Best not, Jack."

I put my face close to the religious madman, I looked him hard in the eyes. "See this stare?" I snarled at him. "That stare comes from killing people before they kill you. Is that God's work? Did God want me to butcher an old man or rip the throat out of…" Simon pulled me away.

We gathered any of our men we could find and returned to our front trench, which was now our reserve trench because the recent German front trench… Oh never mind, you know how it goes.

When we got back to the rear marshalling fields, intended to house troops awaiting immediate deployment and receive the wounded and exhausted, we settled down to a few days of rest. It was supposed to be just out of range of the enemy guns. Now, thanks to our magnificent victory it was just out of range and then a little bit. I was told that every so often enemy planes take a pot shot at the place but I didn't see that.

I had a letter. It was not the usual home newspaper, mags and gossip from mum and dad. This was a light pink envelope addressed in a practised and well presented hand.

"Oh la la," said the post master as he handed it to me. The lads around me laughed.

"Lucky ol' you, mate," cried one of them.

It was from Sarah.

[Letter glued onto the pages of the journal]

My Dearest John. My fine man, Jack.

I hope this letter finds you well and uninjured. How is Simon? I hope the same for him. I shall also write to him. Your letter shall be the more intimate since the peculiar circumstance of this terrible time embolden me.

My life is about to be destroyed. Mother has introduced me to a wealthy lawyer and informs me I shall marry him. I will not.

He is not a bad man but he is too old, at least thirty, and while he is pleasant, I do not love him

I love you, Jack John, John Jack.

This is not the mere outpouring of some foolish emotional immaturity from a silly young girl, I really do love you. I remember our arguments, our laughter, our walks. Please come to me, please rescue me, brave bold Jack.

Mother may not approve of you but I know that Simon also loves you. Between us we shall convince mother. Simon has written that he intends to have you, and your mysterious friend Speedy, promoted to a commission. This may provide her with the necessary social acceptability. She is such a snob.

I should write no more, the war office strictly limits letter sizes. Please come to me, Jack. Please save me from a materially rich but an emotionally inadequate future.

With all of my love,
Your Sarah. Your forever Sarah
XXXXXXXXX

[Journal reverts to Jack's handwriting]

Dear Diary… what the blazes should I do?

It's now six years since I wrote the line above. I stopped making occasional entries when life took its fateful turn. I lost the will to continue this journal but now feel I'm able to and shall tell the rest of my story.

Simon was shot by a sniper while we were in the front trenches. We weren't there for an attack, just holding.

The bastard hit him in the front of his shoulder but the bullet bounced off the shoulder blade and down through his torso, ripping up some organs on the way. Speedy and I pushed everybody out of the way to hold him. He smiled at us both, he said it was bad luck for him. He thanked us both, I have no idea for what. I remember his last words to me. "Go to her, Jack. Make me proud." He died easily and without convulsions or massive pain.

251

We ignored standing orders, the dead should lay where they fall until the proper medic teams recover them. Speedy and I were not prepared to allow our friend to become another macabre backdrop to war, he would not decorate nor fertilise this cursed land. We lifted him and took him back to the marshalling area. We left him in the casualty tent. The doctor objected but we made it clear that Simon would be afforded all respect. He could have called the military police but I think he sympathised. We returned to the front trench.

Speedy and I hatched a plan. That night we slid out into no man's land and found a German rifle. We used the bayonet to run through my left calf. We concocted a story about an encounter with the enemy while out reconnoitring. Most of our lads knew it was a sham but nobody said anything. They and we knew that we'd be executed if this ruse was discovered.

I was duly sent back to Blighty as, yet again, a wounded hero. I was a bit embarrassed that we got more medals for neutralising the fictitious enemy reconnoitring team. Still, one Military Cross for fibbing to go alongside the VC for panicking. In all seriousness, we earned the VC but had to accept the silent embarrassment of the MC. We could hardly send them back with an explanation.

In the drawing room of Penn Court Manor, stood me and Sir Jonathon Metcalfe, MBE, betrothed to the young and unwilling Sarah Penn. Sarah and her mother were seated. It was an awkward meeting. I gave the family

Simon's personal property. Sir Jonathon Metcalfe, MBE, asked how he died.

"It was quick and clean," I partially lied.

"Boldly facing the foe, I hope," stated Sir Jonathon Metcalfe, MBE. I considered punching him but this moment was difficult enough already.

"Who are you with, sir?" I asked him.

"The treasury, I thought you knew. I advise on fiscal and planning laws."

"No sir, I mean your wartime activities, not your civilian occupation."

Sarah's mother glanced at me, she looked a little annoyed. Sarah giggled softly.

"Sir. Mr Adams. I have a reserved occupation. I am obliged to remain in my civilian position."

He was tall, lean, expensively dressed and with a quick attractive smile. In another time and place I may have liked this man. In this time and place I did not. I learned from the conversation that he had recently been promoted due to the death of a senior colleague.

"How did he die?" I hoped to sound innocent but the look from Sarah's mother told me I did not. I did notice that the corners of her mouth momentarily curled upwards. She was inwardly grinning at my insolence.

"He was not young. In his bed overnight, or rather in the bed supplied by his host, he had spent the evening being entertained in Belgravia."

"Ah," I smiled and kept my voice low. "Dead drunk in the bed of some whore, no doubt." I wasn't as low-voiced as I'd hoped to be. Sarah giggled, her mother looked disapprovingly at me. Sir Jonathon Metcalfe, MBE, invited me to walk with him in the garden.

The garden was huge, I would have called it a park. We strolled side by side.

Sir Jonathon Metcalfe, MBE, spoke. "I'm a little cross with your disrespectful comment about my friend. You are impressively prescient, he was indeed in a brothel, a high class one I might add. The needs of men, as you know, are complicated and insistent. We should protect his memory and the sensitivities of his family and friends."

"I'm sorry. I mean that, I apologise. It's the needs of men that underlies this situation we're in, don't you think?"

"I've considered beating you, do you know that?" He spoke a kind of non-threat intended to be threatening.

"I've killed a lot of men who have tried to, did you know that?" I hoped this was a suitable warning for him. Don't pick fights with men just back from the trenches, they won't be able to restrain themselves. In your head you're just punching a man, in his you're a deadly threat and he'll respond on that basis.

"I intended no threat, sir. Your martial prowess is not required. I shall marry Sarah, you shall return to your old life after the war and never bother her again. I have contacts in places that can ensure you find good well paid work. What do you say?"

We stopped walking. I moved close to him and looked him in the eye. "I say that your world is changing. I say that you won't for long maintain the benefits you perceive as your right by birth. I say that if Sarah will have me, I shall have her. I say that you disgust me. I say that I invite you to strike me so that I may strike you back. I say that you will not bully me. I say that your day is done, if not now then soon. I say that you may not control me nor may you buy me."

Sir Jonathon Metcalfe, MBE, thought about it for a while. He would have gone up in my estimation if he had hit me. He turned and strode away. I followed him back to the house.

Back in the drawing room, Sir Jonathon Metcalfe, MBE, made his excuses to leave. He insisted he had business to attend to and that today would decide his future marital status.

"Sarah," he said, rather pompously, "you must make a decision. John is a good man but he is not one of us, no offence intended, John. Sarah, should you decide to marry me our wedding shall go ahead as planned. Should you make the bizarre decision to partner with John, I shall refer to the trustees and leave you to your fate."

Trustees? I learned that rich people don't own much. They apparently rely on wealth and property trusts held for their benefit as a named group or class, such as the family Penn, and therefore may not pass on or dispose of their own assets, which are not theirs but held by trustees who are duty bound to permit the beneficiaries to use them. In this way they avoid several tax obligations. How the other half cheat, eh?

The implication in the words of Sir Jonathon Metcalfe, MBE, was that Sarah would be removed from the class of beneficiaries. Welcome to poverty and reduced life span like the rest of us.

All of this left Sarah's mother with a problem. She liked me, I knew that. She also needed to ensure Sarah's future. Sarah was now insistent that she would have nothing to do with Sir Jonathon Metcalfe, MBE, and he was a cad. My epithet for him would have been a bit stronger.

Sarah's mother agreed that Sarah and I should go away for a short while to discuss our options. Part of the Penn family trust included a small riverside house in Devon. We travelled there by train and coach. Sarah's mother said it should be a clandestine journey and sojourn since Sarah's reputation should be maintained.

"I rather suspect your reputation is perhaps already challenged, but probably rescued by your heroism," Sarah's mother told me with a knowing grin. Sarah remained inscrutable but I later learned she knew exactly what her mother meant.

"I shall try to emulate the gentleman," I sought to reassure her.

"Oh, don't do that. Behave properly instead." We all laughed at her comment.

The faith displayed by Sarah's mother was, I'm sorry to admit, misplaced. The needs of young men are complicated and insistent. It turned out that so are the needs of young women. Sarah became pregnant as a result of our earnest discussions about our options. We didn't know until a month or so later.

The bayonet wound would not heal properly. The army placed me on a reserve list. This meant that I would only be required again if we started losing and the Germans made dangerous headway.

I was not dismissed from the army but would have my pay reduced to 9d a day plus 3d for being brave in the past. Obviously courage is worth less on the home front. I was placed as military supervisor at a factory in Stratford, making bullets. The army felt that experience of the front made munitions workers more conscientious, the army was correct; it's one thing to know that each manufactured round is important, it's another to feel it in your heart, to feel that each round may represent a British life saved. I wrote to Speedy and wished him well. I told him I'd keep an eye on his family.

As a result of my new role, I was able to return to Penn Court Manor when news of the pregnancy arrived by letter. Sarah and I had made no clear plans but it was now obvious that decisions needed to be made and acted on.

I hugged Sarah and meant all of the affection implied by the contact. We were in the drawing room again, tea and sweet cakes were laid out as if I were making a small social call.

Sarah's mother stood in front of me.

"I have to do two things," she said, a little mysteriously. Then she slapped me around the face. I deserved that and didn't flinch. Then, to my surprise, she kissed me on the cheek.

"What do you think Simon would say?" She asked.

"Honestly? I don't think he'd mind. I think he'd berate us for our foolishness but I think he would support us."

"So do I, and so shall I."

The family history was explained, it surprised me. The family were of American descent but the American Penns are originally of English descent. I was informed that they were one of several branches originating from William Penn himself, Quaker activist and founder of Pennsylvania.

Sarah's mother made it clear that we, to her great annoyance, were now estranged from the Penns. She was sorry but Sir Jonathon Metcalfe, MBE, had instructed the board of trustees that our bastards, his words, were an illegitimate line and should not benefit from the trusts nor be considered worthy of inclusion in the line. Furthermore, since Sarah had chosen to impurify her pedigree with seed from a lower order, she too now failed to qualify as a beneficiary. Sir Jonathon Metcalfe, MBE, should hope we never meet again.

Sarah's mother eventually had him dismissed from the board of trustees but the damage was done. I never met any other Penns but Sarah sometimes received letters from some of them. She said they were friendly and morally supportive.

Sarah's exclusion from the trust meant she adopted my working class life style. We set up home in Old Ford, my little income assisted by money often sent from Sarah's mother. The child was a beautiful girl who we named Lilly. It is with deep sorrow that I record she died at the age of four, she just developed a high temperature, went into convulsions and defied the best efforts of doctors and nurses to revive her. When it happened I ran her through the streets to the hospital shouting for a clear way, everybody gave way. I love her eternally and miss her every day.

Sarah and I stayed together. Her mother took up residence in a small cottage in the grounds of Penn Court Manor and we visited often. The main house was now occupied by another part of the Penn family. Any other children we have will be excluded from the trust. Neither Sarah nor I care about that. We are happy. We intend to have more children.

Speedy survived. He lives near us. We meet up regularly to talk and laugh together. We often talk about Simon; we call him our mate the gent.

My mum and dad help us to the best of their limited ability, bless them. Sarah's mum continues to send money and advice which we appreciate very much. I hope that our children and their children and their children are able to continue the unequal fight to achieve more than the world wants to give.

∞ ∞ ∞ ∞

So that's the big secret, I'm in a bastard line. I can live with that. I acknowledge and welcome that. I am proud of Jack and Sarah. I thank them for their genetic input, it may be where the steel and gravel in my soul originates. I bless them. There were no further entries in the journal. I think that Jack had decided enough was enough and he didn't want to continue it much beyond the war's end.

This time I walked the couple of miles from Whitechapel underground to the hospice in Hackney. I passed Bethnal Green underground where many died in one evening during the blitz. They didn't die from the bombs directly, just the crush and fright as planes dropped a series of bombs that marched towards the people entering the shelter. Panic did the rest as they tumbled down the stone staircase and were trampled. I was imagining the lost and the people they didn't make and who they in turn did not make.

Close by, the national toy museum, the Victoria & Albert Museum of Childhood, seemed to mock the thought; here are the toys they couldn't have because they didn't come to get them, now the toys live in glass cabinets untouched. This led to an unpleasant thought, as if the last one was cheerful.

In nearby Victoria Park is a large boating lake. Now a tranquil pretty environment, during wartime fire bombing it had water pumped from it by fire fighters. The lower water level revealed many, maybe hundreds, of cloth wrapped or boxed aborted foetuses. They also were victims of the war, unwanted results of melancholy and hurried liaisons with soldiers, often American or Canadian but also British. The illegal backstreet abortionists gained good trade from the transient warriors and local girls, all of them expecting to die themselves at any moment. London has many park lakes and canals, I didn't want to think about them.

Down this road lives the potential for depression, I decided. I concentrated on walking and casually observing the multi-ethnic cultural babel that now occupied this place.

From the park I heard children laughing, a tonic at any time. I noticed that the kids were herded into their own tribal groups by the adults, mainly women. I also noticed that the kids showed a healthy disrespect for parental authority and played together anyway. Up yours, tribal cultural restrictions, your offspring have reached beyond your miserable restrictive world. I cheer and applaud them.

It was a long walk and by the time I reached St. Joseph's I was clear in my mind what I wanted. I wanted Dave to read the journal, I wanted his reassurance that I was respecting those who went before. I just needed to talk with a friend. I'd been calling his number but he just wasn't answering, I thought that maybe he'd lost his phone.

The hospice receptionist was somebody I'd never seen before. An olive skinned young man who greeted me warmly.

"I need to see Dave Thompson," I informed him. He looked at me enquiringly, which is never a good sign after you've said what you want.

"I'm sorry, he's not available at the moment. Can I take a message?"

"No." I hesitated for a second, "Yes, could you please

let him know Steve is waiting for him in the chapel. He knows me, my mother was here. I'd like to use the chapel to wait for him if nobody minds."

He directed me to the chapel, I didn't bother telling him I knew the way well, he was trying to be helpful. I'm grumpy enough without being churlish as well. I bought a coffee from the Klix machine before I got there, chemical beverage to sear the throat and destroy the taste buds.

I'd been sitting in the chapel for about twenty minutes when a young RC priest came in and asked if I was Steve. He was of Philippine ethnicity but with an English received pronunciation accent. Clean cut and well presented with manicured nails, slim weak hands, shockingly white teeth and a faint smell of cologne. I grinned as I wondered what he made of Dave.

"Will Dave be long?" I asked. "I can wait or come back another time. I tried to phone him but couldn't get through, I was hoping he'd be around."

"How do you know him, are you close?" Asked the young man.

I must have changed my demeanour a bit at that question because he took a small step back. I know the world and I know people and I know what things mean. That question could only mean bad news. I didn't need this well meaning but undoubtedly inexperienced youngster pussy-footing around me.

"Is he alive?" The boy seemed surprised at that direct question.

"He will live forever in the company of…"

"Don't fuck with me, boy." I showed my palms

because he seemed alarmed at that. "I don't mean to sound angry with you. Dave is my friend and if something's wrong, just tell me. Me and Dave understand each other, just talk to me the way you'd talk to him."

I felt a bit guilty because the lad was intimidated. I decided I needed to manage his discomfort in order to get the information out of him. I stood and invited him to sit. At the same time a tall athletic looking priest came in. He was English with a Northern accent. He introduced himself as Donald Pope.

"Pretentious," I chuckled and he smiled. I suppose he's heard a million jokes about his name and I shouldn't really add to that. The young priest took the opportunity to escape. Donald Pope told him he'd see him later and turned his attention back to me.

"Dave told me about you. I spent his last hours with him. He gave me instructions about his family and left a message for you. He told me about your grandfather's journal but didn't know what was in it. He said that I should treat you like a relative."

"What happened?"

"Heart. One attack that did most of the damage. He fought back," I noticed that he smiled when I grinned at that. "He fought back and survived it but was weakened. Examination showed that no operation would save him and there was no available transplant organ. Besides, he said he wouldn't accept a transplant organ and it should go to somebody younger if one came available. He was put to bed to await the inevitable. The doctors kept a crash cart by the bed but he sent it away. The second attack took him almost immediately when it occurred."

"He wouldn't have liked to hang about. He was a great man."

"Yes, he was. We prayed together, obviously. I administered his last rites. He'll be buried in Ireland. I can give you the details if you want to attend. Whatever it was you needed from him I will do for you. He said I was to help with anything you wanted."

"I don't mean to be rude, but no. I trusted Dave because he was Dave, not because he wore a dog collar. Please apologise to the young priest for me, I think I might have frightened him. He just took me by surprise, that's all. It was obvious to me that he had bad news for me and I just need that done, I don't need to be gently led into it."

"I know," he touched my arm. "Dave said you were birds of a feather."

"What was the message he left me?" I asked. He drew a small piece of paper from his pocket and handed it to me. There, in Dave's handwriting was, 'Fuck you. Never give in. Respect the ghosts.'

I smiled. "Did you read this?" I asked.

"Yes," he said, "but I didn't understand it. I don't need to, it's between you and him. He told me not to bother trying to offer you spiritual guidance, he said you'd do that yourself."

I thanked the man and left.

I had planned to get Dave's advice on the way forward. Should I try to contact the Penns? Should I go to Ware? Should I go to the States to find relatives?

I had little to go on. I had a photograph of Sarah Penn with Jack, taken just after the first war. They were so young. I googled a picture of an engraving of William Penn and imagined I could see some likeness. I found Cold Christmas on google maps but I couldn't find the big country house. I racked my memory. I had visited the place when I was about five, there I met my great grandmother. All my memory holds from that time is the bus we used to get there, the tall green iron gates guarding the estate's entrance, walking through woodland, a row of cottages and a big house my dad went into before we went to the cottages.

I remember being told we were going to see mum's gran but there was no other explanation. I remember the old lady, my great grandmother, and the small cottage with its narrow twisting staircase and nothing more. All I could find on maps was a big country hotel, with a golf course, that may or may not have been the house. I remember the old lady kissing my cheek when we left. She held my small hand for a long time.

Ultimately, I decided not to pursue the Penn connection. Sarah had decided to throw in her lot with Jack, it was not for me to seek to undo that decision. The Penns will have to remain my lost family branch. Since I live in Sussex, William's old stomping ground before Pennsylvania, I occasionally see places and signs indicating his work and life. It makes me smile. In a way, for him, I'm one of the ghosts that shouldn't be here.

That thought made me smile as well. There are a lot of people who now exist only because of this history, they are all valid people but wouldn't be here without the wars that brought about some unlikely liaisons. Do they in some way counterbalance the lost millions?

I am not a remnant of the future that did not occur, I am an alternative born from its destruction. 'Sloppy,' I imagined I heard the priest say.

I spent the journey home thinking about William, Sarah, Jack, mum, dad, Dave, everyone I've ever known. It was probably the most introspective journey I've ever taken and that's saying something.

It was still quite sunny when I got home. It had been a while now and I decided to check the ant tin. I lifted it up and sure enough it was filled with larvae and panicking workers. I used a small blow torch to burn them all then replaced the tin to get some more. It only took one more tinning and the nest was so depleted it was reduced to ineffectiveness.

My reasonably content existence continued on its course and occasionally I became aware of the ghosts. From time to time I'd think about the people I've personally lost. In the midst of life we are in death, blah blah blah. I left the journal for my daughter to read when she feels like it.

I did go to Ireland for Dave's funeral. I just hung about at the back, paid my respects and left. I returned later in the day and prayed over the grave, he would have liked that. As I left, I noticed a few middle aged men drinking and smoking outside the pub facing the graveyard. A couple of them raised their glasses to me and I waved as I walked away.

The following summer I looked again at the ant's nest to see if it still constituted a threat. It had changed. There appeared to be another, but not unrelated, species there. A slightly different size and colouring but also recognisable as last year's ants, strange. I'm no entomologist and didn't even try to explain this. The nest was busy and foraging lines were marching out in various directions but not towards the conservatory.

Afterword

In some ways this was an easy book to write; the stories were given to me by those I have known and loved, it is the history of my people. Yet, in other ways it was painfully difficult to write because it felt as if I were exploring the souls of those who lived it.

This is fundamentally a work of fiction. Nonetheless, it is born from the stories that I was told and the people that I knew. It is therefore a work of fact-based fiction where I have given myself licence to fictionalise gaps in the stories. I've aged my dad a bit, just so that I could use him as the vehicle by which I might amalgamate and tell disjointed war stories, sorry dad. He's every bit as tough as the character in the book.

The parts of his story dealing with evacuation and POW repatriation were him. He really did enter Belsen but after the liberation. The rest is from other stories that he told me.

Manny Cohen was real, the short story I tell about him was directly from my dad. I don't know what became of him.

Albert and Findlay are based on real people. The core

of their stories was given to me by family. Albert's ack-ack gun is as described to me by the person on whom he is based.

He was old and I was young when he told me and something may have been lost in translation. I can find no other reference to the adapted gun. I have a photograph of the real person which was taken during the battle of Caen. In it he and his team have a standard lightweight artillery style ack-ack with them. Nonetheless, I've chosen to stay with the description the man gave me.

Sade Morgenthau was real but had a different name.

Aleksandra Ivanovna Barantceva is my own invention since the real individual in the life of the person on whom Findlay is based is unknown to me. Her characteristics are constructed from a couple of real Soviet heroes.

Dietrich von Choltitz was a real figure and, in my view, does deserve more recognition for his brave decision to declare Paris open and undefended. A reader might correctly infer that I also love Paris. I understand how this man could be seduced and improved by her.

After the war he is reported by one source as saying: "We all share the guilt. We went along with everything, and we half-took the Nazis seriously instead of saying to hell with you and your stupid nonsense. I misled my soldiers into believing this rubbish. I feel utterly ashamed of myself. Perhaps we bear even more guilt than these uneducated animals."

Johann Waldheim is based on a man the real person behind Findlay wrote about in now lost letters to my dad. The Polish women and Findlay's children are real but I know nothing else about them.

Friedrich Jagemann is fictional but loosely based on an amalgam of real people, none of whom were noble characters.

Nonetheless I here declare that this odious character has no relation to or bearing on any other person, living or dead, who may coincidentally have the same name. I used the name because it means 'hunter' and suits the predatory nature of the fictitious character.

Jack and Sarah were real. I hope my take on their story does them justice.

At some point in our lives we all come to the realisation that it's never over. Even when we have drifted our slow uncomfortable way to our end it is apparent that we go on; in what we have done, our children, our work or those we have influenced. For good or ill we create the future.

I didn't understand that when I began this book. As I now reflect on it I see that it is true. From the elderly statesperson to the new born child, we all influence events and people in ways that live on. Our deaths are merely the point at which our active input is complete.

Those who were affected by our existence, deal with the passing or mourn us are the meme by which our life extends into eternity. They remember us and our actions and pass it on to those who they in turn affect. Our influence survives long after our names are forgotten, our actions, our mere existence, last forever. It may be that idiosyncratic habits, which we all have, originated in some long forgotten ancestor and in that way they still are with us.

The opening poem, which for the purposes of the story I ascribe to John 'Jack' Adams, is intended as both a tribute to the original work and a post script to it. I don't think John McCrae would object. I've mainly kept his syllabic metre but did not copy his verse structure.

Insofar that anyone may think it worthy of use, I here state that the poem, the copyright of which I retain, is placed on perpetual public licence for free use or performance by anybody, especially in remembrance ceremonies, except that this licence does not extend to commercial, profit making, political or non peaceful uses and excludes publishing or copying the poem except in an educational setting or as part of a scripted performance. The nature of public performance varies, so if you want to use it as part of a play or other presentation for which the audience pays... contact me first to see if we can agree the use is acceptable.

This licence for use of the poem further contains two conditions: first that the source, this book, be acknowledged, and second, that if you are able you should make a small donation to the Royal British Legion, if within the UK, or to your national equivalent association if outside the UK.

Please use it in your school, British legion or church with my blessing. If you use it to make money or promote nationalist hate, I will sue you.

As a post war child the bombsites and derelict buildings of east London were my playground. It makes me chuckle to imagine what modern risk-averse authority would make of the games we played igniting unexploded incendiary bombs. 'Firesticks' we called them, when thrown at the correct angle they were effective and free fireworks. On one occasion a passing police officer chastised us for exploding one of them too close to the road. He sent us further into the bombsite to carry on, how times change.

We often sire late in my family so each generation can be forty or more years separated from the next. Consequently, I only need step back one generation to be with relatives from both world wars. Some of them fought in both. All of them experienced the blitz.

So it was that I spent my early life listening to the stories of the traumatised. I didn't know any adult who was not in some way damaged by their experiences. My family had experiences from most spheres of the second war and some of the first. My teachers included veterans of Arnhem and Normandy as well as the Far East. My headmaster was partially blind because his eyes were damaged by a depth charge when he was a sub mariner.

Today we label it PTSD and offer treatment. In the London of my childhood we just accepted the eccentricities, were not much bothered by the fist fights that sometimes broke out and, most importantly, just accepted that those who fought lost something more than their peace of mind; they lost something indefinable and nebulous that enables contentment.

It is very sad that we have recently, yet again, seen people so damaged return to our land from distant wars.

Therefore, this book is intended as a tribute to everybody who has been lost, failed to exist or damaged through war. This includes the soldiers, of all nations, the civilians and especially the innocent. I have no doubt that humanity will continue its talent for conflict. I have no doubt that more nutcases will occupy positions of power in the future just as they did in the past. I have no doubt that each new war will be considered justifiable and promoted by deluded politicians.

It won't carry much weight with these people but if I could say one thing to everybody involved in all of the current conflicts around the globe, it would be this: "Stop it, please. Just stop it."

The fictional character Dave Thompson started out with a standard Irish name. That probably made him a bit of a cliché but I was OK with it.

My intention was to use the involvement of the feisty priest as a foil in order to progress what I wanted to say. The character's intelligence, general street smarts and all round good-guyness were based on a friend of mine called Dave Thompson.

Sadly, the real Dave died from a heart attack while I was writing the book. In tribute to him I renamed the character. Our relationship was not unlike that with the drinking, swearing, caring, fighting clergyman. Dave was an atheist and it amuses me to give his name to a priest. It would have amused him too.